SLEIGHT OF PAW

A Klepto Cat Mystery

Patricia Fry

Matilija Press
PMB 123
323 E. Matilija St.,Ste 123
Ojai, CA 93023
www.matilijapress.com

Sleight of Paw

A Klepto Cat Mystery
by Patricia Fry

ISBN 978-0-9911065-4-7

Cover Art: Bernadette E. Kazmarski
Cover layout: Dennis Mullican
Page layout: Dennis Mullican

Printed in U.S.A. by: Create Space

Other Novels by Patricia Fry

Catnapped
Cay-Eye Witness
Undercover Cat
The Cat Colony Caper

A Klepto Cat Mystery

Sleight of Paw

by Patricia Fry

Chapter One

Something caught Michael's eye. "Get out of there, Rags!" he scolded. "We don't want to lose you in this maze of walls."

Savannah stopped sweeping for a moment and looked toward her husband's latest sawdust-producing project. She smiled at her cat's appetite for adventure. "Curious creature, isn't he?"

"Sure is, and always willing to help," Michael said, shaking his head from side to side.

Savannah heard a hint of annoyance in his tone, so she walked over and lifted the oversized grey-and-white cat from inside the open wall. Just then, she saw something float down and land at her feet. "What's this?" She leaned over to look more closely, placing Rags on the floor beside her. He followed the item with his eyes as she picked it up and stood to examine it. The cat wasn't about to let this fascinating object go, and he reached up in an attempt to retrieve his latest treasure.

"No, you klepto. Just you never mind," Savannah reprimanded. She turned the piece of paper over in her hands a time or two and then unfolded it and more carefully examined it.

Michael glanced up. "What is it?"

"It's some sort of note or letter."

He made a pencil mark alongside his tape measure before glancing her way again. "Looks like it's been in the wall for a long time."

"Yeah, and it's written in a foreign language." She creased her brow in contemplation while murmuring to herself, "…maybe German."

"Really!?"

She stared over at her husband. "Michael, it looks ominous."

Hearing the apprehension in Savannah's voice, he quickly stood and released the lock on his tape measure. Once he heard the tape snap into place, he slipped it into his leather tool belt. "What do you mean 'ominous?'"

Savannah's eyes met his. "Michael, do you remember the night we approached Auntie Marg about buying this house?"

He cocked his head. "Yesss. What about it?"

"That night, she told us there was something in the house—she wouldn't tell us what it was, but it sounded like something rather…sinister or creepy." She hesitated. "And then she brought it up again a few months ago, remember?"

"Yeah, but I didn't think it was anything to be concerned about. I mean, she never told us what it was." He walked over to take a closer look at the time-worn paper in Savannah's hands. "What is it, anyway? What does it mean?" He then stepped over to the wall opening and peered in. "How did Maggie know about it?" he asked, not expecting an answer. He tilted forward a little and squinted down amidst the framing and drywall. "Wait," he said, "there's something else in here."

Savannah watched as he pulled a small box out of the wall cavity. "Wow! What is it?" she asked, recoiling just a bit.

"Heck if I know." He blew some of the dust off the top of the box and then lifted the lid. "Well that's odd." He held it out so Savannah could see inside. "It's a broken eggshell."

Savannah looked in the box and then down at the letter. She gasped. "It's a curse, Michael! This house has been cursed!"

He frowned. "Now, how do you know that?" Then, raising one eyebrow in her direction, a hint of a smile on his lips, he said, "Hey, don't tell me I married a witch."

"No, but I do read," she said. "When I outgrew my *Nancy Drew* mystery phase, I started reading stories about witches and gypsies." She narrowed her green eyes in his direction.

"Michael, I believe this is a gypsy curse." She stared into space for a moment before asking, "Now who do we know that reads German?"

"A curse? Savannah, that's absurd, don't you think? We're happy in our home and Maggie and Tom and other members of the Forster family all had a good life here."

Savannah thought for a moment and then reminded him as if reciting a mundane laundry list, "My great uncle Jed Forster died in a fire on this property. Auntie and I were kidnapped from this house. A man was killed in Auntie's bedroom upstairs. You were brutally assaulted. You were accused of murder..."

Michael waved a hand toward Savannah. "Okay, I get it. Let's see if we can find out more about this…this, supposed curse thing."

Michael watched as Savannah walked out of the room carrying the box and the note…Rags trotting along beside her. Once they were out of sight, he shifted his gaze to the open wall where he was about to add a couple of new electrical outlets, and began thinking about the most recent challenges he and Savannah had faced as a married couple. It seemed to start several months after their wedding…

***

It was mid June. Savannah had just returned from an early morning jaunt on Peaches and he had walked out the back door and met them at the hitching post. "How was your ride?"

"Oh, hi Michael. You startled me," Savannah said as she slid the saddle off her mare's back.

"Here, let me take that." Michael reached for the saddle and easily carried it into the tack room which he had converted from an old shed on the property. He plopped it on the closest saddle rack. Savannah soon appeared behind him and laid the pad and blanket over the saddle. She hung the bridle on a nearby hook.

Grabbing her rubber grooming tray, she walked back out to join her horse. "I had a wonderful ride," she said over her shoulder. "It's just a gorgeous day and Peaches is such a good girl. I think she enjoys these early morning rides as much as I do." She patted the mare on the neck, turned toward Michael and smiled, her green eyes twinkling under side-swept bangs. "When are you going to ride her?"

"When will you give me a chance?" He laughed. "You're always on her back or brushing her or giving her carrot tops."

Savannah grinned over at her husband. "Yeah, I do kind of hog her, don't I?" Her smile widened. "Hey, we should get you a horse. Then we can ride together."

Michael looked down and shook his head. "I don't think so. Looks like too much work to me."

"Work? You call this work? I love it. It's fun! I really enjoy spending time with her." She made swirling motions over the mare's back with the rubber currycomb. "I guess not everyone has a passion for riding."

"Right. Like not everyone has a passion for renovation."

She turned sharply to look at him, her blond ponytail whisking to one side. "I like some parts of renovation—just not the dust and the noise and..." she hesitated..."the sawing and hammering..."

"Well, pray tell what parts do you like?" he asked, a wide grin transforming his handsome face.

Her eyes lit up. "Decorating. Iris has taught me a lot about decorating and I do love it." She cocked her head slightly. "...choosing fabrics and wallpaper, rearranging things..."

"Buying furniture and doodads..." Michael laughed.

"Yes!" she said. "I like that, too. And that's what makes us a team." She dropped the currycomb into her carry tray and picked up a soft brush. "I ride and you handle the saddle and..." She paused and looked at Michael impishly. "...clean the corral?"

He leaned his six-foot frame against the hitching rail, crossing his arms over his chest. "Your horse, your poop."

"Then, how come I have to clean up *your* sawdust?" she asked.

"Because, dear wife, you jump the gun."

She shot a quick look at him while brushing long strokes along Peaches's neck. "What do you mean?" she challenged.

"You start sweeping and vacuuming before I'm even finished with my project."

She turned to look squarely at Michael, her left hand on her hip. "So when you go off to read the paper, have dinner or go to bed, you aren't actually finished?" she asked.

He pursed his lips and looked askance. "Not always."

"Well, I don't want that dust around any longer than it has to be, even if I have to sweep up every hour on the hour."

"Okay, then." He walked over and gave her an affectionate pat on the fanny as he moved around to the other side of the horse.

"Have you been making more sawdust behind my back?" she teased.

"Just a little; don't worry, I cleaned it up. Just wanted to finish the woodwork in that upstairs bedroom so I can install the new closet doors."

She glanced up while brushing the mare's back and rump. "That room is really shaping up, Michael. You do beautiful work. Before long, our home will qualify for the *Better Homes and Gardens* centerfold."

Michael laughed. "Maybe the *Klutzy Amateur Woodworker's Weekly* or the *Weekend Wannabe Builder's Rag*."

Savannah shook her head. "You're too modest." She leaned over the back of the horse toward him and gazed up into the sky. "I just love what you've done in our bedroom and master bath. It's so luxurious, yet…" She thought about her choice of words. "…still in harmony with the period of this old house." She dropped the brush into the tray, tugged at one leg of her size-eight extra-long jeans and gave her horse a hug around the neck. She then made eye contact with Michael while releasing the lead rope from the railing. "I'm so glad you're almost finished with Adam's room. He's going to love having his own room when he comes to visit. …one that looks like an eight-year-old boy's room, not an old-fashioned room designed for elderly guests."

"Yes, I hope to have it finished when he visits in two weeks—or at least have the painting done and his toys organized." He winked. "You know, the important things."

"Yeah, the most important thing here for that little boy is his dad. He does love you, Michael."

Michael smiled. "Sometimes I think he loves you more. You're always coming up with fun things to do with him." He stared off into space for a few moments. He then walked up behind Savannah and kissed her on the back of the neck. "I really get a kick out of watching the two of you together. You know that?"

Suddenly, he pulled back, edged his cell phone from his jeans pocket and looked at it. He turned toward Savannah. "It's a text from Bud." When he looked back at the screen, his demeanor turned sullen. "Oh no. There's a problem with Pete Gamble's dog. Bud says he doesn't look so good this morning. He seems kind of worried. I'd better go over to the clinic and have a look. Wanna come?" Before she could respond, he said with a smirk, "Or do you have more sweeping to do?"

Savannah feigned a disgusted look in Michael's direction. And then she said, "Okay. Give me just a minute while I put Peaches away and wash up. I'd like to check on Marsha Ralston's cat."

***

"Dear God."

"What?" Savannah asked as she walked into the animal recovery area carrying the chart for Rufus Ralston.

"This dog is dead," Michael said, his voice thin and weak.

She stopped and peered into the pen where Michael crouched. "My gosh, what happened?"

He shook his head back and forth slowly. "I don't know. I just…don't…know." He glanced up at Savannah. "He tolerated the surgery. His recovery was right on track. He was awake and doing a little tail-wagging when I checked on him late yesterday; vitals were excellent. What could have happened?"

"Looks like a young dog."

"Yes, right around two years." Michael stood and faced Savannah, who was still looking down at the dog. "You know, we went in to retrieve a piece of plastic he had swallowed. It could be that part of it or something else had perforated the bowel." He looked over at the dog. "When Bud called with his symptoms last night, they seemed consistent with a common infection after surgery. I instructed him to administer a higher dose of antibiotics." He hung his head. "This is awful. I feel just terrible."

Savannah put her hand on his arm. "Such a shame. This part of veterinary work never gets easier, does it?" She glanced over at Michael. "Will you do an autopsy?"

"Probably not…unless Pete wants it. You can never tell what he's going to do." He ran his hand through his straight dark-brown hair. "Gosh, I hate to call him."

"I'll call him, if you want," Savannah offered.

"Naw, I'd better do it," Michael said as he looked at the dog's chart to locate Pete Gamble's phone number. He walked into the lab across the hall while dialing.

"Is Pete Gamble there, please?"

"Yes, let me get him for you."

Within a few seconds, a gruff voice responded, "Yeah?"

"Hello Pete; Dr. Ivey here." He hesitated. "Pete, I'm awfully sorry to tell you this, but we lost your dog, Brute. We don't know for sure what happened…"

"He's dead?" There was silence for a few moments. And then Michael heard, "You jerk! You said the surgery was no big deal…that he would be okay. How many other dogs have you killed doin' this *easy* surgery?" he yelled. "You told me yesterday he was doin' just fine. Was he dead then? Was he dyin'? Were you lyin' to me?"

"No, Pete, I didn't lie to you. The surgery *was* a success, his recovery was normal. He was doing just fine when I left last evening."

"You left him alone all night to die?"

Michael took in a deep breath. In a calm voice, he said, "There was no reason to monitor him. When we came in this morning, we discovered a problem and he died a short time later."

"So if you'd stayed with him, he might have made it?" Pete growled.

Michael hesitated. "I can't say, Pete. I can do an autopsy to see if we can figure out what happened. No charge to you, of course."

"Hell no! You ain't doin' no more cuttin' on my dog." He paused and then continued, "You better believe my customers will hear about this. I'll ruin your business. Everyone needs to know what a…a…butcher shop you run over there, you moron."

Michael grimaced. "Now Pete, please. I know you're upset, and frankly, so are we here at the clinic. This is an awful waste of a good dog and a fine pet. But yelling won't…"

"Don't you tell me how to behave, you butcher. You killed my dog!"

Michael gritted his teeth and spat into the phone, "And anger won't bring him back."

There was silence and then Pete said, "I'm comin' to get him."

"I'll have him ready," Michael said quietly before noticing that Pete had hung up.

He looked down at his cell phone, pushed "end call" and shook his head slowly from side to side.

"Not taking it well, huh?" Savannah asked while closing the door to the pen where she'd been examining the Ralstons' cat.

"You heard?"

"I could practically hear him shouting from his store two miles away." She walked across the hall to the room where Michael sat and put her hand on his shoulder. "I'm so sorry, honey. I know how hard it is to lose a patient."

"He's so angry. He's blaming me." He stared ahead for a few seconds and then swiveled in the chair toward Savannah. "You know, I've seen a lot of emotions expressed when I've given a client bad news, but anger isn't usually one of them." He took her hands in his. "Savannah, this guy has me kind of scared. I don't know what he might do." He looked over at the dog. "He's coming to get him."

"Does he want you to do an autopsy? Does he want to know what happened as much as we do?"

"No. He said emphatically, no." Michael leaned over and rested his head in his hands. "Gosh, this is awful—just awful."

Savannah ran her fingers over his head and down the back of his neck. "I'll go unlock the front door and then let's get him ready for Mr. Gamble," she said, patting his shoulder a couple of times.

***

"Where are you, you lousy vet?"

Savannah looked over at her husband. "Oh

my gosh," she said under her breath. "He sounds furious." She grabbed at Michael's lab coat as he moved toward the booming voice. "Don't go in there, Michael," she begged.

"I'll be okay," he said, and he continued walking down the hallway toward the front of the clinic. Savannah rushed after him. There, just inside the slightly ajar door, his face contorted with rage, stood Pete Gamble, a sturdy-built man of fifty-one wearing faded jeans and a dark blue polo shirt with his store logo above the pocket—*Gamble Pet Supply*. He held a small wooden baton in his right hand, which hung at his side.

When he saw Michael, he raised the bat and made a move toward him. Savannah rushed forward, putting herself between the two men. She tried to control her voice. "Mr. Gamble, be reasonable."

"Get out of the way," Pete hollered as he pushed Savannah aside. "I'm going to kill him." She felt herself stumbling toward a small table. Before she could stop the forward motion, she slammed into the table, tipping it. A display of sample dog treats crashed to the floor along with a few magazines. Savannah landed hard on her left knee. She barely noticed the pain. She was too terrified for her husband. "NO!! NO!!!" she screamed, as she watched Pete rush toward Michael. The attacker held the baton over his head ready to strike.

Michael put his hands up in an effort to calm the distraught man. "Now, Pete, settle down," he said. But the outraged man charged Michael, a menacing look on his face. Pete's agility and speed proved to be detrimental, however, as he stepped on some of the kibbles that had spilled over the waxed linoleum and his feet went out from under him.

Savannah looked over from where she still sat and watched as he landed hard on his back.

"Gawd damn it," he growled, struggling to his feet. He glared over at Savannah, who had scurried up off the floor. She stood against a wall, frozen in place. "I oughta kill you, too!" he yelled. "You butchers…dog killers!!" He raised the bat and ran at Michael again. He swung at Michael's head just as he ducked, grabbed Pete's arm and twisted it behind his back. Pete shouted profanities.

Savannah thought she heard another voice. It was Michael's. "Call the sheriff, Savannah!"

Stunned by the horrifying reality of the scuffle going on in front of her, and aware, now, that her knee was throbbing, it took her a moment to comply. *This just can't be happening. I'm so scared for Michael. This maniac really does want to do damage,* she thought to herself. She pulled her cell phone out of her jeans pocket and began to dial. Suddenly, Pete freed himself from Michael's grip. He rushed toward Savannah and knocked the phone out of her hands. She stood there helpless, watching it scoot across the floor to the other side of the room. Michael took the opportunity to grab the baton the attacker still gripped, and the two men struggled hard in an attempt to take control. Suddenly, Michael lost his footing and fell over a chair against the wall. Pete lifted the bat and began pounding it savagely against Michael's back and head. Savannah couldn't contain herself. She ran over to Pete, grabbed his shirt, and pulled on the fabric. "Stop it, stop it, now!" she screamed.

He reached behind him, slapping at her with the small bat. Just then, Michael spun around to face his opponent. "Out of the way, Savannah!" he shouted. He dove for the enraged man, hitting him hard in the stomach with his left shoulder and knocking him to the floor. He fell on top of Pete and the bat went flying. Pete broke loose from underneath Michael and scrambled to his feet. Michael promptly jumped to a standing position. However, before Michael had his balance, Pete swung at him with his fist, making contact against his cheek. Michael staggered backward, giving Pete time to reach over and pick up the baton.

"I'm going to kill you, you butcher!" Pete lunged again and Michael was fast enough to grab the man's wrist. Remembering a move he'd learned while on the wrestling team in college, he hooked his right foot around the back of Pete's legs and slammed him face down on the floor. Michael straddled him and grabbed his other wrist. As Pete thrashed around, Michael moved up and placed his knee in the middle of Pete's back. Michael had him pinned to the floor; now he strained to twist one of Pete's arms behind him, making sure to bend it back far enough so that it hurt, rendering him virtually helpless.

In the meantime, Savannah had made her way behind the reception desk and used the phone to call for help.

"Are you all right?" Savannah screamed.

"I think so," Michael said, his chest heaving with each breath. "Did you call the sheriff?"

"Yes, they're on the way. Wait, I think I hear them now—gosh, that was quick."

"Dr. Ivey?"

Savannah and Michael looked toward the voice. There, peering wide-eyed through the open door was a pudgy teenager. "Steven, what are you doing here?" Savannah asked, her voice shaky.

"Just walking by with Princess." Steven stared down at Michael and Pete in disbelief. "You know, we live just down the street. I heard yelling and got worried. I called 9-1-1." He took a step inside and his little Aussie came into view.

“Thank you, Steven,” she said. And then she quickly added, “Don’t come in here. Stay out there, okay?”

Pete lifted his head and looked up at the boy, blood covering his nose and mouth. Noticing the dog, he yelled, “Don’t let these butchers operate on your dog, kid. They’ll kill it like they killed mine.” He began squirming and kicking his feet.

“Just be still, you lunatic,” Michael snarled.

“I’m gonna sue you two and drag your name through the mud. I’ll ruin you,” Pete said through gritted teeth.

Steven stared down at the angry man. Suddenly, he turned and moved aside. Michael and Savannah heard another voice. “Okay, what’s going on in here?” Deputy Jim asked as he pushed the door open and entered the room cautiously, his hand on his gun. Deputy Ben followed. Upon surveying the situation, Ben quickly walked over, put his foot on Pete’s right arm until he released the bat he still held in his hand. He then said, “We’ll take it from here, Dr. Ivey.”

Michael stood and walked slowly and stiffly toward a chair; Savannah rushed to his side. She took his arm and helped him sit down. “Are you all right, hon?” she asked.

“He got me a few good ones,” he said, lowering his head and patting it with one hand. Savannah examined the area and Michael cringed under the light pressure of her touch.

“No blood, but I do feel a knot.”

“Yeah, so do I.”

“And your pretty face, Michael…” Savannah said, holding back tears. She slid her fingers along his cheek ever so gently.

“He killed my dog, Sheriff,” Pete said. “And then he tried to beat me up—came at me with that weapon; I had to take it away from him. Look, he bloodied my nose with that thing."

"Yeah, Michael bloodied his nose before Pete could kill him with that bat," Savannah yelled sounding close to hysterics.

"Okay, everyone calm down. You'll all get a chance to tell your story."

"He killed my dog, man," Pete bellowed as Ben cuffed him and helped him to his feet. Jim patted him down.

"Let's go, Gamble," Ben said, walking him out the front door.

"You're arresting me?" Pete screamed.

"Just taking you outta here for questioning," he said.

Jim looked over at Steven who had backed away from the door for a moment to let Ben through and then stepped back in. "Are you a witness?"

"Yes, sort of," the teen said.

"Wait, I know you, don't I? You're Steven Byrd," Deputy Jim said. "It was your dad…"

"Yes, my dad was murdered at Dr. Jordan's house."

"So what did you witness here today, son?"

"I was walking by with my dog and heard banging noises and loud yelling coming from inside here and screaming. Dr. Jordan screamed."

"Yes, I did." She smiled weakly at the boy. "It's Dr. Ivey now, Steven."

"Oh, I didn't know that." He looked down at his hands as he fidgeted with the end of the dog leash for a few seconds. Taking a deep breath, he continued, "I could see Dr. Ivey—um—the guy vet, and this dude fighting through the window."

"Did you see who started the fight?"

"No."

"Did you hear what they were saying?"

"Yes." He pointed in the direction that Ben had taken Pete Gamble and said, "He was swearing at Dr. Ivey and accusing him of killing his dog." Again, looking down, he ruffled the fur on Princess's head while mumbling, "That's about all I heard."

"Did you hear either of these men threaten the other?"

Steven promptly raised his head, his eyes wide and riveted on the deputy's. "Yeah," he announced. "The other guy said he was going to kill Dr. Ivey. Um, I think he meant the guy Dr. Ivey."

"Okay, Steven, thank you. Can I have your phone number in case we need to ask you any more questions?"

"Sure. And I'm the one who called you."

"Yes, I guess we got two calls. You made the first call. Thank you for doing that."

"Yes, thank you so much, Steven," Savannah said as she limped over to the boy, giving him a hug and petting his energetic Aussie with affection. "How's she doing?" she asked.

"Great!" Steven smiled. "She's a super dog. Thanks for finding her for us."

Savannah looked over at Steven. "Thank *you* for taking such good care of her."

The boy's round face brightened. "Wanna see a trick I taught her?"

"Sure do." Savannah glanced back at Michael and Deputy Jim before hobbling after the boy and dog out into the parking lot. Once outside, she noticed that Pete Gamble was sitting in the back of a patrol car. She led Steven off to the other side of the large parking lot.

In the meantime, Jim pulled a chair around to face Michael, sat down, and asked, "So what happened, Dr. Mike?"

Michael looked up at him. "It was surreal. I performed surgery on his dog. Everything was going well. But something happened overnight—we don't know what—and the dog died." He took a deep breath and then coughed. He hugged his middle and bent over a little. "Dang, I guess I have a bruised rib cage."

Jim winced. "The paramedics are on their way." He looked down at his notes. "So the dog died..."

"Yes, and when I called to tell Pete the bad news, he came unglued...began swearing and making awful accusations. He wanted to come and pick up the dog, which was okay with me. I figured he'd calm down by the time he got here. But, no. He came in here bent on hurting someone—namely me." Michael leaned forward a little in the chair, his left arm wrapped around his rib cage. Several strands of his straight dark-brown hair hung over one brow.

"What did he say to you?"

"He said he was going to kill me." He choked up a little. "He also threatened Savannah." Taking a ragged breath, he looked up at the deputy. "He said he would ruin our reputation in this town."

"Who struck the first blow, Dr. Mike?" Jim asked, pen and pad poised.

"I think he did. I mean, he came at me with that club and I couldn't do much except try to protect myself. When he pushed Savannah and threatened her, that really got my blood boiling and I knew I had to find a way to stop him or one of us...or both...well, someone was going to suffer some serious damage. So I tried to remember some of the moves from my old wrestling days and went from protection mode to, you might say, combat mode. Somehow, I was able to take control and, well, then you got here."

"Ever have anything like this happen before?" Jim asked.

"Never!" Michael said. "Like I told Savannah earlier, I've seen a lot of emotions when I've had to deliver sad news to a pet owner, but never such outrageous anger."

"Did you offer any sort of consolation?"

Michael frowned and looked the deputy in the eyes. "Consolation? Do you have pets, Jim?"

"Yeah, the kids have a dog and a cat."

"There's little consolation when it comes to losing a beloved pet. I know the pain and I have great empathy for our clients who lose pets." He looked down at the floor. "I suggested we do an autopsy to see if we could find out what happened. I offered to do it at no charge." He looked up, a questioning look on his face. "Is that the kind of thing you're talking about?"

"Yeah. What did he say?"

"Hummph. He just kept spouting profanities, as I recall."

Jim scribbled on his notepad and then looked up at Michael. "Do you want to press charges?"

"Absolutely," Michael said, reaching back with his hand and touching the goose egg on his head. "That savage belongs in jail."

"Okay, then." Jim glanced through his notes.

Michael stared at him for a few seconds. "I take it you guys know Mr. Gamble. I heard the other deputy call him by name."

Jim sneered and nodded his head. "Oh yes, we know him." He stood and walked over to look out the door into the parking lot. He then turned to face Michael. "I'd like to speak with Savannah now. Is there some place I can question her while the paramedics look at you?"

"Sure. She has an office in the back."

Jim disappeared out the door and promptly returned with Savannah, who had been talking to some of the neighbors congregated outside. Michael stood when he saw Savannah limp through the door. He rushed over to her. "Oh honey, you're hurt."

"Just my knee—no big deal."

Jim glanced down at her knee. "We'll find out how big of a deal when you get looked over by the paramedics."

Savannah scrunched up her face at the thought of being examined. She looked at Michael. "Have you been checked out yet?"

"No, I'm going to do that right now while you go with Jim to your office for questioning." Just then, he noticed a petite blond woman probably in her late twenties walk into the room lugging a paramedic's bag.

Jim motioned toward Michael. "There's your first patient, Sarah. Dr. Michael Ivey."

She nodded in his direction. "Hello. Want to sit over here for me?" She set her bag next to the chair Jim had vacated and she sat down. Michael took the chair opposite her. She looked at his face. "I hear you had quite a commotion in here this morning."After examining Michael, she said, "Sir, you have a pretty nasty bump on your head and a contusion on your cheek there. You don't have any loose teeth, do you?"

Michael shook his head. "No."

"It appears that you have some bruising around your ribs. And your ankle is a little swollen." She began to clean and dress a couple of cuts she discovered on his hands and one elbow. "Sir, I don't see anything life-threatening here, but I recommend that you get checked out at the emergency room over in Straley. We can take you over by ambulance or you can have someone drive you. I would rather you not drive until you've been seen."

"Why not? I feel okay. I don't think I need any treatment, do you?"

"You're a veterinarian, you know the problems that can accompany a head injury."

"Well, I've never prescribed that any of my patients refrain from driving," he said with a chuckle.

Sarah gave him a sideways glance and handed him a piece of paper. "It's up to you. Here, take this list of danger signals. If you experience any of them, see your doctor, okay?" She looked in the direction she'd seen Savannah and Jim go and then stood up. "I'll come back for your wife in a few minutes. Would you make sure she waits in here for me?"

"Sure will. And thank you."

Sarah appeared to be rather surprised at the gratitude. "Not a problem."

In the meantime, in Savannah's office, she blotted her eyes with a wad of tissues. "I don't know why I'm so weepy."

Jim tilted his head a little and stared into her face. "You were assaulted. That's traumatic." He looked down briefly. One corner of his mouth twisted upward. "I don't imagine this is something you encounter on a daily basis."

Savannah laughed a little through her sobs. "No. Sure don't." She blew her nose into the tissue and took a ragged breath. "Now what was it you just asked me?"

"Uh, you said that Michael lost his temper. At what point did that happen?"

"Michael was wonderfully calm. He tried to talk to the guy. So did I. But he wasn't having any of it." She thought for a minute. "I don't think Michael started really fighting back until that monster threatened me." She paused. "Yes, I think he got angry at that point." She looked over at Jim. "He didn't want to fight. He did his best to defuse the situation. He had no choice other than to take a beating and…" She began to choke up. "I'm so glad he didn't do that." She sobbed into the tissue in her hand. Her next words were muffled. "He could have been killed."

"Okay, Savannah," Jim said, "what I get from your statement is that Pete Gamble was pretty much riled up when he walked in and he began issuing threats at that point. He was armed and he struck the first blow." He looked down at his notes. "Maybe all the blows."

"Yes, I don't think Michael ever did hit him." She smiled a wicked smile. "But he sure slammed Pete down on the floor a good one."

Jim looked up at Savannah—a slight grin on his face. He then became serious again. "And do you want to press charges?"

"Yes! People can't go around hurting other people like this. It's uncivilized."

Jim chuckled. "Yes, uncivilized, indeed." He looked over at Savannah. "Are you okay now? Ready to have Sarah check you out?"

"Yeah. I'm okay," she said without emotion.

As Savannah walked into the waiting room, she heard Sarah say, "Sir, you were lucky. This could have been much worse for you."

Savannah slid into a chair next to Michael and put her arm around his neck, pressing her cheek against his shoulder. "Yes, my husband is quite the scrapper, as it turns out. I didn't know he had such he-man skills."

She pulled back and Michael turned to face her. He managed a strained smile and repeated, "Scrapper? He-man?"

Sarah chuckled right along with Michael and Savannah.

"And you ma'am, looks like you got nicked a little there." Sarah reached over with her gloved hand and touched near a scrape on Savannah's arm.

"Oh yes, I guess I caught it on something when I went down."

Sarah's eyes widened. "He hit you, too?"

Savannah shook her head. "Pushed me."

"Same thing," Sarah said while moistening a gauze patch with an alcohol solution and dabbing at the fresh cut. "It's assault. Any other cuts or bruises?"

"Well, my knee's sore," she said, rubbing it gently. "I think I went down on it."

"Let's take a look."

Savannah began to pull up her pant leg when she stopped and said, "Darn, feels like it's swelling." She carefully worked the fabric up to her thigh to reveal a skinned knee that was already puffy and turning purple.

"Oh hon." Michael's tone was sympathetic. He then twisted his face into a scowl. Through gritted teeth, he virtually growled, "That damn…"

Savannah reached over and patted his knee. "It's okay, Michael. I'm okay."

"I can't stand that he hurt you."

"Oh nooooo," Savannah said.

"What?" Sarah and Michael asked in unison.

"Blood on my favorite jeans," she wailed.

"Now the woman knows her priorities," Sarah quipped. "Hematoma on the knee—no big deal; blood stains on the clothes—problem." She laughed, as she dabbed at the scratches with alcohol and taped a patch with ointment over the scraped knee. She looked Savannah in the eyes. "Any head trauma?"

She shook her head slowly from side to side while working her jeans back down over her knee. "I don't think so."

Sarah continued to stare at Savannah. She then glanced over at Michael. "You should both be seen."Addressing Savannah, she asked, "You can drive, can't you? Your right leg is okay?"

Savannah nodded.

Just then, a male paramedic walked in and addressed Sarah. "We're taking the other guy to the hospital with a police escort."

Savannah grabbed Michael's arm, shaking it a little. Her face brightened into a wide smile. "Did you hear that, Michael? You put him in the hospital. My hero."

"Naw, honey. He just wants to go there instead of jail; right Jim?"

Jim, who had been standing against the reception desk going over his notes, tilted his head in their direction. "Could be, Dr. Mike. Could be."

The three of them watched as Sarah packed up her equipment. "Can we go?" Michael asked Deputy Jim.

"Yes, but I recommend you do as the medic suggests. Go get checked out. This is partly for your health, Dr. Ivey, but you may need a report if this case goes to trial." He winked. "Just a little off-the-record professional advice, sir."

Savannah sat up straight. In her most authoritative tone, she said, "That's where we're going right now, then." She looked toward the hallway, a hint of sadness crossing her face. "…as soon as we put that poor dog in the cooler."

After locking up the back area of the clinic and grabbing their belongings, Savannah and Michael returned to the waiting room. Just then, Jim stepped in and spotted them. "You might want to wait until they load Gamble into the wagon. He's pretty angry. I don’t think you want to hear his tirade.”

Savannah felt suddenly weak-kneed. She took a deep breath and then pressed her lips together in an attempt to hold back another barrage of tears.

Chapter Two

"It was like watching a barroom brawl on the big screen with Sylvester Stallone," Savannah said, her green eyes widening as she relived the scene. She became somber. "Only it was my gorgeous husband out there. Oh Auntie, I was so scared."

"*You* were scared?" Michael challenged as he set his sandwich down on the plate in front of him and took a sip of sun tea.

"Yes. I was really scared." She looked over at him, cocking her head. "And you weren't?"

"Sure was," he said picking up his sandwich and taking another bite.

"Well, you didn't act like it. You were so courageous. Made me swoon."

"You swooned? I thought you just tripped over something."

"Yeah, when that guy pushed me," she said, looking down at her leg which she had elevated on a kitchen chair. She adjusted the icepack.

"You two checked out okay at the emergency room, didn't you?" Margaret asked, concern taking over her round face.

"Yes. Well, Michael got a pretty good wallop on the back of the head and he needs to take it easy for a few days. My knee is throbbing like heck."

"And we're both stiff and sore," Michael said. "We move like old people."

Margaret's husband, Max shook his head slowly from side to side. "I can just imagine." He looked across the kitchen table at Michael. "So what's he charged with?"

"Probably assault."

Max poked at the small portion of coleslaw left on his plate. "Really too bad all the way around. You lost a dog—that's gotta be hard to start with—

and then his owner goes berserk and threatens your life. And then you get beat up."

Margaret cocked her head, her brown bobbed hair dancing across one shoulder. "But look at the bright side."

Savannah creased her brow. "Bright side?"

"Yeah, what bright side?" Michael challenged, squinting his clear blue eyes.

Everyone waited to hear Margaret's reasoning. She looked around the room and then said, "You're still here. You live to treat more dogs and cats, have some kids, and finish the renovation of this old place."

"Yes, we're still here." Michael reached over and squeezed Savannah's hand. "I'm definitely thankful for that."

Margaret blotted her mouth with her napkin, folded it onto her empty dinner plate, and addressed Michael. "What you're doing with this house is wonderful. I'm so glad you two were able to buy it. It's perfect for you."

Max shoved his plate toward the center of the kitchen table. "Yes, Michael, you are quite the craftsman. I had no idea."

"We do love it here," Savannah said, reaching out to stack the dinner plates, "where Adam can come, where I can have Peaches, where Mom and my sister can stay when they visit. It's great."

Margaret stood. "Stay there, Vannie. I'll take care of that. You two need rest. Isn't that why we came over and fixed supper for you?"

"And it was delicious," Michael said. He addressed Savannah, "Honey, see if you can get the recipe from Max."

"Yes, Max. That is the tastiest grilled cheese sandwich I've ever had. What is your secret ingredient?" Savannah asked.

"There are several of them—like the Texas sliced bread…" Max started.

"That's right, you have to use fresh thick-sliced bread," Margaret agreed. "I like to bake my own or buy it fresh-baked and cut it into thick slices."

"And then you use pepper-jack cheese, right?" Michael asked.

"Yup." Max nodded. "Or any cheese of your choice. Two slices on each slice of bread. And in between, before putting the sandwich on the griddle, we spread a mixture of roasted tomatoes, lime zest and juice, red or green onions, and chopped cilantro. I like to roast the tomatoes with a little olive oil and garlic."

Savannah tilted her head toward Max. "That's it?" She then looked over at her husband. "I think we could do that, don't you, honey?"

"Yeah, we should be able to manage it. Sure was good." He addressed Max, "Did you learn this recipe at the culinary academy?"

Max thought for a moment and then said, "No. I think one of the restaurants I worked at in Chicago had one similar to this on the menu. This is a copycat recipe."

"Berry cobbler anyone?" Savannah offered. "And coffee?"

"When did you make that?" Margaret asked.

"Early this morning. I thought we'd have some for breakfast, but we got kinda side-tracked. After my ride, we hot-footed it to the clinic and… well, you know the rest of the story." She reached up and whisked her long bangs to one side. "So any takers?"

"Sure." Max nodded enthusiastically.

"Yeowza!" Margaret said from where she stood rinsing dishes at the sink.

Savannah started to move her leg off the chair. "I'll heat the cobbler and set the ice cream out to soften. That will give the coffee time to brew."

"I'll do it. You just sit, will ya?" Margaret scolded.

"Thanks, Auntie," she said while rearranging the icepack again.

"It hurts, huh?" Margaret asked, concern in her voice.

"Yeah, a little. Trying to keep the swelling down."

"What's that?" Margaret jumped back and looked down toward her feet. "Well, hello Walter. Where's your sidekick?"

Just then, the jangle of a dog collar could be heard and everyone looked over in time to see Lexie rising up from a nap in her bed near the kitchen door. When the dog saw the furry black cat rubbing up against Margaret, she rushed over to him and began bumping him with her nose. Walter laid down and froze in place; Lexie pawed at him.

"Watch out Lexie, he's going to get you," Michael warned.

Suddenly, Walter swished his tail once and then twice. His ears went back and the game was on. The cat and the Afghan-mix dog began chasing each other through the kitchen, into the dining room and living room and then back into the kitchen where they tore around the table—Walter in the lead during one go-around and then it was Lexie. Finally, amidst laughter, the duo raced into the living room and up the large staircase where they disappeared.

"What a pair," Max said, still laughing.

"Yes, they are entertaining," Savannah agreed.

"So how does Rags and the little Himmie fit into the scheme of things here?" Max wanted to know.

"They stay out of the way when those two decide to play," Michael said.

Savannah chuckled. "Rags and Buffy have teamed up. But they're quite the odd couple. Buffy is so prim and fastidious. Rags is lackadaisical. She likes routine and loves to laze around in someone's lap. He thrives on adventure and, as you know, has bundles of energy and some rather creative habits. She was kind of a loner, wasn't she, Michael, before Rags came along?" He nodded and she continued, "Now she follows him around, plays with him and even lets him sleep in her pink canopy bed."

"Now there's a vision I can't quite wrap my brain around—that long-legged cat of yours curled up in a pink foo-foo bed…" Margaret said with a laugh.

"Yeah, it is rather humorous," Michael agreed. Then he explained, "He's still king pin around here. It was Rags's home first, you know."

"Oh yes, I know," Margaret said. "He took over as soon as he and Savannah moved in here with me last year." She placed the cobbler in the oven and turned to face the others. "He wouldn't leave my stuff alone—had to get married and move it all over to Max's place."

Max stiffened and frowned at his wife. "You married me to get away from Rags?"

Margaret laughed, walked over behind Max and put her hands on his shoulders. "Just kidding." She looked at Savannah and asked, "Does he still steal things?"

"Uh, sure does, Auntie." Savannah grimaced. "In fact, I think I see him snooping in your purse."

"Drats." Margaret dashed into the living room. Everyone laughed. "Oh no you don't," they heard her say. "What do you have, Rags? Bring that back, you bad boy."

"Oh dear, I'd better go intervene," Savannah said, preparing to move her leg off the chair.

Max stood. "No stay here. I'll go."

"So what did he take?" Savannah asked when she saw Margaret and Max return with big grins on their faces.

"Nothing," Margaret said, walking into the pantry in search of ground coffee.

Max sat down, leaned back and stretched his long legs out in front of him. "Nothing, my eye. You could have poisoned him with that thing. You really shouldn't be leaving something like that down where a cat like Rags can get it. He did save your life once, you know."

Margaret set the canister of coffee on the counter. She stood silent for a moment, remembering. No, she would never forget Rags's part in saving her and Savannah from that crazy kidnapper. "Yes, he did," she said.

She turned to face the others, tugging a little at the hem of her loose-flowing, purple-print blouse. "No. I would not want to harm one whisker on his little face." She then tightened her mouth in staunch determination. "But I don't need him stealing my stuff, either."

"Then put your stuff out of his reach," Max scolded good naturedly, his brown eyes twinkling under heavy, dark brows.

Margaret raised her arms. "And where is that? Where is, 'out of his reach,' pray tell?"

Max looked across the table at Savannah. "Good question. Do you have an answer?"

She addressed her aunt: "Sure, inside a closet or one of the rooms where you changed those lever door handles to knobs. He could certainly open the lever-handled doors, but not those with knobs."

"We'll have to build a closet just for women's purses," Michael joked.

Margaret, who had finished making the coffee, took her seat. She looked over at Michael. "Speaking of your projects, how's the renovation going?"

"Good. I'm really enjoying the work." He smiled. "This place is a tinkerer's dream house."

She leaned forward and looked squarely in his eyes. "Now tell me, have you found anything… well, unusual while tearing out walls and floors and such?"

He narrowed his eyes. "Um, no." And then he chuckled. "Like what? Pirates' gold or a lost Rembrandt?"

"Noooo, maybe something sinister."

"Sinister?" the trio repeated.

"In what way?" Michael asked. "Dead body?"

"Been there, done that," Margaret quipped with a shudder, remembering the day she found Marvin Byrd's body in an upstairs bedroom of the old Forster home—her former home. "No, let's don't go there. No more dead bodies. No, Michael, from what I hear tell, it's something a tad more… let's say…eerie."

"A ghost?" Savannah asked. Her face lit up. "Auntie did you sell us a haunted house? How cool is that?"

"No, I don't think it's haunted—unless old Jed Forster is still around." Margaret thought for a moment and then smiled, her brown eyes sparkling under dark-brown bangs. "But his spirit would be gentle. He would fit in nicely with the two of you."

"Well, I don't want anyone else living here with us and peering in on our private life," Michael said emphatically.

"The house isn't haunted, Michael," Margaret insisted.

"Then what?" he asked.

"To tell you the truth…"

"Helllloooooo, anyone here? Michael? Savannah?"

"Oh, it's Iris," Savannah said, rising carefully from her chair and hobbling toward the living room. She saw Iris peering through the open door and called out, "Come in, girlfriend."

Iris stepped inside and closed the door. She looked at Savannah, concern on her face. "I heard about the…trouble and came to see if you two are okay." She glanced around behind Savannah. "Where's Michael?"

"He's right in here." Savannah grabbed Iris's arm and began leading her along. "Come on in; have some cobbler with us."

Iris stopped. "Just a minute, let me find a spot for my purse—somewhere away from that thieving cat of yours." She laughed.

Savannah shook her head, grinning slightly as Iris reached up and tucked her large purse into a space on a bookshelf. Just then, Iris felt something against her leg. She looked down, a few curly wisps of red hair bouncing alongside her face. "Hi there, Lexie. How are you, girl?" She stooped over and ruffled the dog's fawn-colored fur before entering the kitchen.

Michael stood. "Hi Iris. Have a seat—join us."

Margaret reached out for Iris's hand and the two former graduates of the Hammond High School class of 1973 greeted one another warmly. Iris patted Max on the shoulder. "Hi there, Max. Good to see you." After sitting down in the chair Michael had pulled out for her, Iris looked over at Michael and Savannah, scrutinizing them carefully, and then frowned. "So how are you two? Sounds like you had an awful situation at the clinic this morning."

"How did you hear about it already?" Savannah asked.

"Craig told me."

"Oh yes, your honey. We can't keep anything from you anymore since you're dating Detective Craig Sledge." Michael laughed.

"You were going to keep this from me? Why?" Iris looked hurt.

"Noooo." Savannah slapped her hand in the air in front of her. "He's delusional." She leaned toward Iris and whispered loudly, "…got a wallop on the head, you know."

Iris looked over at Michael again and noticed the purple swelling on the side of his face. "Oh Michael, you look like you took a beating. How are you feeling?"

He grimaced slightly, took a deep breath, and coughed. "Not too bad—a little sore here and there."

"I would imagine." Her eyes darted from Michael to Savannah. "So what happened?"

The couple repeated the details of the story once again.

"What does the doctor say?" she asked.

"Just to take it easy, use icepacks—general stuff like that," Michael said. "Oh honey, you'd better get that pack on your knee."

"Your knee?" Iris looked over at Savannah.

"Yes, Iris," Margaret said—her voice accelerated, "he hit Savannah, too and knocked her down. She has a messed-up knee."

"My God!" Iris exclaimed, looking down at Savannah's legs. "He attacked you, too?"

"He pushed me, that's all."

Iris sat up straight, revealing a hint of black lace from beneath the low neckline of her fitted green and black blouse. "That's assault, kiddo."

"Oh I forgot, you know the lingo now," Savannah said as she started to stand up. "Ouch." She grimaced, reaching down and cupping her hand over her knee.

Margaret quickly stood. "Sit down, Vannie. I'll serve the cobbler."

Iris joined Margaret at the kitchen counter. "Here, Maggie, let me get those," Iris said when she saw her struggling to reach the dessert plates.

"Thanks, Iris. Everything in this house is organized for giants. I need a stepstool or stilts to get anything out of these cabinets." Margaret glanced over at her husband and said, "I'm trying to train Max to store everyday things we need for the shelter cats where I can reach them."

"Or you could just grow, or wear platform shoes," Savannah quipped.

Margaret smirked in her niece's direction. "Spoken by the only Brannon to get the tall genes."

Once the cobbler was served and the coffee poured, Michael asked Iris, "So is Craig on the case?"

"He didn't say." She took a sip of coffee, looked down at her dessert, and shook her head. "This is an awful thing to have happened. I was so scared for you two when I heard about it." Tears filled her eyes.

"We're okay, Iris," Savannah said, setting her fork down and patting her friend's arm. "Thanks for caring."

"Iris, what do you hear from Damon?" Margaret asked. "Is he getting along okay?"

Still dabbing at her carefully made-up eyes, Iris said, "It seems so. He's over at the state prison. Craig thinks he may get out early." Her eyes brightened a little. "We can visit."

"You visit that place?" Margaret scrunched up her face. "I've never set foot in a prison or jail. It must be dreary and drab. And then there are all of those…criminals." She shuddered.

"It's not my favorite place to spend a Sunday afternoon; that's for sure," Iris agreed. She took a bite of her cobbler, swallowed, and said, "But they do have a grassy area with picnic tables where you can visit. So it's not too bad." She looked off into space for a moment. "If I want my son back, it's something I have to do." She glanced over at Margaret. "You know, Maggie, Damon and I get along better when he's in jail than any other time. It's almost like the relationship we had when he was twelve. You remember those days, don't you? He was a cool kid. Things didn't go bad until he was in his senior year at high school." She became sullen for a moment. And then she smiled. "He's a very different young man when he's not with those so called friends of his."

Margaret shook her head in disgust. "Iris, my dear, you can't blame his friends. He made his own decision to do drugs. It was the drugs making him so difficult, don't you know that?"

Iris lowered her eyes. "Yeah, you're right, Maggie." She looked up and said, "They tell us at Al-Anon that we have to fight going into denial. I've been in denial for much too long." Smiling brightly, she said, "Craig is really helping me change my thoughts—my way of thinking." She became serious for a moment. "Makes a big difference. It really does."

"That's cool, Iris," Max said, while scooping up more of the dessert with his spoon. "Sounds like you and Damon are turning over a new leaf."

"Yes," she said, glancing around the table, "and the relationship between the younger boys and

Damon is getting better, too. You know, Damon was eleven when I married the boys' father. Chris and Brett were just toddlers. Damon was rather fond of his new little brothers at first, especially Brett. It wasn't long after that two-timing man left me and his sons that Damon started getting into trouble and things went sour with him and the younger boys." She stared off into space for a moment and then said, "As you know, his lifestyle affected all of us." Her bright-red lips curved into a smile, revealing her carefully whitened teeth. "Now he and Brett write back and forth—real letters—no cell phones or texting for prisoners. And the boys go there with me to visit sometimes."

"How long were you married to Jack Clampton…four or five years?" Margaret asked.

Iris frowned, narrowed her eyes. "Five miserable years. Damon was nearly seventeen when he left, and Chris and Brett were seven and eight." She hesitated. A grin washed over her attractive face. "Craig is working with Damon."

"Really?" Michael set his fork down and wiped his mouth with his napkin.

"Yes. He visits him alone, you know, using special cop privileges, and he's helping him to work a drug program right there in the prison. It's a sort of all-around confidence-building, distraction sort of technique he's using. It's a healing program and it also involves creativity. I had no idea how important creativity is to a human being." She paused before sharing, "Did you know that Damon has an interest in writing? He's been writing poetry and short stories. Says it makes him feel real good when he's writing." She leaned back in her chair, holding her hands palm-up in front of her. "Who knew?"

Michael smiled across at Iris. "That's really great news."

Margaret shook her head, a pensive look on her face. "Iris, I still can't believe you're dating the cop who was going to arrest you for murder last year."

"Yeah," Iris let out a forced laugh. "I've met some interesting men in some interesting ways, but this was definitely a first for me." She took a sip of coffee before adding, "And something new for Craig, too."

Savannah leaned forward in her chair and addressed her friend, "Iris, you do believe in fate, don't you? I mean, how else would the universe have put the two of you together unless you were a suspect of some sort?"

She scoffed. "Hell, kiddo, I can think of a lot of ways—he could be a customer at the diner, he could save me from a pickpocket, he could be having a drink at a local club when I walk in, he could come to the boys' school and talk about police work…" She took a breath, her perfectly made-up eyes flashing with mischief. "He could run out of gas in front of my house, bump into me in the produce aisle at the grocery store, come to my door selling tickets to the policemen's ball…"

"Be serious, Iris," Margaret scolded. "Things never happen the way we expect. Look at me and Max. He came all the way from Chicago, moved in next door, and started a cat-rescue shelter."

Max straightened his posture. "Yeah, and you wouldn't give me the time of day until I rescued you from that relative of yours."

"Well, I was waiting for you to come riding in on a white horse," she said, faking innocence. Before her husband could respond, Margaret continued, "And look at Savannah and Michael. I broke my foot so Savannah would get her cute little butt up here and start kanoodling with our handsome veterinarian."

"Kanoodling? Auntie, that sounds vulgar," Savannah complained amidst a kitchen lively with laughter.

Margaret tilted her head, a wily grin on her lips. "Wellll?"

"Yeah, Auntie," Savannah said, smiling briefly at her handsome husband, "I guess it was fortuitous that you broke your foot and that I came to help you out. How else would Michael and I have found each other—with me down in LA and him up here in Northern California?"

"Wait," Michael said, frowning, "are you telling me this was some sort of conspiracy? I thought it was my idea to fall for my beautiful wife." He looked suspiciously at Savannah. "You tricked me?"

Savannah reached out and slapped playfully at Michael.

"Ouch, that hurt. Be careful, I was injured fighting for your honor, you know." He pretended to sulk.

"I'm sorry, honey. Kiss kiss," she said as everyone laughed.

Michael grinned. "Finally, I get some sympathy.

***

The Monday evening headlines of the small-town *Hammond Daily* screamed, "Veterinarian Brutally Beaten by Dead Dog's Owner."

Savannah heard the front door open and close. "Where are you?" Michael called out.

"Kitchen!"

"Did you see the paper tonight, hon?" he asked as he approached her. He slapped it down on the kitchen table. "It looks like Gamble's out on bail."

"Yeah, I saw it," Savannah said somberly, turning away from the counter to face her husband. "My cell phone has been ringing like crazy all afternoon."

He lowered his brow. "Why? Who's been calling?"

"Well-wishers mostly. You know, our friends."

With a sigh of relief he said, "Oh, I thought maybe it was clients concerned about their pets."

"Noooo, Michael." She walked over and put her arms around his neck in a hug. Pulling back a little so she could look at him, she asked, "You don't think this is going to scare people away, do you? No one's going to believe you were negligent. You have a great reputation in this town, honey."

"Savannah," he said taking a deep breath, "it can take years to build a good reputation and a few minutes to ruin it." He released her hands from around his neck, squeezed them, and turned away.

"But you did nothing wrong."

"I hope I didn't make a mistake with that dog." He stood leaning with his hands on the back of a kitchen chair, his head down.

"Of course, you didn't."

He turned toward her. "It doesn't really matter what did or didn't happen; an accusation like this can be damaging." He paused and then began to tear up. "I'm worried about our practice."

"This really does have you shook up. I'm so sorry it happened. But I don't think we should go through life with such heavy regret that it interferes with living."

Michael lowered himself into the chair and put his head in his hands. Savannah looked down at him with sadness in her heart. *How can I help this man?* she wondered. *I just hate to see him so beaten down.* Finally, she said, "Michael, don't let one unreasonable jerk spoil even one minute of your life. Sure, you feel badly about losing the dog. This is every veterinarian's nightmare and one that we all must live through more times than we care to think about. Losing Brute is something you will need to come to terms with. And you will. You've had situations like this before. You grieve, you try to figure out what happened so it never happens again, and you move on. The equation that's in the way for you now is that horrible, unbalanced man. His opinion is wrong! His opinion doesn't count. You can't take it seriously. You can't take him seriously."

Savannah moved around and stood in front of her husband. "Michael, look at me. You didn't do anything wrong. The guy's off his rocker. No one's going to believe what he says against you—you have loyal clients who have trusted you for a long time."

"Yeah, I know. I guess I'm overwrought and overreacting." He put his arms around her and pulled her onto his lap. "What would I do without you?" he asked into her hair.

She chuckled. "Sure wouldn't want to find that out."

"Neither would I."

They held each other for a while and then Savannah pulled back and said, "Now, I have good news."

He took a deep breath…coughed a little. "I could use a dose of that. What is it?"

She smiled. Using her most enticing tone, she said, "Adam's coming this weekend."

Michael perked up immediately, his eyes bright; a smile on his face. "Really?" And then he cocked his head and asked, "Why? I thought they were bringing him over next week."

"Marci called to ask how we are. One thing led to another and we decided you could use some cheering up." Her ever-so-slight frown lines suddenly became obvious. "Adam heard his parents talking about what happened and got concerned about us." Her face brightened as she explained, "Marci and Eric thought it would be good for him to see you, if you're up to it."

"Up to it! Gosh, that would make my day—my weekend—my whole week." The couple stood and he hugged her to him. "Thank you," he whispered.

"What for?"

He held her at arm's length and looked deeply into her eyes. "For being my wife, for loving my son, for getting along so well with Marci, for caring so much about me." He wrapped his arms around her again and said, "For being you. I love you, Savannah."

"I love you, too Michael. And thank *you.*"

"For what?"

She choked up a little. "For saying all those nice things to me." Gaining her composure, Savannah turned to her husband and asked, "Are you hungry? I put together a nice chopped salad and I can make some cheesy toast points or heat up some soup to go with it."

"The salad sounds fine. I don't know about you, but I'm pretty tired tonight. I'd like to eat light and go to bed early."

"Sounds good to me."

"Meow. Meow. Meeeooowwww."

The couple looked over in time to see Rags pacing back and forth on the perch Michael had installed for the cats so they could view the out-of-doors through the large kitchen window.

"What's wrong with him?" Michael asked.

"I don't know. Something outside has his interest." She started to walk toward him to look out the window when he scampered down the kitty staircase and darted into the dining room, through to the living room. Savannah followed him. "What is it, Rags? Did you see a critter?"

When she caught up with the cat, he was standing next to the front door in the living room, his front paws on the small sill. He seemed to be trying to peer out through the stained glass window. Savannah could hear a low growl coming from him. "Rag's, what's wrong?" Then she called out, "Michael, something's wrong!"

Unbeknownst to Savannah, Michael was right behind her. He had also observed the cat's odd behavior and he opened the front door and stepped out onto the porch. Suddenly Savannah heard her husband yelling, "Let her go!" He then shouted, "Savannah, call the sheriff! Call the sheriff!"

She quickly followed Michael out through the door while dialing 9-1-1 on her cell phone. She didn't know what the emergency was until she looked up and saw someone carrying Lexie down their long driveway toward the highway. She felt as if her heart jumped up into her throat as she watched Michael run after the person who was sprinting away, his arms wrapped tightly around the thirty-five pound dog.

"Let her go! Let her go!" Michael called.

Upon hearing Michael's voice, Lexie began squirming and flailing her legs, making it difficult for the person to hold onto her. Finally, the dognapper tripped and fell, losing his grip on the dog. Lexie hit the ground hard. She yelped and then jumped to her feet and ran as fast as she could toward Michael. "Call Lexie!!" Michael shouted as he continued his pursuit.

"Come, Lexie! Come!" Savannah yelled, leaning over and slapping her right thigh with her free hand. She was just finishing up with the 9-1-1 operator when she saw Lexie slow toward Michael. The dog spotted Savannah and rushed past him to her. "Good girl, Lexie," Savannah said as she pocketed her phone, lowered herself to the porch step and began petting and hugging the dog. Lexie wriggled and licked at Savannah, obviously happy to be safe. But the dog didn't have Savannah's entire attention. Her eyes were on Michael, who was still chasing the person they'd seen running away with their dog.

Not again, she thought. *Please God, don't let him get hurt.*

Michael was gaining on the sprinter. But just before he could get his hands on him, the would-be thief jumped into a waiting car. The passenger door slammed shut, and the driver drove off, spraying gravel up at Michael. He rubbed his eyes as he walked back to the house.

Savannah headed out toward him, Lexie at her side. "Who was it, Michael? Why did he have Lexie?"

"I don't know." Michael shook his head; he was breathing hard. "I don't know who it was, but I'll bet," he said with venom in his voice and gasping for breath, "it was Pete Gamble. An eye for an eye. That's about his speed, the jerk." He then turned to Savannah and asked, while still trying to catch his breath, "How did he get his hands on her?"

"I let her out in the pen this afternoon not too long before you came home. I forgot about her." She grimaced. "Gads, how could this happen?"

"It's not your fault. We leave her in that pen all the time. There's never been a problem before." He reached down and ruffled the dog's fur. "Come on, Lexie, let's go in and get your supper." The dog danced alongside the couple as they walked toward the house.

"I just hate this," Savannah said, her eyes filling with tears. "Now our animals are in danger." She momentarily took her eyes off the ground in front of her and looked toward the porch. Her limp-along pace suddenly quickened. "Oh no you guys don't."

Michael's eyes followed hers and he, too, began walking faster. There, sitting on the top step, were Rags and Walter. Buffy was standing in the open doorway. "Come on kitties," Savannah said, "the excitement's over. Everyone inside where it's safe." She looked over at Michael. "At least I hope it's safe for them. Oh Michael, now I *am* scared."

"I'm flat-out angry," he said, his face still red from exertion and emotion.

Savannah put her hand on his arm. "And you're supposed to be taking it easy."

"Would you rather they got away with Lexie?" he snapped.

"Of course not, Michael. I'm sorry." She held her breath in an attempt to stop the tears she felt welling up. It was too late. She was too frightened. The tears spilled over and flowed freely down her cheeks.

Michael promptly turned away, rubbed both hands through his hair, and said, "I didn't mean that, honey. I'm sorry. I'm going to take a shower. Maybe I'll feel better about things. Just keep the doors locked and the animals in." He started down the hallway and then stopped. "Gotta feed the mare. I'll do it, hon. I don't want you going out there by yourself this evening."

Savannah followed Michael into the kitchen and watched him leave through the side door. That's when she remembered she hadn't fed the cats. She grabbed a paper towel and dabbed at her eyes while murmuring an apology to them. After filling the cats' bowls, she placed them on their mats and stared down at them for a moment as each cat engaged in their individual methods of approaching their food. Suddenly, she noticed that Lexie was also watching them. "Oh, you're hungry too, aren't you, girl?" She picked up the dog's bowl and began preparing her supper.

Knock, knock.

Someone's at the door, Savannah thought. She glanced out through the window. She could still see Michael in the dimness of dusk as he closed the tack room door and headed toward the house. She placed Lexie's food dish on the floor and then waited for Michael to walk into the kitchen. "Someone's at the door, Michael."

A look of apprehension crossed his face and he headed boldly toward the living room. He peered through the stained glass side panels and saw a blurred shape. He asked, "Who is it?"

"Craig Sledge."

Michael swung the door open wide and invited the detective inside.

"It's Craig," Michael called out to Savannah, unaware that she had followed him to the door and was standing right behind him.

"I can see that," she said, an impish smile dancing momentarily at her lips.

"Oh," he said, jumping a little. "I didn't know you were there."

"Sneakin' up on you, is she, Michael?" Craig laughed.

"Yeah, she does that." He then looked over at the detective, motioned for him to come inside and asked, "What brings you out here?"

"I hear you had a problem just now," Craig said as he entered the room.

Michael looked puzzled. "Oh yes, Savannah called. I didn't expect *you* to answer the call personally. They don't usually dispatch you, do they? But then I guess nothing is kept secret from you."

"Not if you're gonna to flirt with the law." He laughed. Then furrowing his brow, he asked, "So what happened?"

Michael gestured toward a chair. "Here, Craig, sit down."

Once they were seated, Savannah looked over and saw Lexie cautiously entering the room. "Come here, girl, it's okay." The dog walked slowly toward her and sat down, resting her chin in Savannah's lap.

Michael reached over and petted the dog before saying, "Someone tried to take Lexie."

"Lexie?"

"Our dog," he said, motioning in her direction. "I chased him down and he dropped her, thank heavens."

After Michael told the story, Craig asked, "Did you get a plate number?"

"No," Michael said, lowering his head. "I was just so focused on getting our dog, and then I went for the guy. Didn't look at the license plate. Damn, should have done that. I can tell you the car was a small, dark-colored, four-door, like maybe a Toyota or Nissan—an older model. It had tinted windows—at least the one in back. I couldn't see inside."

"Do you have a description of the guy who took the dog?" Craig asked.

Michael grimaced and shook his head. "I'm not even sure it was a guy. He was wearing a dark knit beanie down low on his head…I guess jeans and a sweatshirt. Yeah, a hooded sweatshirt, black or dark blue, maybe."

Craig addressed Savannah. "Is that pretty much what you saw?"

"Yes." She nodded.

"Come to think of it, I did notice some sort of emblem or writing on the back window." Michael thought about it for a moment, struggling to remember. Finally, he cocked his head and said, "You know, I think it might have been one of those memorials. I couldn't read what it said, but it looked like a lot of writing across the lower middle section of the back window…like with a name and date of the deceased."

"An 'in memory of' decal." Craig nodded. "You see a lot of those these days. You couldn't read the name, though?"

"No." Michael jumped to his feet and walked across the room in front of Savannah and Craig. He then turned toward Craig. "I'd bet that freak Gamble is behind this, don't you think?"

Craig nodded. "I wouldn't be surprised."

"But it sure has us spooked, as you can imagine." Michael walked back toward his chair. He thought for a moment and then sat down. "My son was coming for a visit this weekend, but you know what? I think I'd better tell him not to come. I just can't risk something happening to him…"

"Maybe Gamble will be in jail over the weekend. Would you feel safer?"

Michael's eyes lit up. "You can do that?"

Craig stood and moved toward the front door. He stopped and turned. "Possibly. I'll let you know if we find out the car belongs to him or that he had something to do with this. Don't change your plans yet, Michael. Let me see what I can do, first."

Michael reached out and shook the detective's hand enthusiastically. "Okay. Thanks, Craig."

Craig glanced over at the dog. "By the way, is the dog okay?"

"Seems to be," Michael said.

"Good." He started to exit, but then looked back at Michael. He scratched his head. "So where was the dog when this…person got his or her hands on it?"

"She was in the dog run in the backyard."

"You don't keep that locked?"

"She's not out there very often or for very long." Michael thought for a minute and then said, "I'm going to start locking that gate when she's in there—the horse corral, too."

Savannah stood and walked toward the men. "Rags saw the guy take her. He's the one who alerted us."

"Rags?" the detective repeated. "Oh, your cat. How did he…alert you?"

Michael responded. "He was looking out the window and started meowing and getting all upset. He must have seen the whole thing and he…well, he told us there was something wrong."

"He told you, huh?"

"Yes," Savannah said. "Animals have a lot to say if humans will only listen to them."

"No kiddin'?" Craig said, only partially hiding his skepticism. And then he let out a breath through pursed lips and added, "Your cat sure had a hand…er…a paw in solving our last big case, didn't he?"

"Sure did," Savannah agreed.

Craig started to turn toward the door again, but changed his mind. He looked from Michael to Savannah and said, "If we find out it was Gamble, you may want to get a restraining order against him."

"Good idea," Savannah said. "Honey, let's do that for sure."

Michael's face grew rigid. He looked down at his feet. "Yeah, what good does it do?"

"If he comes around, you can have him arrested. You don't want him anywhere near you or your property, do you?" Craig asked.

"Sure don't want him near me, my family, or my animals," Michael said defiantly. He then looked Craig in the eyes and said, "That reminds me; he wants his dog. I have him on ice. Can I arrange to get the dog back to him through a police escort or something?"

"Yeah, talk to Jim about that—I'm sure he'll arrange it for you."

***

"Gosh, I can't believe it's only Tuesday. A lot has happened these last few days," Savannah said while standing at the stove stirring a cream sauce.

"Yeah, too much. How's that knee feeling?" Michael asked.

She reached down and touched her left knee, then bent and flexed her leg a couple of times. "It's better, I guess. I think the swelling is down some."

"You probably aren't resting it as much as you should be," he said.

Savannah turned toward her husband. "Well, treating animals for a living isn't something you can do sitting down with your leg elevated." She creased her brow. "You aren't still having headaches, are you?"

"No. And the swelling in my face is going down. I guess we'll survive, babe."

"I'm counting on it. We have things to do and babies to welcome into the world."

"Babies?" Michael walked over to Savannah and repeated, "Babies?"

"Well, yeah." She tilted her head and raised her nicely arched eyebrows. Her highlighted hair draped over one shoulder. "You want babies, don't you?"

"Sure. You know I do, but I don't hear you bring it up much." He stared over at her for a moment. "Does this mean…"

She waved a hand in the air in front of her and shook her head. "It doesn't mean anything, Michael. Of course, I want children. But no, I'm not pregnant and I don't intend being pregnant anytime soon."

Michael sighed deeply and walked across the room. He turned back toward her, his voice deeper now. "When, Savannah?"

Savannah felt as though her heart was about to break. "Oh Michael, I'm sorry. I know how important having our child is to you. I didn't mean to..." She turned off the stove burner, walked over and wrapped her arms around his neck. "We've only been married for a few months."

"Nearly six months."

She pulled back and saw signs of brooding on his face. She ran her fingers through the straight hairs that stubbornly fall over one of his eyebrows. "Actually, honey, I was thinking about suggesting I stop the birth control sometime in the fall. What do you think?"

Michael's posture straightened and his face lit up. "Really, Savannah? Really? August? September? We could have a baby by this time next year."

He put his hands on her shoulders and looked into her eyes. "What do you say, Savannah? Shall we shoot for a spring or early summer baby?"

"Uh, well, I guess…" she started, when he bent down a little and kissed her hard on the lips.

She slid her hands up around the back of his neck and held him to her, kissing him back, gently at first and then passionately.

"Savannah, you make me so happy."

"This really does mean a lot to you, doesn't it, Michael?"

"It means everything to me, Savannah. You mean everything to me and to have a baby with you…" He choked up and didn't finish the sentence. They held each other tightly for several moments before Savannah pulled away with a gasp.

"What's the matter?"

She rushed toward the oven and began to laugh. "Can't you smell it? I just made Gladys Jordan bread." She yanked the oven door open and began fanning at the thin ribbon of smoke that wafted past her.

Michael looked puzzled. "Gladys Jordan bread?"

"Mom has this knack for burning bread when it's under the broiler. I guess I've inherited the curse." She laughed.

"So what are we having tonight, hon," he asked, "besides burned bread?"

"Creamed eggs and asparagus on…only slightly scorched English muffins. Sound yummy?"

"Sure does. Only…"

"Only what?" she turned to look at him.

"Only I've never had it before, but I'll try to like it."

"So what do you think?" Savannah asked after they'd been eating for a few minutes.

"It's pretty good. Creamed eggs, huh?"

She nodded.

"Yes, I like it."

Savannah scraped more of the burned parts off an English muffin and placed it on her plate. She ladled some of the egg sauce over it. "Michael I'm so glad you got that restraining order against Pete Gamble. I hope he follows it. Did you get his dog back to him?"

"Yes, he had a sheriff escort and Bud took care of things. They recommended I just stay out of the way."

"Good." She picked up her fork and cut through an asparagus spear. Before lifting the bite to her mouth, she said, "I'd rather see him in jail, though."

"All in good time, I imagine. I spoke with Sondra Blair and it looks as though he could go to trial sometime in October. Don't know why they drag these things out."

"Do you like Sondra as an attorney?"

"Yeah, I guess. Never had one before, except to help me when I established the clinic. I haven't seen her in action—you know in the courtroom—so it's hard to tell." He then looked intently at Savannah. "So far no leads on who tried to take Lexie."

Upon hearing her name, Lexie raised her head up off her paw and stared over at Michael from her bed near the kitchen door. When no one made any further gestures toward her, she settled back down and closed her eyes.

"I'm convinced that Pete Gamble had something to do with it, aren't you?"

"Sure am," Michael agreed while cutting a piece of English muffin and swirling it around in the creamed eggs on his plate.

***

The next morning, Savannah got up first. She was in the shower when Michael opened the frosted glass door. He peered in at her, an impish smile on his face. "Want company?"

"Why sure, sleepyhead." She reached out and pulled him to her.

Fifteen minutes later, Savannah was blow-drying her hair. "What an exhilarating shower," she said with a sigh.

"Sure was," Michael agreed, a wide grin on his face. He walked up behind her, reached around and started to untie the belt on her terry robe.

She pointed the dryer in his direction saying, "Don't even think about it, buddy. We've got to get to work."

"Awww, you're no fun." He walked into the bedroom and began to dress. He then returned to the bathroom wearing jeans and a lightweight flannel shirt. He looked over at Savannah, who was braiding her hair. "I'll go feed the herd—what do you want for breakfast?"

"Just yogurt and fruit. We still have blueberries and raspberries left, don't we?"

"I think so." He turned to leave the room, stopped, and added, "I think I'll have some of that creamy egg stuff we had last night."

"Cool. Then you did like it."

"Yeah."

"Michael," she called, "I'm going to take my own car today. I have to run a few errands after work." She stepped into the bedroom and asked, "By the way, did you hear a ruckus last night?"

Michael stopped and looked over at his wife. "No, what sort of ruckus?"

"A cat ruckus. Some cat—probably Rags—was upset about something. I heard his thunder paws racing around the house and he was meowing. Something had him upset."

"Nope, I didn't hear a thing. Maybe you dreamed it."

"Maybe, I guess. I really was sleepy, couldn't wake up enough to figure out what was going on. Next thing I knew, it was morning."

Savannah returned to the bathroom and finished primping in front of the mirror and then she headed in to straighten the bedroom and dress. She was pleasantly surprised to see that Michael had done a pretty good job of making the bed. She pulled a clean pair of jeans and a sweater out of the closet and quickly dressed. She was tying her sport shoes when Michael entered the bedroom. She took one look at his face and asked, "What's wrong?"

"I guess you weren't dreaming, after all."

"Huh?"

"Your cat *was* upset about something last night."

"Why? What happened?"

"Damn tires have been slashed."

Savannah frowned. "What tires?"

"Your car and my truck. All flat." He paced across the floor in front of Savannah, slammed his palms down on a chest of drawers on the other side of the room, and said, "Damn that Pete Gamble!"

Chapter Three

"So what do we do, Michael?" Savannah asked. "How do we get to work?"

"We get new tires. That's what we do. As far as getting to work, maybe we can borrow Maggie's or Max's car." He took his phone out of his pocket. "I'll call and ask."

Savannah picked up her phone off the bedside table, unplugged it, and called the sheriff's office. "Hi Ben, this is Savannah Ivey. I'd like to report vandalism. Yes. The tires on both of our vehicles have been flattened. No kidding. This *is* getting old. Okay, sir, we'll do that."

They hung up their phones at about the same time. Savannah spoke first, "Ben wants us to leave everything as it is until they can come out and look around. If they miss us here, they want one of us to come in and fill out a report."

"Okay. What's your schedule like today?"

"Not too bad. Why?"

Michael said, "Why don't you go with your aunt over to that car-rental place this morning and rent a car for us. When Ben or Jim gives us the go-ahead, I'll call and have the vehicles towed and arrange for the new tires." He shook his head and thinned his lips. "My tires were almost brand new and yours were in good shape."

"Isn't this covered under our insurance?" Savannah asked.

"Possibly, but then there's the deductible." He started to pace again and then he stopped and said, "Since it happened here, this might come under our homeowner's policy. Can you call and check on that? I'll take your patients this morning." He stopped and looked over at her as she picked up her jacket and scarf. "Anything I should know about your schedule?"

"No, I don't think so…oh wait, Edie's coming in with Sally. I was talking to her recently about a new treatment for cats with Sally's condition and she wanted to consider it. Do you know the one I mean?"

"Uh, yes. You showed me that case history you were reading. I actually prescribed the treatment for the Montgomerys' cat and he seems to be doing better. I'll talk to Edie about it and maybe we can start Sally on a low dose. Is that what you had in mind?"

"Yes—she's so fragile, we don't want to introduce her to anything too abruptly. But I do have a good feeling about this treatment, don't you?" Savannah asked.

He looked at his watch. "You'd better get some breakfast; your aunt will be here in twenty minutes. She's going to drop me off at the clinic before taking you to the car-rental place."

Michael followed Savannah into the living room. She walked over to one of the windows and looked out at their vehicles, which were parked in the circular driveway in front of the house. "Yup, flat," she said upon seeing the car and truck both sitting on their rims. She started to let the curtain drop into place when she pulled it back again. "What's that?"

"What?" Michael peered over her shoulder.

"There's something sticking in the front tire of your truck."

"Shoot, I didn't see that. I'll go look."

Savannah stepped out onto the porch and watched as her husband approached his veterinary truck. "Better not disturb it, Michael," she yelled. She watched as he squatted down and looked more closely at it. He then stood up, scratched his head and headed back up the porch steps.

"Well, what is it?"

He walked past her through the front door. "It's an ice pick sticking in the tire with a note attached." He turned to her, his face slightly contorted in anger. "It says, 'You will die, too.'"

Savannah put her hand to her mouth and gasped. "My gosh, Michael, what does this mean?"

"It means that we could be in some danger. Or, it's an empty threat." He paced the length of the living room, turned, and said, "Whatever it means, I don't like this. I don't like it one bit! I'm going to call the sheriff's office."

"Don't you remember, I told you I called and talked to Ben?"

Michael continued pacing. "That damn Pete Gamble," he snarled. "Hasn't he done enough damage?" He stopped in front of Savannah, looked over at her and ran his hand through his hair. "Why don't you go ahead to the clinic. I want to stay here and talk to Ben or Jim—whoever shows up. I'll hitch a ride over to get a rental car." He looked up at Savannah, who was clutching her hands to her chest, a look of terror on her face. "Oh, honey. I didn't mean to scare you," he said, walking toward her. He put his arms around her in a bear hug just as she started to cry. "It'll be all right, honey. I'm sorry if I scared you. It just makes me so mad, that's all. I feel so helpless." He put his hands on her shoulders and moved away, looking her in the eyes. "Now, you go eat something, will you? I don't want you to wilt away." He spun her around and gave her a nudge toward the kitchen.

She walked a few steps and then turned and looked at her husband. He motioned for her to go on and she disappeared into the kitchen.

***

Later the same day, Michael stepped into the lab where Savannah was viewing a set of x-rays. "Hi honey," he said hugging her from behind.

She placed her hands on his arms for a moment and then turned to ask, "How did things go today?"

"Ben and Jim came out and did an investigation. They hope to get prints off the ice pick, of course. They said they will question Pete, but they doubt they'll learn much. It would be hard to prove he was there, although they did find some tire tracks on the grass beside your car. And they took the note to see if they could find matching paper in his home or office. Whoever did this wasn't smart enough to use plain typing paper—oh no—they used paper with a logo. Part of the logo was visible."

"Let's hope he left behind some good clues. I'm ready for this nonsense to stop. He's really scaring me." Savannah reached over and turned off the light on the x-ray reader. She looked at her watch and said, "Ready to go home? It's nearly six."

"Yes."

She removed her lab coat and hung it up on a hook on the back of the door. "What are we driving today?" she asked.

"It's a surprise," he grinned. And then he added in a beguiling tone, "It has a seat warmer."

"Cool."

"No, warm," he joked. He reached into his jeans pocket. "My phone," he said as he pulled it out and put it up to his ear. "Hello?"

"Hello, Michael. Craig Sledge here. I hear you had more excitement over at your place."

"Yes Craig. We sure did have some excitement this morning—and not the happy kind.

Do you know how much tires cost these days?"

"Not really—and you need—what, eight of them?"

"Yes, all four on both cars."

"So how are you getting around—on Savannah's horse?" Craig chuckled.

"We have a rental car. Ours should be ready tomorrow."

"Where are you now?"

"At the clinic. We're just heading home, why?"

"I have some paperwork I'd like Savannah to sign. Can I come by—say in an hour and a half?"

"Okay, I think we can do that. Let me ask Savannah." He took the phone away from his ear. "Craig says he wants to talk to us. And you need to fill out a report. He said he can come by our house around 7:30."

Savannah nodded and he put the phone back up to his ear. "Yes, that's fine."

Savannah and Michael turned off the lights, locked up the clinic, and left through the back door, veering to the right toward the parking lot.

"Oh, this *is* a nice feature," Savannah said as the passenger-side seat of the rental car began to feel warm.

"Nice, huh? And look at this—it tells you the outside temperature, how much gas you're using, all sorts of things," Michael explained.

"It's only fifty-one degrees outside?" Savannah remarked. "Brrrr. Sometimes it's best not to know."

"Kind of chilly for this time of year, isn't it?"

Savannah let out a sigh. "Yeah, nothing's quite as it should be right now."

Michael tightened his lips—reached over and patted Savannah's knee. "Hey, was there anything you needed to do today that we can do now? You had planned to run some errands."

"Sure did. I'll have to do the banking tomorrow. I was going to get a few groceries, but I think we have eggs and bacon, if you don't mind breakfast for dinner."

Michael nodded. "Sure, that's fine. We never have time for that kind of breakfast for breakfast anymore, so why not for dinner?"

***

"Come on in, Craig. Savannah's just finishing up in the kitchen." Michael motioned for the detective to be seated. "So, any news?"

"Not much, I'm afraid. The prints on the pick are smudged. We did find tire marks in the grassy area, but they're pretty nondescript. Appears to be from a small car or pickup. And we didn't get a match for the paper used for the note—not yet, anyway." Craig looked past Michael, stood, and greeted Savannah with a nod as she walked into the room.

"Hi Craig," she said, walking over and hugging him briefly. She sat on the sofa next to a snoozing Walter. She ruffled his luxurious black fur while asking, "So have you traced any clues to Pete Gamble, yet?"

"Nothin' concrete." He pulled out a form from a folder and handed it to Savannah. "Here, do you want to sign the report?"

"Sure do."

After a few minutes of conversation, Craig yawned. "It's been a long day. I'd better go get somethin' to eat and head for bed."

"No date tonight?"

Craig laughed. "You know, I've discovered that dating is for the younger set. Iris and I do well to share a meal together once in a while at her house and then we fall asleep watching TV or listening to music. We're not very exciting."

"Yeah, you had all of the excitement together you two could stand when you were accusing her of murder." Savannah laughed.

Craig turned sullen. "Sure glad that case didn't go the way I expected it to. I would have missed out on the company of a wonderful woman."

"We tried to tell you that," she said. "Remember when you were trying to get us to say bad things about Iris?"

The detective creased his brow. "Oh, I wouldn't say that. I was just trying to get at the truth and, man, that striking redheaded woman sure seemed to fit the killer profile." A smile softened his face. "Like I said, I'm sure glad she wasn't our man…er…uh…you know what I mean."

Michael and Savannah laughed as they followed Craig toward the front door. "That wind is really blowing tonight," he said as he opened the door and stepped out.

Savannah wrapped her sweater tightly around her. "Oh, Michael, we'd better pick up the cushions off the porch furniture."

"Already did," Michael said with a big smile.

"My aren't you Johnny-on-the-spot," she remarked. "Good job."

***

"It sure howled last night, didn't it?" Savannah said as she brushed her hair in front of the bathroom mirror the next morning. "I had trouble sleeping. Kept hearing strange noises."

"Yeah. Sure was a strong wind. I wonder if we still have a horse out there," Michael quipped.

"Well, I'm sure she was cozy in the nice stall you built for her. Horses know to face away from the wind, anyway." She glanced over at her husband, who was shaving. "I can't tell you how many times I've seen that silly mare stand out in the rain, though. What's up with that?"

"Dun na."

Savannah twisted toward him. "What?" She laughed. "No wonder I couldn't understand you—your face gets all contorted when you shave—makes your speech unintelligible."

He rinsed his razor. "I said, 'Don't know.'"

"Oh, I thought you were asking for a donut or something."

"No, that was my shaving vocabulary. You never heard my shaving vocabulary?" He winked. "I have quite a rapport."

She laughed. "You mean repertoire." She pulled her blond highlighted hair back into a ponytail and said, "So you don't know why horses stand in the rain when they have a perfectly good shelter?"

"I think it's some innate response to the elements, I guess, going back to their origins."

Savannah stopped and stared over at him, hands on hips. "You just made that up."

"How do you know?" he asked playfully, wiping the excess shaving cream from his face.

"I know," she said. And then changing the subject, she suggested, "Hey, Michael, we have a light load at the clinic tomorrow, how about we drive over and pick up Adam in the afternoon when he gets out of school."

His eyes lit up. "Do you think Marci would agree?" He then looked over at her, a worried expression on his face. "What if…"

"Look, I know what you're going to say. Michael, we can't be absolutely sure about anything. But I do know that it would do you and that little boy a world of good to be together right now. I'm going to call Marci."

"Not this early, are you? It's only…" he looked at his watch. "It's not even 7:30."

"Yeah, I'd better wait a while."

"Great!" He smiled. He then frowned. "You know, we have to work Saturday morning."

"I know. Adam can either come hang out with us at the clinic or he can go over to Max's and Auntie's. You know how he loves helping them with their cats; and they have kittens now. Someone brought an abandoned litter to them a few days ago."

He ran his hand through his hair. "Yeah, I guess you're right. Is his room ready?"

"I think so. I put that horse-print bedspread on that we bought for his room. I hung the curtains. I cleaned up the sawdust. I think we're all set for our favorite little visitor, aren't we?"

"I guess so," Michael said hesitantly.

"Just relax, honey. It will be a good visit."

"Do we have enough toys in there?"

"Well, let's just go see."

"And we'd better go to the grocery store and get his favorite food," Michael suggested. He stopped midway up the staircase. "What is his favorite food, Savannah?"

"Never mind, Michael. I'll take care of the food situation. I think we ought to stop for dinner on our way home tomorrow evening. We can go to that chicken place that has kids' meals. He likes that. He also likes hotdogs on a stick and hamburgers. Oh, he ate two helpings of my Texas hash last time he was here and he loves Jello. I'll make him lots of Jello."

"And mac and cheese," Michael added as they walked through the door into Adam's newly renovated bedroom.

"That's right," Savannah agreed. "I still have some of that crunchy cereal he likes and we can make Mickey Mouse pancakes."

Michael's face lit up. "No, remember, he wanted *horse* pancakes last time."

"Oh yeah," she said with a laugh. Then she frowned as she recalled, "It wasn't easy making pancakes into a horse shape."

Michael laughed. "And after you made them, he didn't want to eat the horse." In a more serious tone, he added, "What a neat kid."

"He sure is," Savannah agreed. "You just gotta love him." She then thought of something else. "Bananas and carrots. Must have carrots."

Michael made a face. "Carrots? I don't remember him liking carrots."

"He doesn't, but he likes to feed them to Peaches."

"That's right." He looked down to see which of their household pets was asking for attention. "Hi there, Rags," he said, reaching down and giving the cat a body rub.

Rags saw Savannah sitting on Adam's bed, one foot tucked under her, and he jumped up to join her. "So, what toys do we have here for him?" she asked while scratching the cat behind one ear. She grabbed the fur on both sides of his face, looked into his eyes and said, "Besides, you, Mr. Rags?"

Michael walked over and looked at the books and puzzles stacked neatly on the wall shelf. He pulled out a drawer on a low chest and appeared to be taking inventory of the coloring books, crayons, and marking pens inside. He noticed a plastic box sitting in the middle of a child-size table off to the side, full of colored paper, pencils, plastic shapes, safety scissors, and other craft items. "Where's his train set?" he asked.

"You mean *your* train set." Savannah chuckled. "I'm convinced you enjoy that more than Adam does. He only plays with it to humor you."

Michael looked stunned. "No way."

"Yes, way. He'd rather play with that farm set Auntie and Max gave him with all of those horses, cows, stock trucks, and stuff."

"Where's that?"

"Right up in the closet with the train set and race-car set." She smiled. "I have a surprise for him this time. I borrowed a child-size saddle from Bonnie. I tried it and it fits Peaches—just barely."

"He'll love that," Michael said. He then turned abruptly and grabbed at Rags as he ran past him and out the door toward the staircase. "Uh-oh, what's he got?"

Savannah was busy wiping the carpet with a tissue and didn't see her cat make his rapid exit. "What did it look like?" she asked.

"Um, not sure." He looked down at the spot on the carpet. "What happened there?"

"One of the cats urfed up a fur ball." She stood, deposited the tissue in a waste basket, and said, "I'll go see what Rags has."

Michael walked out of the room behind her and they headed down the stairs. Rags had dropped his treasure at the bottom of the staircase. When he saw the couple moving toward him, however, he grabbed it and took off down the hallway, waking a sleeping Lexie along the way. The dog jumped to her feet and took off after Rags.

"I think he went into our room," Michael said. Sure enough, the couple found him sitting in their bathtub staring up at them. Lexie pranced excitedly around the room, looking at the cat and then up at the couple.

"What *is* that?" Michael asked, looking down at the item lying in front of Rags.

Savannah took a closer look. "Oh no. It's what's left of the beanbag Adam made for your birthday. Darn it, Rags," she scolded as she reached in and picked up the empty pouch Adam had decorated with his indelible marking pens. "Pretend you didn't see it. I'll fix it up so Adam won't know Rags tore it open." She looked over at the cat, who had his front paws on the edge of the tub, his eye on the contraband. "No, you can't have this, Rags," she said sternly. She looked down at the piece of cloth and asked no one in particular, "I wonder what he did with the beans?"

"He made me something for my birthday?" Michael said. "That is so cool." He wiped at his eyes with his palms. "My first gift from my son."

"It's not yours yet. You have to wait until your birthday."

"When is my birthday?" he asked.

She turned to face him. "You don't know when your birthday is? What, were you raised by wolves?" She laughed.

"Well, I know it's June twentieth, but when is that—what is today's date?

She thought for a moment before saying, "Gosh, it's already the fourteenth."

"Yeah, that's what I thought. Close enough. Let's have birthday cake…and a party."

She looked at him for a moment before saying, "Yeah, we could do that."

"I mean just you, me, and Adam—nothing big. A small celebration."

"Sure—then I'd better go fix the gift he worked so hard on so he can wrap it for you when he gets here."

***

Saturday morning came on the heels of a busy Friday. "Good morning, Adam. How'd you sleep, buddy?" Michael asked, ruffling the boy's stick-straight dark-brown hair as he walked past him.

"Good. I like my new room, Dad. It's rad."

"I'm glad you like it. What's that you're drinking?"

"Orange juice and lemonade."

Michael looked over at Savannah. "Orange juice and lemonade?"

She shrugged her shoulders. "That's what he wanted."

Michael chuckled. "And what are you having for breakfast?"

Adam smiled up at Michael. "Scramble' eggs and horse toast."

"Oh good. My favorite." Michael poured a cup of coffee and sat down across from his son. He glanced up at Savannah, who was standing at the counter beating two eggs in a bowl. "Scramble' eggs and horse toast for me, too."

"Savannah has a horse cutter," Adam said.

Michael looked askance. "A horse cutter?"

"A cookie cutter shaped like a horse," Savannah explained. She then said, "It's such a gorgeous morning, I thought maybe Rags would like to go out for a while. What do you guys think?"

"Yeah," Adam said, excitement in his voice. "Can I put his harness on him?"

"Sure."

"And hold his strap?"

"The leash? Sure can."

"Rad," the boy said before picking up his horse-shaped toast and spreading it with apple butter. "Hey, horses like apples, so I'm putting apple butter on my horse toast."

Michael laughed. "Good idea. Me, too."

After helping Savannah put the dishes in the dishwasher, Adam went in search of Rags. Michael and Savannah heard him calling throughout the house, "Rags, time to go outside. Here Rags." As he walked, he shook the cat harness, making the fasteners jingle. Soon he returned to the kitchen, a downtrodden look on his face. "I can't find him. Where is he?"

A knowing smile passed between Michael and Savannah. "Well, buddy," Michael said, squatting down so he was at eye level with his son. "Rags doesn't really like his harness all that much. He'll wear it, but he would rather go outside without it. So I think he knows you have the harness there and he's probably hiding from you."

Adam looked down at the harness." Oh," he said, "then I'll leave it here and go look for him again."

"Good idea."

Adam walked out of the room calling, "Rags, I don't have the harness anymore. Come here, Rags. Wanna go outside? See, I don't have your harness." Within a few seconds, they heard Adam exclaim, "There you are, Rags! Come on, boy."

"I found him," he announced as he walked into the kitchen struggling to hold the cat in his arms. Savannah couldn't help but notice that Rags's feet were almost dragging on the floor. "Whew," Adam said, upon releasing the cat, "he's heavy!"

"Yes, he is." Savannah laughed.

"Now, can I put the harness on him?" Adam asked with enthusiasm.

"Let me hold him for you," Michael offered. He picked up the cat and placed him on his lap.

"Okay, now, buddy. Let's get him dressed."

"Get him dressed…" Adam repeated with a chuckle. "That's funny, Dad."

Once outside, the threesome watched as Rags explored through the tall grass and random bushes, jumped in the air after grasshoppers and batted at butterflies. Suddenly, Rags stopped. He seemed to be looking at something in front of him. He crouched into a typical cat's stalking pose and stared ahead. With Adam right behind him holding onto the long tether, he took a few steps forward, carefully, slowly.

"What does he see?" Savannah asked.

Adam looked over at the clump of grass in front of the cat. "I don't know—maybe something's hiding in the weeds."

Suddenly, the cat leaped high into the air and landed on a clump. He began pawing at the grass and rolling around in it.

"What is that he has?" Michael asked.

Adam walked over closer to the cat, looked down. "It's just a piece of paper. That's all." He reached over and took it from Rags. "See?" He held it up to show Savannah and Michael, who both laughed upon seeing Rags stretching and pawing in an attempt to take his "catch" away from Adam.

"Wait!" Michael shouted.

Adam turned quickly, a somber look on his face. "What?" he asked as if he'd been caught doing something wrong.

"It's okay, son. I just want to get a look at Rags's treasure. Savannah," he said after studying the slip of paper briefly. "This looks like it was torn from that piece of paper with the note on it. Take a look at it." He held it up for her to see.

"Gamble Pet Supply," she read out loud. "Well, I'll be. And you think this could be the missing piece from that note?"

“Yes. Call Craig, will you? And then we’d better get going to work.” Michael looked over where Adam sat on the grass, Rags right next to him, both staring back at him—as if waiting to get the treasure back.

“Adam, do you want to go to work with us or help over at Aunt Maggie’s and Max’s place this morning?”

“Can Lexie go with us to work?”

“Sure.”

“Then I want to go with you guys.”

“Cool.”

Chapter Four

"It's a perfect match," Craig announced that evening when he called. "So you found it in the backyard?" he asked Savannah.

"Yes. Well, the cat found it."

Craig chuckled. "Oh yes, the cat." He then asked, "How do you suppose it ended up back there? Weren't your cars parked in front of the house?"

"Yes. But remember, we had that big wind."

"Yeah, right."

"So what happens now, Craig? Can you arrest him? Is it enough evidence?"

"Well, I'd like to have a match on that car you saw the day they tried to take your dog. There's nothin' registered to Gamble matching that description. We can certainly bring him in for questioning about the vandalism and see if we can put him at the scene of the crime." He paused for a moment and then said, "We'll keep you posted, guys."

"Sure. Thanks, Craig."

Savannah rejoined Michael and Adam, who were going over one of Adam's school lessons. She smiled when she saw Buffy curled up next to the boy. He had a pencil in one hand and was gently petting the little Himalayan-mix cat with the other. "I still can't believe they give so much homework in third grade," she said.

"Yes, times have changed, haven't they?" Michael looked up at Savannah. "Everything cool with Craig?"

"Yes, it was a match and there will be some questioning," she said trying to relay the message to Michael without alerting Adam to any potential problems. "How much more homework do you two have?"

"After this page, no more!" Adam announced.

"Then after this page, how about we have a birthday party for your dad?"

***

"Happy Birthday to you, Happy Birthday to you…"

"Open my present. Open my present," Adam begged jumping up and down.

"Okay," Michael said with a wink in Savannah's direction. He then looked over at Adam. "Who wrapped this present, anyway?"

"I did!" the boy said excitedly. He glanced at Savannah, and added, "Well, I did most of it."

Savannah reached out and smoothed his hair. "You sure did, Adam. And you did a great job."

"I'll say," Michael agreed. "I never saw such a creative wrapping. Just look at all this tape." He smiled over at Adam. "Good job, buddy." He started to rip into the package and then looked up again. "Gonna need some help here."

"Okay, I can help," Adam said as he began tearing into the wrapping.

"What is this?" Michael asked enthusiastically.

"It's a beanbag game. I...er…Savannah and I made it for you."

"You made this?" Michael asked.

"Yes, I colored on the beanbags and filled them with beans." He looked at Savannah. "Savannah helped me sew them."

"This is great. I really like it." Michael looked up at Adam. "So the point of the game is to toss the beanbags, is that right?"

Adam reached over and pulled a folded piece of cloth from the wrapping that still lay across

Michael's lap. "Yes," he said. He unfolded the cloth and pointed to the circles, squares and triangles with numbers inside. "You throw the beanbags and get points!"

"Cool. This is super, Adam. I'm going to enjoy playing this game…a lot." He grinned over at his son. "Wanna play now?"

"Sure."

Savannah stood. "Why don't you boys go play in the living room while I dish up some cake and ice cream."

"Okaayyyy," Adam said, racing off toward the living room.

What a great kid, Savannah thought as she watched him scamper off with his father. *And to think that we've only known him for six months. I'm so glad his mother decided to tell Michael he had a son. And for her to bring him to our wedding; it just made our day that much more special. It's obvious that he was hungry to meet his real dad and Michael has been thrilled to get to know the boy. I love that Adam and I get along so well, too. We have great fun together. And the relationship is so easy between us.*

She cut three pieces of cake and began scooping the rainbow sherbet onto the plates. *I can't wait to give Michael my birthday gift. Michael is going to be so pleased. If only this awful problem with Pete Gamble would blow over and we can go on with our wonderful life together.*

"Who wants cake and ice cream?" Savannah asked as she entered the living room.

Adam jumped up from his spot on the floor next to Lexie. "I do! I do!" And then he said, "Hey, Savannah, I beat Dad. I had 175 points and he only had 70. That makes me the winner, huh, Dad?"

"It sure does, son. You're the best, my man." Michael's smile widened as he offered knuckles to his son.

After a few minutes, Adam asked, "Are you finished with your cake, Dad?"

"Almost, why?"

He leaned across Michael's knee. "Wanna play my beanbag game again?"

"*Your* beanbag game?"

Adam blushed. "I mean your beanbag game. Want to, Dad, huh?"

"Sure do," Michael said taking his last bite.

"I'll get it ready." In a few seconds, Adam asked, "Hey Dad, where's the other beanbag?"

"Well, it should be around here somewhere. Have you looked under the furniture? You chucked one under the sofa a while ago."

"I got it out. I found just one beanbag. We're missing one."

"Adam," Savannah said, "do you know where Rags's stash is?"

"Um, his toy box? Yeah."

"His toy box. Yes, that's a good name for it. I'll just bet if you go look, you'll find your beanbag in his toy box."

"Oh Rags…" he scolded as he dashed up the staircase. Within a few moments, Adam could be heard hollering, "Here it is!" He rounded the top of the staircase and started down the stairs. "Rags took it when we weren't looking. It was right up there in his toy box."

Everyone laughed. Adam walked over and handed Michael the beanbag, and then he looked up at Savannah, a slight frown on his face. "Why does he do that? Why does he take things that aren't his? Tiger doesn't do that."

Savannah stared into the boy's blue eyes. "That's a good question, Adam. Not very many cats do. Walter doesn't. Buffy doesn't. I don't think any of Uncle Max's and Aunt Maggie's kitties do it. There are just a very few cats in the whole world who take things that don't belong to them and hide them like Rags does." She leaned into Adam as if she was sharing a secret—her eyes glistened with intrigue. "Maybe…just maybe now…he's the ancestor of a cat that belonged to a pirate hundreds of years ago. It could be," she said, exaggerating her facial expressions, "that the pirate taught his cat to steal jewelry and gold coins from the wealthy people in the village. Just imagine Rags's great-great-great grandfather cat wearing an eye patch and carrying a loot bag."

Michael didn't even try to conceal the kick he was getting out of watching Adam, who was fully entranced by Savannah's story.

The boy's eyes were big as saucers. "Do you think he had a hook paw and a wooden leg?" Adam looked over at Rags, who had just entered the room. The cat spotted him and walked up to rub on his legs. The boy petted the cat affectionately. "How would you like to have a hook paw, Rags, and a patch over your eye?" He covered one of the cat's eyes with the beanbag he still held in his hand.

Michael piped up, "It could be that Rags just thinks certain things are way cool, like the beanbags you made, and he wants one."

Adam knelt down next to Rags, his demeanor now serious. He showed the cat the beanbag. "Rags, these are Dad's beanbags, not yours. They go to Dad's game. Now you leave them alone." Suddenly, his face brightened and he turned to Savannah. "Hey Savannah, maybe we could make a beanbag for Rags."

"Well now that's a nice idea. I think we should do that. How about tomorrow before church?

But now, I think you'd better get ready for bed."

"Awwww, already? But Dad was gonna play me another game of beanbag," he whined.

"Yeah," Michael whined.

"You two are something else," she said. "Okay, one more game and then how about a story and off to bed."

"Okay." Adam looked over at Savannah. "Would you tell me more stories about Rags great-great...great grandfather?"

"Sure, kiddo."

***

"Hey this is the church where I first saw you guys," Adam said, looking out the car window as they pulled into the parking lot.

"It sure is, buddy," Savannah said. "We come here sometimes on Sundays and we thought maybe you'd like to come here with us today before we drive you home."

"You mean to my other home. I have two homes. My home with my mom and other dad and my home with you and my real dad."

"That's right. You are one lucky boy." Michael reached back and gave him knuckles.

Adam opted to sit in the pew with his dad and stepmom rather than join the other children for youth Sunday school. After the services, the threesome walked out to the foyer toward the refreshment table, when they heard a familiar voice say, "Hi Thavanna. Hi Dr. Mike. Hi Adam."

Savannah turned. "Charlotte, Reba, good morning. How are you ladies?"

Charlotte smiled shyly at the greeting and stared over at Adam.

"Nice sermon, wasn't it?" Reba said. She leaned toward Savannah saying, "I think Pastor was speaking to me today."

"Oh no," Savannah said with a chuckle, "that message was for me."

Michael leaned into the conversation. "It was for all of us." He smiled. "A universal message."

Adam reached over and pulled on his dad's shirt sleeve. "Hey Dad, can Charlotte and I go get a cookie?"

"Oh, you already spotted the cookies, did you? Sure, if it's okay with her mom. Just stay right out there on the patio."

"Can you come with me?" he asked Charlotte.

The girl looked over at her mom. Reba smiled and nodded.

"Yeth," she said.

Adam took hold of her hand. "Okay, come on."

Savannah and Michael watched the children rush toward the refreshment table. At the same time, Reba turned and spoke to an elderly gentleman who was walking toward her.

"They let dog killers inside the church?"

"What?" Michael turned around quickly to see who the angry voice belonged to. There, standing in front of him was a pudgy, well-dressed woman in her mid-seventies. She stared intently at Michael with dark, deep-set eyes. She hissed, "You killed my son's dog, you miserable excuse for a veterinarian." She glanced over at Savannah, scowled, and then turned and walked away.

"What's wrong?" Reba asked as she returned to where the Iveys stood. "Has something happened?"

"Reba, do you know who that woman in the blue coat is?" Michael asked.

"That's Mrs. Gamble." She looked up at Michael. "Was she rude to you? Don't pay her no mind. She's always unhappy about something. She often has an insulting remark to make about someone's child. She has been rather cruel to Charlotte a time or two. What did she say to you, anyway?"

Michael and Savannah glanced at one another. He responded, "Oh nothing. Nothing of any importance." All he had on his mind now was gathering up his little family and leaving. "Adam; where's Adam?" He excused himself, took Savannah's hand, and led her toward the patio. He scanned the area quickly. When he didn't see the children, he started to panic. "Where is he?" he asked, his eyes darting back and forth.

"I hear him," Savannah said. "Sounds like he and Charlotte are having fun just on the other side of that table. Michael rushed over and saw the two of them sitting on a rock wall eating cookies and sipping punch.

"Hi, Dad," Adam called out when he spotted Michael and Savannah. He began to giggle. "Hey Dad, you shoulda seen it. A lizard just took a bite of Charlotte's cookie."

***

"What a super weekend," Savannah said as she and Michael drove home after delivering Adam to his mom and stepdad.

Michael reached for his wife's hand, looked over at her with a smile, and said, "It sure was. It sure was." He laughed a little. "I got a kick out of your conversation with Adam about Charlotte. It was cute when he asked you why she talks funny."

"Yeah, he said, 'she talks like a little kid, but she's a big kid.'" Savannah laughed.

"I thought you handled his question very well. He understood when you explained she has Down syndrome, since his little sister also has it."

"But Rose isn't saying words yet. Reba told me once that many people with Down syndrome have speech impediments because of the way their tongue is formed or the way they use their tongues."

"Interesting. I didn't know that."

The couple drove in silence for a while, each with their own thoughts, when Michael glanced over at Savannah briefly and asked, "How do you think the new girl, Alyce, will work out?"

"Oh, seems okay. Too early to tell, really," Savannah said. "She's been with us for…what… four days?"

"As long as she does a good job of

disinfecting pens and keeps our offices and waiting room clean, I'm happy," Michael said.

"Well, yes, but you want her to fit in with our office family, too," Savannah reminded him. "And it appears as though she's getting along with Bud and the gals in back okay. Scarlett seems okay with her, too, as far as I can tell."

Michael took a swig of water and set the bottle back down in the cup holder. "It's hard to replace someone like Cindy. She's a good worker and knows her job."

"She sure does. I'll miss her." Savannah sat quietly for a moment and then said, "It's really odd how Alyce came to us, don't you think? I mean we'd been interviewing for several weeks and had so few applicants. And then to have this girl just show up out of the blue when we were so close to making a decision…it seems almost too fortuitous."

"Yeah, it was odd the way it happened. But she lucked out—came in at the right time with what seem to be the right credentials."

***

The next morning as they prepared for work, Michael asked Savannah, "By the way, honey, do you think we should take the cats to the clinic this morning?"

"What?" Savannah asked, switching off the blow dryer.

"I think we should take the cats to the clinic."

She spun toward Michael. "Why? Are they sick?"

"No, but the termite people are coming today, remember?"

"Oh that's right." She faced the mirror again and looked at Michael's reflection. "I thought they worked without chemicals."

"Yes, but they'll be all over this house, in the attic, under the house, in all the rooms."

"Yeah, I guess we'd better not leave the cats here. What about Lexie?"

"We'll take her, too. The staff likes it when she comes to work."

"They sure do. Everyone spoils her with treats."

"You finish doing that foo-foo stuff you do to yourself and I'll go get the carriers ready and feed the gang. What do you want for breakfast?"

"I'll just fix a bowl of oatmeal and fruit. Want me to cook you some eggs?"

"No. I'm going to have one of those muffins you made."

***

"I feel kind of bad leaving the kitties behind tonight," Savannah said as she climbed into bed next to Michael. "But you're probably right, they'll be fine. They all seemed relaxed and contented in that big pen. How smart of you to build that community pen at the clinic—sort of reminiscent of Max's outdoor runs for his rescued cats."

Michael smiled. "Yeah, that's where I got the idea. They did have fun playing in that kitty playhouse didn't they, with all of the different levels and cubby holes to zip in and out of?"

"And Buffy was in her element with the hidey places," Savannah said, snuggling close to her husband, her head on his outstretched arm. "She likes to just observe from a safe place. Yeah, they'll be okay tonight. But I miss them."

"You were with them all day."

She rolled toward him. "Not the same; I was working. Only got to see them a couple of times." She laid her head back and looked up at the ceiling. "They seem to like the placement of that pen, too—lots of activity, people coming and going. Good location. You did remember to close off the outside area, didn't you?"

"Yes," Michael said. "I secured the kitty door. They're tucked in for the night. And Lexie has us all to herself. She seems to be enjoying that luxury, doesn't she?" Michael looked over at the dog, who was lying stretched out at the foot of their bed.

"She sure is—looks like she's going to sleep with us tonight unencumbered by the fur kids."

Well, good night, honey. I love you," he said, rolling over and kissing her on the neck and then the lips.

"I love you too, Michael," she said dreamily. They fell asleep in each other's arms, Lexie snoring quietly at their feet.

***

Brrrrrriiiing, Brrrrrrriiing.

Michael opened his eyes and squinted at the bedside clock. 5:50 a.m. He reached up and pulled the chain on the lamp, picked up his phone and, still sounding groggy from a good night's sleep, answered it. "Hello? Hey Bud, what's going on?" Michael quickly sat straight up. "Oh my gosh," he said. "Are you sure?" He kicked at the blankets to free his legs and swung them over the side of the bed. "Bud, have you called the police?" He stood and walked toward the bathroom. "I'll be right there."

A look of panic spread over Savannah's face. She rose up off her pillow. "What happened, Michael?"

He walked back toward her, stopping to grab his jeans off the chair where he had left them the night before. He rolled his head from side to side. "Unbelievable," he muttered.

"What?" she demanded. And then she asked, her voice shaky and shrill, "Are the cats okay?"

He stepped into his jeans and fastened them, then sat on the edge of the chair and slipped on the socks he'd worn the day before and his sport shoes. He stared into space, took a deep breath, and said, "Bud found a body at the clinic."

She was sitting up now. "What?" She threw the covers back and slid out of the bed. She looked down at her husband. "What kind of a body? Who?"

"I don't know. Bud…" He hesitated. "How could this be happening?" He finished tying his shoes and then stood and ran his fingers through his hair. "The sheriff's on the way. I've gotta get over there."

"I'm coming with you." Savannah raced into the bathroom and closed the door. When she returned, Michael was still standing in the middle of the room. She rushed over to the chest of drawers, grabbed a T-shirt and threw it at Michael. "Put this on," she said, peeling off her nightgown and pulling on a pair of jeans and a sweater. She looked over at her husband while slipping into her Uggs. "Michael, are you all right?"

"No," he said moving his head back and forth slowly. "No, I'm not all right. Someone is lying dead in our clinic."

Chapter Five

"My gosh, there are a lot of cop cars," Savannah remarked as they turned the corner toward the clinic. A synchronicity of red and blue lights flashed against the building, silhouetting the array of uniformed officers who had congregated in the large parking lot. A few neighbors, still in robes, stood watching. Some had their hands wrapped around hot cups of coffee.

"Hey, Michael, what's going on?" Dave Taylor from across the street hollered as Michael climbed out from behind the wheel of Savannah's Honda Accord.

"I don't know, Dave. Just got here." He headed toward the front door of the clinic. "Jim, what happened?" Michael asked when he spotted the deputy.

In the meantime, Savannah stepped gingerly out of the passenger door, still babying her injured knee. Before she could close the car door, she spotted something on the ground in front of her. *Keys—it's a ring of keys.* She picked it up and examined it. *Hmmm, that's odd,* she thought. She looked ahead of her and saw Michael approaching Deputy Jim. Eager to hear what he had to say, she tossed the keys into the car and pushed the door shut. She walked away, not noticing that the keys had slid across the seat and slipped down between the seat and the console. She caught up with the two men just in time to see Jim shake his head and hear him mumble, "Doesn't look good, Dr. Mike. Doesn't look good." He walked past Michael and Savannah over to where some of the other uniformed officers stood.

They both followed Jim with their eyes and watched as he gave the officers some instructions.

"Michael, can we go in?" Savannah asked.

"Don't know. They have tape across the door." He glanced toward the door and then back at Jim. Finally, he reasoned, "I don't know why not. It's our clinic." He started to move in that direction, but stopped when he saw Jim walking briskly toward them. "Jim, can we go in? We have animals in there that may need attention."

"Including our own cats," Savannah said, her voice quivering a little.

"Yes," Jim said. "We need to ask you some questions. Let's go inside." He opened the door and led the way.

Michael caught up with Jim and asked, "Where's Bud? He called me."

"I think they're questioning him."

Michael swallowed hard, frowned. "Jim, Bud said someone died."

"Yes," Jim continued leading Michael and Savannah into the waiting room of their veterinary clinic. "Please sit down here, will you?" He looked over at Michael, who was still standing. "Looks like you're healing up pretty good. Feeling okay?"

"Yeah," Michael said. As if he were on automatic pilot—not totally in the moment and apprehensive about what was going on around him, he added, "Savannah's still hobbling around with that knee—can't ride her horse." He fiddled with something in his pocket, and asked, "Can we go back and check on the animals?"

Jim thought about his request for a few seconds and said, "I guess that would be okay."

Before they could move forward, a man in street clothes walked into the waiting room from the back offices and motioned to Jim. "Wait here," Jim told Savannah and Michael. He strolled over and talked quietly with the man for a few moments before saying to the couple, "Okay, I'll walk with you to the pens now."

Michael and Savannah followed Jim through the waiting room and down the hallway. Before they entered the doorway to the recovery room, Michael stopped and looked in the direction of some commotion. He saw a yellow tarp covering what appeared to be a body just inside the back door to the clinic. The door was open and several sheriff deputies and other officials were milling around in that area—some talking on cell phones, others talking among themselves. Suddenly, his eyes connected with those of Craig Sledge, who nodded somberly toward Michael and Savannah. "Come on," Jim said, hastening them into the recovery room.

The veterinary team checked on the two patients, scooped out a litter box, and gave the animals clean water and a gentle petting to reassure them. As the couple closed the doors to the pens, Jim asked, "Everything okay?"

"Yes, seems to be," Michael said. "Now we'd like to see *our* cats—they're out near the… commotion…in that large pen. I didn't know there was all that activity out there. I'd like to bring them in here away from…all that."

Jim thought about it for a few moments and then said, "Yeah, go ahead."

As the trio walked toward the cordoned-off area, Savannah looked down at where the body lay under the yellow tarp. She slowed her pace, stared.

"Let's get the cats out," Jim said, in an attempt to keep the couple focused.

"Who is it, Jim?" Michael asked. "Anyone we know?" His speech accelerated, as panic gripped him. "It's not one of our employees, is it?"

The deputy frowned. He took in a breath and said, "No, it's not one of your employees." He looked over at the cats in the pen. "Let's move the cats and then we'll talk."

As they walked toward the large pen, Rags jumped up on the platform closest to them. "He's happy to see us," Savannah said. "Hi Ragsy. I missed you, too, boy." Walter sat on top of a small carpeted cat tree closest to the activity, watching intently. "Where's Buffy?" Savannah asked.

Michael looked around inside the pen from a series of different vantage points. "Oh, I see her in that pink tent thing over there." He then said, "Savannah, get Rags, would you? I'll take Walter. We can put them in separate pens in recovery. I'll put Buffy with Walter."

Savannah followed behind Michael toward the door to the pen. "I think she should go with Rags."

"Why?"

"She and Rags are closer now than she is with Walter."

Jim, who had been leaning against a wall across from the pen, took a couple of steps forward. "Okay, we can't stand here and argue—get the cats situated. I need to question you. You might also want to put a notice on the door that you're closing today."

"Oh, we are?" Michael said as he took the clasp off the pen gate. He looked over at the activity near the back door again and shook his head in disgust. "I'll have Bud call the clients with appointments today." He started to enter the pen and then stopped. "Where is Bud, anyway?"

"I told you, they're questioning him. He should be along shortly. I'll let them know you want to speak with him."

"I can make the calls, Michael," Savannah said as she entered the pen. Michael stepped in after her and closed the gate. He stood in the center of the pen, trying to digest what was happening around them. Just then another deputy walked toward Jim and called him out of the room. Savannah watched him join the other authorities as they all huddled near the body.

She tried to ignore the sick feeling she had in the pit of her stomach. *A kitty hug—that's what I need*, she thought. *Kitty hugs always seem to make things better.* She looked over at Rags—*What's that he has*? She walked closer and saw him pick up something with his teeth and shake his head with it in his mouth. He then put a claw in it and pulled while holding onto it with his teeth. "What do you have there, Ragsy?" she asked as she grew nearer. The cat dropped it again. This time it floated down to the floor. Rags jumped down, snagged the object in his mouth and leaped back up onto the perch, where he continued to paw and claw at it. Savannah reached over and picked up the large cat. "I missed you boy. Are you okay?" Suddenly, she felt overcome with emotion. She buried her face into his fur and started to cry.

"Awwww, honey," Michael said. He walked over and put his arms around her and the cat. He kissed the side of her head. "I know, honey—awfully close to home. Another tragedy. It…it just sucks." He gave her a squeeze and then rubbed Rags's head. "He seems to be okay, don't you think?"

"Yes, I think so." Before she turned to carry him into the recovery room, she looked back at the item on the perch. She wiped her eyes with her sleeve and took a closer look. *It's a piece of cloth from something.* She looked around the pen and saw nothing in there made from this swatch of fabric. *Hmmm*, she thought to herself, *it's a light-weight woven tweed fabric in browns with a little dark blue running through it. I wonder where it came from.*

Just then, Deputy Jim walked back into the room. Savannah pushed the cloth swatch deep inside her jacket pocket and carried Rags out of the pen. Michael followed her with Walter in one arm and Buffy in the other. Once Savannah had placed Rags in a clean pen already supplied with a litter box, kibbles, and water, she turned and took Buffy from Michael.

"Hi there, sweet girl," she crooned, while hugging the little Himmie mix to her. "Here, you keep Rags company," she said as she set her gently inside the pen. After latching the gate, she walked over to a cabinet and opened it. She rummaged around for a few moments, eventually retrieving a soft flannel pad. She tucked it into the pen for Buffy to lie on. Only Rags thought it was for him and he promptly walked over and sat in the middle of the cushy blanket. Savannah smiled and shook her head. "Okay, I get it. You want to be pampered, too." And she went back to the cabinet, found another section of blanket and scrunched it into an opposite corner of the pen. She watched as Rags claimed that bed for himself, leaving the original one for Buffy, who immediately ambled over and settled down for a nap.

Savannah pulled a small pad out of the cabinet for Walter. After placing it inside his pen, she peered in at the black cat and he stared back at her through yellow eyes. "All set?" Jim asked, as he led the couple out into the hallway. Michael closed the door behind them. After taking only a couple of steps, Savannah looked back at the scene at the end of the hallway. She promptly bumped into Michael, who had stopped to stare in that direction. Without a word, the two of them turned and followed Deputy Jim back into the waiting room.

"Let's sit here, shall we?" Jim suggested. Savannah and Michael sat next to each other against the wall and Jim pulled a chair out of the line-up and sat down facing the Drs. Ivey. "Michael, I need you to account for your whereabouts last night."

"What?" he barked.

Savannah's posture stiffened. She frowned at the deputy.

"Where were you last night, Michael?"

Michael squirmed in his chair, a scowl on his face. "I don't believe this. What's going on, Jim? Who is that back there?"

Jim stayed on track. He spoke without emotion. "Just answer the question, please."

Michael stared over at Jim, shaking his head in disbelief. "At home."

"All night?"

Michael could tell the deputy was serious. He knew he had nothing to hide, so he took a deep breath and said, "Yes. Let's see, I left the clinic around six, stopped at the deli for some sandwiches, and got home around…he hesitated…six-twenty, I'd say. Savannah and I had the sandwiches for dinner, we worked a little on my remodel project upstairs, and went to bed around ten."

"And you were home all night. You didn't go out at all?"

"No. What is this all about? Are you accusing me of something?"

Jim ignored the question. Looking over at Savannah, he asked, "Were you home, too?"

"Yes. I left the office at five-thirty. I brought the dog home with me. Oh, I did stop by my aunt's place to drop off some pharmaceuticals for their cats. Then Lexie and I came right home."

"Who's Lexie?"

"The dog."

"And you were home all night? Neither of you went out?"

"No," Savannah snapped. She clenched her teeth and pressed her lips together lest she say something she might regret.

"What's going on, Jim?" Michael asked. "Why all these questions? Who is it back there—under that tarp?"

Deputy Jim looked Michael in the eyes. He hesitated before saying, "It's Pete Gamble. He's been murdered."

Savannah's hands shot up to her mouth. Her eyes widened and she gasped. "Oh my gosh. Here? How…?"

Michael sat back in his chair, feeling as though the wind had been knocked out of him. Finally he asked, "What happened? What was he doing here?" He looked off into space as if in a daze. And then he stood. He stepped into the center of the room and began pacing, raking his hand through his hair. He turned and said, his voice raised, "And you think that I…" he looked down, trying to gather his thoughts. He then stared directly at Jim and said slowly, "I am not a murderer." He pointed a finger at Jim. "You should know my character by now. I wouldn't kill someone just because they got in my face. What are you thinking?" He put his head in his hands and rubbed his forehead hard with his palms.

Savannah stood and walked over to him. "I'm sure he doesn't suspect you—he just has to ask these questions. It's his job, Michael."

Jim swiveled in his chair to face the couple. "That's partially correct, Savannah. It's my job. But dang, it looks suspicious finding him here, after all he has done to you in the past week. How do you suppose he came to be here—inside your clinic?"

"He was inside right there when you found him?" Michael asked.

"Yes and the door was wide open when Bud arrived this morning, or so he says."

Savannah walked over and sat down opposite Jim.

"Who has keys to the clinic?" Jim wanted to know. He picked up his notepad and pencil.

Savannah responded. "Michael and I, of course. Bud—he checks on the patients early each morning and, when advised, throughout the night. Scarlett, our receptionist, has a key, as do our cleaning people. That would be Iris and Cindy." She then caught herself and said, "No, not Cindy. She's out on maternity leave. Our new cleaning gal is Alyce." Savannah turned toward Michael. "Did you give her a key?"

"Yes," Michael said. "So it's me, Savannah, Bud, Iris, Scarlett, and Alyce who have keys."

"And Lisa has a key," Savannah said. "She's Bud's backup."

"Now why does…" Jim looked at his notes, "Iris have a key?"

Michael walked over and sat back down in his chair. He took in a deep breath. "She comes in and cleans the clinic a couple times a week after hours."

"And the new cleaning gal? What does she do, what is her schedule?"

"Well, she cleans and sanitizes cages, examining rooms, and so forth on an ongoing, as-needed basis throughout the day." Michael explained. "She sometimes comes in early to make sure things are ready for patients or she might stay late to prepare for the next day."

"Hmmmm," Jim said, rubbing his chin and fixing his stare on his notepad. "I'll need contact information for Scarlett, Lisa, and Alyce, if you don't mind." He looked up at Michael. "We have Bud here now and I know how to find Iris."

Savannah rose from her chair. "I'll get that for you," she said as she walked over to the reception counter.

Jim looked down at his notes again. "Now wait. Does the one out on maternity leave—Cindy—still have a key?"

Michael thought for a moment. "Um, yeah, I guess she does."

"I'll need her contact information, too, if you don't mind, Savannah."

Michael leaned forward, rested his elbows on his knees, his hands clasped in front of him, and asked, "How?"

"Huh?"

"How did he die?"

"Stabbed," was all Jim would say.

Michael sat somber, a look of disbelief on his face. He then straightened his posture and asked, "What I want to know is why is he in my…" he turned his head and looked over at Savannah briefly and then continued, "our clinic? What was he doing here?"

Jim pursed his lips and shook his head slowly from side to side. "That's what we're trying to figure out. Why was he here, how did he get in and who was with him?"

Savannah walked over and handed Jim the piece of paper with the information he wanted. She took her place next to Michael.

Suddenly, they heard a familiar voice. "Good morning, folks."

Savannah and Michael looked up. "Hi Craig," Savannah said, her voice strained.

Detective Craig Sledge didn't look like he was there for a visit. He walked over to where

Michael and Savannah sat and faced them, saying, "Michael, this doesn't look good."

Michael squirmed in his chair, rubbed one hand through his hair, and said, "Yeah, that's what Jim says. I'm some sort of suspect, it seems."

Craig stared down at the floor. "Gotta start weedin' people out. That's what we're doing now."

"I'd think this was some sort of a frame job," Michael said. "But the only one I can think of who would do such a thing is dead." He rolled his head slowly from side to side. Finally, he said, "This is insane." He looked up at the detective and then over at Jim and asked, "So did someone break into the office or use a key?"

"Looks like they knew their way in," Craig said matter of factly.

Savannah sat silent, tears welling up in her eyes. *This must be how those innocent people I read about, who are sitting in prison, feel,* she thought. *Helpless. Absolutely helpless.*

She looked up at the clock behind the reception desk and then jumped to her feet saying, "Oh! It's after seven. I'd better call the staff and then make calls to the morning appointments," she said. She hesitated and then asked flatly, "Can I do that, Craig?"

"Sure, go ahead." Craig then looked over at Michael. "I'd like to ask you some questions."

"Gosh, Craig, I can't think of anything that I haven't already told Jim."

Craig thought about it for a minute. He conferred with Jim and then addressed Michael. "Okay, buddy. You and Savannah don't have plans to go anywhere, do you?"

Michael stared at Craig, anger rising to the surface. He stood abruptly. "Well, hell!"

Savannah looked up from the reception desk, phone to her ear, concern on her face.

Michael then turned toward Craig and said, "Do you know where Bud is? I need to talk to him about the patients. We do have a business to run here, you know."

"I think they're just about finished with him in there," Craig said while craning his neck to peer down the hallway. "Oh, here he comes now."

Michael walked over to the hallway entrance. "Bud, are you okay?"

"Yeah, I guess," he said, looking a little shaken. "Did you see that dead guy?"

"No," Michael said." He looked over to see Craig and Jim walk out the front door with a couple of officials—from the crime lab maybe, or the coroner's office. Michael wasn't sure.

"He's an awful mess," Bud continued. "Someone sure must have hated him bad. Blood all over. I couldn't believe it when I walked up to the back door and found…" He shivered. "It was horrible."

"Bud, how's the sheltie? Did she do okay last night?" Michael asked.

"Oh yes, they let me do rounds, but only quickly, so I haven't done a full assessment yet." He paused and looked behind him before saying, "They're calling this whole area a crime scene, you know."

"Yes, I know, Bud. And the Kenton's cat, did you check his vitals? Is he eating?"

"Yes, he's doing real good. I was glad to see it after our rough day yesterday with him. Everyone looks okay, Dr. Mike. Your three cats included." He chuckled. "They seem to enjoy a night away from home once in a while." He lowered his eyes. "Except for Buffy. I think it's all rather overwhelming for her."

"Let me in!" a voice shrieked from just outside the waiting room door. "That's my niece in there. This is her business. Jim, tell them to let me in. I want to see Vannie."

"Oh, it's Auntie," Savannah said, hanging up the phone before dialing the next number. She limped a little toward the door. Before she could get there, Margaret burst in, two uniformed sheriff's deputies behind her.

"Let her go in," she heard Jim shout. And the other deputies backed off. Craig Sledge walked in behind Margaret.

"Vannie, are you all right? I heard about it on the radio. What happened?" she asked, looking around the area.

Savannah met her aunt in the middle of the room. They embraced. "We're okay, Auntie," she said, looking down into her face. And then she burst into tears. "Oh Auntie, someone was killed here in the clinic. They're asking us a bunch of questions. They think we had something to do with it," she said, not even trying to hide the fact that she was blubbering.

"Are we through here?" Michael asked, irritation evident in his tone. "We want to take our cats home."

Craig Sledge looked around at the uniformed officers. "Yeah, I guess that's okay." Then he addressed one of the younger officers. "Deputy, would you go with them while they get the cats out?" He then warned Michael, "Just be careful not to disturb any evidence."

As Michael walked back toward the recovery room with the deputy, he noticed little markers sitting here and there with numbers on them—indicating evidence, he supposed. Once in the room with the cats, he picked up one of the carriers stacked in the corner, and brought it over to the pens. Rags seemed most eager to get out, so Michael opened the door to his pen first.

Buffy stayed at the back of the cage curled up on a blanket. He picked up Rags and put him into the larger carrier, secured the door and set it aside. He glanced over at Buffy just as the cream-and-sable long-haired beauty stepped out of her bed. He pushed the pen door closed and walked over to get the second carrier. The deputy saw the cat moving toward the wire door and reached up to hold it closed. "No, kitty. You wait there."

Michael eased Buffy into a carrier just as Savannah walked into the room. She moved a third carrier in front of Walter's pen and Michael loaded him up. The two of them picked up the three carriers and walked toward the waiting room. Savannah stopped at the reception desk and grabbed the appointment book so she could finish making calls from home.

It was light when they stepped out into the crisp morning air with the cats. Margaret walked along with them. "Have you two eaten?" she asked.

They looked at one another. "Actually, no," Savannah responded.

"Yeah, I am kinda hungry," Michael said. "Let's take the kitties home and give them their canned food. Then shall we meet at the diner for some breakfast?"

"Okay, I guess. I'm not very hungry, though," Savannah said.

She set Buffy's carrier in the backseat of her car next to the other two. She looked over at her aunt. "See you at the diner?"

"Okay," she said before walking the few steps to her car.

Before entering the car with Michael, Savannah turned toward the building, saying, "I'd better put up a sign." She walked back into the clinic, wrote a note on a piece of paper, and taped it securely to the front door.

"So how long do we have to stay away?" Savannah asked Michael on the drive home.

"Until they finish their investigation," he said. "I think we can probably open up tomorrow. And Bud should be able to go in and check on our patients." He hesitated and then said, "At least I hope so. I'll talk to Craig."

The couple rode in silence. Savannah felt a chill and put her hands in her jacket pockets. That's when she remembered the scrap of fabric. She pulled it out and said, "Michael, I found this in the pen with Rags. He was playing with it. Do you recognize it?"

He looked over a couple of times as he drove. "Doesn't look familiar to me. What's it from?"

"I don't know. Could be from someone's clothes."

"Why didn't you give it to Craig?"

"Kinda forgot about it. But I probably should make sure he gets it."

Michael parked Savannah's car in front of the house. She climbed out through the passenger door and reached into the backseat for Rags's carrier. "Wait," Michael said. "Trade me places. You come over here and take Buffy. I'll get the guys."As they approached the front door, they heard Lexie barking. "It's okay, girl," Michael soothed through the door. "It's us."

Once inside, Savannah reached out and ruffled the dog's fur. "Want some breakfast, girl?" She released Buffy from the carrier and then Walter. Michael unlatched Rags's carrier. "Come on babies, let's go get something to eat," she said, walking toward the kitchen.

Michael headed for the side kitchen door. "I'll go feed your horse."

When he returned, he noticed that Savannah was snapping Lexie's leash on her collar. She looked up, "Going to take her out for a few minutes," she said. "She hasn't been out yet this morning."

"Oh, that's right."

"Then I need to finish those calls to our clients."

"Here, let me take Lexie out; you make the calls. I'll put the carriers away while you freshen up."

Savannah started to walk away, but stopped and turned. "Hey, do I look like I need to freshen up?"

"No, I just know you. After a morning like we've had, you must be ready to at least wash your face and comb your hair. Am I right?" he asked looking her in the eyes—a knowing grin on his face.

She hesitated—thought about it and then said, "Yeah, right on. You know, it's spooky sometimes, how well you know me."

"Just observant, that's all, and you are pretty predictable."

She stared at him for a moment, pulling her eyebrows together in a frown. "You think I'm predictable? Gosh, I'm going to have to do something about that. Don't want you to get bored with me."

He reached over and grabbed her elbow, pulling her to him. "Not a chance." He kissed her and then said, "Now go—your aunt's waiting for us."

***

"Dr. Mike; Savannah!" Iris said, waving her hand in the air from a booth about midway along one wall in the diner. As the couple approached, Iris moved over next to Margaret, who sat pouring cream into a cup of coffee. Savannah and Michael slid in opposite them. Once they were seated, Iris leaned into them, her brow creased. "Maggie told me what you've been through this morning; that's awful."

"It's been a nightmare of a morning," Savannah said while slipping out of her jacket.

Michael reached over behind her to help, saying, "Sure not the way I expected to spend this day." He looked across at Margaret and Iris. "But things are looking up—here I sit with three beautiful women and access to any food I want." He picked up the menu and began studying it.

"Except blueberry pancakes," Iris said quickly.

"No blueberries?" He collapsed a little into his seat, feigning extreme disappointment.

Savannah nudged him with her elbow. "Oh stop. You don't usually order blueberries."

"Oh, I don't?" he asked. "Okay then." He composed himself and continued studying the menu.

Savannah rolled her eyes toward Iris and Margaret. They grinned back at her and Michael. She then looked around the interior of the diner. "Where is everyone?"

Iris glanced across the room. "It's not usually busy this time of morning. Our crowds come in between six and seven-thirty. You two are usually at work by now petting puppies and kittens."

"Oh that's right," Savannah said. "It's Tuesday."

Michael slapped his menu on the tabletop and said in jest, trying to keep things light on what was proving to be a dark day, "Petting puppies and kittens? Really Iris, is that what you think we do all day?"

Iris and Margaret laughed.

Savannah smiled. "What are you laughing at Auntie? You and Max spend the majority of your day doing just that."

"Do not," Margaret insisted.

Savannah leaned toward her. "Do so…"

"We don't have one puppy on the place," Margaret stated, indignantly.

"Well, excuuuuse me," Savannah said, forcing a chuckle.

The others joined in on the laughter. Just then, Frank walked up with the coffee carafe and two cups. He poured coffee for Savannah and Michael and offered Margaret a refill. He then set the pot down, took a pad and pen out of his apron pocket, and asked, "Ready to order?"

"Yes," Michael said, looking around at the others, who all agreed they were ready. "Go ahead, ladies."

"I'm good," Iris said. She smiled up at Frank. "Gotta come back to work in a few."

Margaret pointed to the menu and then looked up at Frank. "Veggie omelet with a biscuit."

"Oooooh, sounds good," Savannah said. She winced a little. "…but I don't think I could handle that much food today."

When she hesitated, Iris suggested she consider a two-egg omelet.

"Yes, that sounds perfect," Savannah said, handing her menu to the waiter. "With fruit instead of a biscuit, please."

"Meat lover's omelet," Michael said as he picked up his menu. "Make mine with two eggs, too, would you, Frank?" He hesitated and then said, "I'll have a biscuit with gravy—no potatoes."

Savannah rubbed the back of Michael's neck. "You *are* hungry, hon. That interrogation must have taken a lot out of you."

Iris looked over at Michael. "So tell me what happened this morning."

Michael pursed his lips. "Well, the long and the short of it is that someone killed that jerk Pete Gamble at the clinic and they seem to be trying to implicate me—or us..." He glanced over at Savannah.

"What?" Margaret's mouth dropped open. "The dead guy is Pete Gamble? I'm speechless."

"That's a first," Savannah said, her attempt at keeping the mood light obviously failing.

No one spoke for a few moments. Margaret, who continued to stare down at her coffee cup, finally broke the silence. "Gosh, guys, this is unbelievable." She shook her head slowly back and forth.

Savannah took a deep breath and her eyes filled with tears. "It's pretty disturbing, to say the least." She wiped at her eyes with her napkin.

Michael reached over and put his hand on her knee. "It'll be okay, honey," he comforted.

"How can you be so sure?" Margaret asked.

"Well, it's just gotta be, that's all," Michael responded. He then stared past Iris, a look of slight apprehension on his face. "Here comes Craig."

Iris craned her neck to see him, and Savannah finished dabbing at her eyes. She then wadded the napkin and reached over to stuff it into her jacket pocket. That's when she remembered the swatch of fabric. She pulled it out and held it in her hand.

When Craig spotted Michael, he walked over to their booth. Iris stood and smiled brightly. "Hi there."

"Hi, yourself." He looked around the diner and then moved toward Iris and quickly kissed her on the lips. She looked at him, her eyes alive with excitement. Then she said, "Oh, I guess you came in to see the Iveys, huh?"

"'Fraid so."

"Well, I have to get back to work. Can I bring you a cup of coffee?"

"Yeah, that would be great." He then gave her a flirtatious look and added in a sultry voice, "You know how I like it."

"Sure do," she said imitating his flirty manner.

"You two are sickening," Margaret said as Craig sat down next to her.

"Sickening?" Savannah said. "I think they're cute." She leaned in toward Craig. "Don't let her spoil all that fun you and Iris are having."

"Oh, no chance of that," he said. He then took on a more serious demeanor. He looked across the table at Michael and Savannah. "So, how are you two doin'? Rough morning, huh?"

"Yeah," Savannah said drawing out the word in a dull cadence.

He focused his eyes on Michael. "How are you holdin' up, guy?"

"Okay, I guess. The reality of it hasn't quite sunk in."

"I can imagine," Craig said, showing a concern they hadn't seen from him before. "You two are probably still in shock."

"Do you know when we can get back to work?"

Craig looked at Michael and then Savannah. "They oughta be out of the clinic this afternoon." He placed his elbows on the table and tented his fingers before saying, "You may want to call the cleaning company to come in later today, when the investigators are finished."

"Oh, right. Good idea," Savannah said with a sigh. "Thanks for reminding us."

"Yeah, wouldn't want the employees to come in to that mess tomorrow," Michael added. He saw Iris coming toward them with a tray. "Ahhh, food," he said, pulling back from the table. "Thank you, Iris. You have saved a man's life today. I could kiss you!!!"

"Okay," Iris said playfully. She then turned to Craig. "Do you want anything to eat?"

"Naw. I have to get back to work. Just wanted to check in with these folks." He smiled up at Iris. "…and see you." She returned the smile. She started to leave when he called out to her. "Oh, Iris, would you fix me a cup of coffee to go, please?"

"Sure." A minute or two later, she set a covered Styrofoam cup in front of him on the table and picked up the five-dollar bill he had laid down.

He started to rise, when Savannah held her hand out toward him. "I don't know if this is important or not, but I found it at the clinic this morning and neither of us have ever seen it before."

Craig sat back down and took the swatch from Savannah. He studied it for a few moments and then looked up at her. "So what is this, anyway?"

Savannah shrugged. "Just a piece of tweed material, I guess."

Iris walked up, set Craig's change on the table in front of him, and then reached over him while pouring coffee into Margaret's cup. She looked down at the swatch and said, "It's frayed on the edges."

Craig stared up at her as if hoping for more information. "Yeah?"

"Looks to me like it was torn from a larger piece of fabric." She took the swatch from Craig and examined it more closely. "It's kind of old and worn. I can see that it would rip fairly easily."

"Tell him where you found it, hon," Michael said as he poured gravy over his biscuit.

She looked a bit pensive when she said to Craig, "Rags had it."

"Rags..." he said, tilting his head slightly. "Oh, that's your cool cat."

"Yes." Savannah smiled. "When we moved the cats out of the big pen where they had been overnight, Rags was playing with this."

Craig started thinking out loud. "And the large pen where the cats were is darn close to where the body was found." He took the fabric back from Iris, rubbed it between his fingers, and said, "You know, we're pretty sure the body was brought to that spot. I don't think he was killed there. And the door wasn't jimmied, so someone had a key. It doesn't make sense, Michael, that you or any of your employees would open the door and then leave it open like that, unless..."

"Unless what?" Savannah and Margaret said in unison.

"Unless someone scared them off before they could lock up." He appeared to be deep in thought. After a few moments, he said, "I need to speak with the neighbors around there. I met Mr. Taylor. And what is the name of the couple who rent your log house?"

"Giselle Patterson and Robert Martinez," Michael said. "Then the Normans live on the other side."

Craig took out his pad and made some notes. He then picked up the swatch and took one more look at it before tucking it into his jacket pocket. He winked at Savannah. "Tell your cat thanks." He looked over at Michael. "I'll be in touch." He stood and started to walk away, then he turned and looked at Michael and Savannah. "You two take it easy. I know this is hard, but just know that we're going to find out who did this and then you can have your life back. Until then, it may get gnarly."

***

"Dang," Michael said as he turned into their driveway and saw a sheriff's car, an unmarked car, and a van parked close to the house. "What do you suppose they're doing here?" He put the car in park and turned off the key. The two of them stepped out of the car.

Savannah took a sweeping glance around the property. "Sheesh, maybe we should have left the cats at the clinic." As the couple walked toward the front door, they noticed their gardener Antonio approaching them. "Senora, what is this?" he asked, swinging his arm around toward a uniformed officer and a couple of plain-clothed men and women milling around the property.

"An investigation, Antonio. Nothing for you to be worried about. Everything's okay." She looked over and saw two people examining the cab and bed of Michael's veterinary truck. *Well, I sure hope everything's okay,* she thought. *They can't actually believe that Michael would do such a thing.* She turned her attention back to Antonio. "If you'd like to take the day off, it's okay with me. I think these people will be gone tomorrow. Come back tomorrow, if you like."

The slight Mexican man let out a sigh of what seemed like relief. He reached for his cell phone. "I will have Esperanza come get me."

The trio watched as the investigators climbed in and around the truck. After a few seconds, Michael opened the front door to their home and he and Savannah walked inside. "Hi

Lexie," Savannah said as the dog gave them her best tail-wagging reception. "We're happy to see you, too." She couldn't help but smile a little at the dog's enthusiastic efforts; but even Lexie couldn't help her shake the sense of melancholy she felt gripping her. After giving the dog one last scratch behind her ears, Savannah removed her jacket and walked toward their bedroom. She returned wearing a brown cardigan sweater over her cream-colored pullover top. As hard as she tried putting the reality of their morning out of her mind, she was drawn to the front window.

"What do you suppose they're looking for in your truck, Michael?" she asked.

He glanced up from the home remodeling magazine he was reading. "My guess would be, blood."

Savannah closed her eyes, pretending she didn't hear it. She then turned toward him. Her voice raised an octave, she said, "Michael, you hit that deer the other day on your way home from vaccinating Tim Bagley's horses."

"Yes, I did and I threw it in the back of the truck."

"Why? Why did you do that?" she asked, walking across the room and plopping herself down in the overstuffed chair next to where Michael sat on the sofa.

"Well, honey, I didn't want to leave it on that back road. Road crews don't get out there very often," he explained. "I took it over to the preserve for the vultures."

"So they've probably already found blood."

"Certainly, they did. I haven't had a chance to clean my truck in a while." He stared over at her. "Hey, honey. Not a problem. They'll be able to tell it's animal blood."

"Yeah, I know. It's just that…"

He placed the magazine on the end table and leaned toward his wife. "Savannah, you don't think…"

"Oh my gosh, no, Michael. Of course not," she said. "But we both know there are people accused of things they didn't do. It happens all the time." Her voice became more animated. "Just look at what happened a few months ago to Iris. She was accused of Steven's dad's murder and she obviously had nothing to do with it. Things got pretty scary there for a while."

Michael lowered his head and took Savannah's hand. He lifted her face so he could look into her eyes. "There's nothing for us to worry about. The truth—whatever it is—will come out. Savannah, we haven't done anything wrong."

"Yeah, you're right. We don't have anything to worry about."

Michael squeezed her hand before letting go, leaned back on the sofa and picked up his magazine. Just then Rags appeared. He jumped up on the chair and stood on Savannah's lap pushing his head into her, demanding her attention.

Rap. Rap.

"Oh, someone's at the door," she said. "Sorry, Ragsy—come on, jump down, boy." She made her way to the front door. Before she got there, the door opened and Margaret peered in.

"Yoohoo!"

"Oh hi," Savannah said, a puzzled look on her face. "Everything okay?"

"Well, you tell me. I was driving by on my way home." She motioned toward the front of the house. "Looks like the whole police force is out there—swat team and all," she said, obviously exaggerating. "Stopped in to see what's going on."

Just then, there was another knock on the door. Savannah and Michael glanced at one another in disbelief at how complicated their day was becoming. "Oh hi Craig," Savannah said upon opening the door. "Come in. What's up with all these people climbing in and out of our vehicles? Will they be coming in the house?" Savannah asked, near tears.

"Oh I think they're about finished here," he said. He looked over at Michael, who was still sitting on the sofa. "I just came in to tell you, Michael, they found blood in your truck."

"Yeah, I know that," he said.

"You seem surprisingly calm about it. Is there a logical explanation?"

"Sure is."

Savannah heard her aunt gasp and looked over in time to see her turn a little pale. "It's okay, Auntie, really it is," she said.

"It's okay?" Craig repeated.

"Well yeah," Michael said, standing to address him. "I hit a deer a couple of days ago and threw the carcass in the back of the truck."

"What, you butcher road kill now?" Margaret let out a rather nervous laugh.

"No, Auntie. He just didn't want to leave it along the road—he wanted to properly dispose of it."

"Is this true, Michael?" Craig asked.

"Well, yes. Didn't you see the blood and the dent on the front of the truck? I called my insurance company the next day. I'm sure they have a record of it."

"Now, isn't that good news?" Craig said with a half smile. "I'm really glad to hear it. That could make a big difference in the investigation."

"Can they tell the difference between human and animal blood?" Margaret asked.

"Yes," Michael responded. "That's not going to be a problem, is it Craig?"

"No, I doubt it. But I am concerned about… something else."

"What's that?" Michael asked.

He stared over at him for a few moments and then asked, "Michael, do you carry a knife in your truck?"

"Sure," he said matter of factly.

"What for?" Craig asked.

"For emergencies."

"What sort of emergencies?" Craig wanted to know.

Michael grimaced—took a deep breath. "Well, in case a horse gets tripped up in a rope and I need to cut him free. I might use it to cut an embedded halter off." He thought for a minute and then said, "I also have hoof knives."

"Do you keep them locked up in your truck?"

"Yes," Michael said. "I keep things like that locked in the side compartments."

Craig thought for a minute—his eyes studying Michael's face. "Did you use your knife on the deer?" he asked.

"I don't…" Michael started. He narrowed his eyes, scratched his head. "No. I did use it that day to cut a rope. But I'm sure I locked it back in the compartment."

"Well, we're going to need to take a look at the knives you carry in your truck. Would you show me?"

"Yes. Sure," he said, heading for the front door.

Craig glanced over at Savannah and then followed after Michael. He watched as Michael unlocked one of the side boxes on his veterinary truck and started to reach in for a knife. Craig said, "Allow me." He looked into the well-organized bin, spotted a buck knife in a leather sheath and, after slipping on a latex glove, reached in to retrieve it. He looked it over and then dropped it into a large envelope. "I'll get it back to you in a few days."

Michael started to close the box when Craig said, "I'd like to take a look inside while you have it open, if you don't mind."

Michael stepped back.

"Can you unlock the others for me, please?" Craig asked while poking around inside the bin. After several minutes, Craig said, "Okay, I think that's all." He picked up the envelope, stared intently at Michael and said, "I'm sure there's nothing to worry about."

When Michael stepped back into the house, he heard Savannah telling her aunt, "Well, at least, we don't have to worry about that awful Pete Gamble anymore." She turned toward her husband. "Isn't that right, Michael?"

"Yeah, that's a relief," he agreed. "But then, our problem with him is the main reason they're looking at me as a suspect," he added.

"But like you told me earlier, we haven't done anything wrong. We're innocent. We have nothing realistically to worry about."

"Playing devil's advocate here, let me remind you that we didn't do anything wrong to deserve the trauma and fear Pete put us through when he was alive, either."

Chapter Six

"Good morning, sunshine. I guess we have no excuse not to go to work today, right?" Michael propped himself up on one elbow and furrowed his brow. "What are you doing up so early, anyway?"

Savannah was quick to respond. "I think there's something wrong with Rags. He isn't eating this morning—didn't eat much last night. He seems lethargic to me. I'm going to take him to work with me and check him out."

He sat upright to get a better look at the cat, who was lying in a meatloaf position—all of his paws under him. "Oh, he doesn't look as perky as usual, does he? What do you think is wrong?"

"Could be cystitis. Or maybe he got some bad cat food. But the other cats seem fine."

Michael climbed out of bed and walked over to Rags. He reached down and scratched him behind one ear. The cat pushed into his hand with his head, but didn't bother to get up. "Yeah, he's not feeling himself, that's for sure. Sorry Rags. Mommy will have you feeling good in no time. She's a doctor, you know," he added, smiling over at Savannah.

***

Savannah pulled into the parking lot at the clinic a little before 8 a.m. Michael drove in right behind her. It took longer than usual to coax Rags off the car seat and into the carrier. In fact, he didn't want to go in at all. "It's protocol, Rags—you know, policy—the rule here. Cats have to be confined in a carrier when they visit the clinic. You can ride on the seat in the car. But now it's time to get into the carrier. Come on, boy," she urged.

Suddenly she heard a rap on the car window. She looked up and saw Michael staring in.

"Need help there, Ma'am? Is that tiger giving you trouble?"

She rolled the window down about two inches and said, "Doesn't want to get in his carrier. I guess he's feeling better."

"Looks like a two-vet job. Here, let me help," he said as he opened the door and latched onto the large cat. Savannah turned the door of the carrier toward Michael and he slipped Rags in and closed it up. "Voila," he said.

"Thanks. Now I'll let you carry him in—if you don't mind."

"Well hello, Rags. You're becoming a regular here, aren't you, big guy," their receptionist Scarlett crooned. She looked up at Savannah and Michael. "Something wrong with him?" she asked.

"I think he may have an infection—maybe urinary tract…" Savannah explained. She spotted Bud coming out of the recovery room. "Bud, would you find a place for Rags? I'm going to examine him after the morning patients."

"Sure. Come on Rags. We always have room for you," Bud said as he toted the cat in his carrier to the back of the clinic.

That morning patients came and went. It was a steady stream of mostly routine exams, inoculations, claw-trimming, new kitten and puppy checkups, and a few cats and dogs that stayed for neutering and teeth cleaning. It wasn't until noon that Savannah could work Rags into her schedule. She went back to get him. After opening the pen, she took a look to see if he'd used the litter box. She did, in fact, find a small wet spot. *Good, but not great,* she thought. *He could be blocked or just nervous. Some cats actually resist urinating when they're away from home.* "Well, let's take a look," she said, picking up the cat and carrying him into an examining room. They arrived just as Alyce had finished sanitizing the table.

"Oh, what a cool cat," Alyce said upon seeing Rags. "He's big!"

"Yes, this is Rags—he allows us to live with him," Savannah joked.

"Well, aren't you something?"Alyce said as she moved closer to him. She then said, "He was in the kitty playpen a few days ago with two other cats, right? I remember seeing him in there."

Savannah nodded. Suddenly she could feel the cat tense up. He began pushing his paws against her arms as if he were trying to escape. "What's wrong Ragsy?" she asked.

Just then, Alyce reached her hand out toward the cat and he began to growl. He hissed.

"Ouch!" Savannah cried, as Rags dug his back claws into her arm and freed himself. He landed on the examining table and then jumped down onto the floor. He turned around once and stared at Alyce, his ears back and his tail low to the ground, before slinking under a chair in the far corner of the room.

Suddenly, the door opened and Michael peered in. "Everything okay in here?" he asked. "Did someone get bit?"

"No, scratched," Savannah said as she dabbed at the wound on her arm.

"Did Rags do that?" he asked, stepping in and closing the door.

Savannah nodded. She looked over at their employee, while holding a tissue against the cat scratch. "Alyce," she said, "I don't know what this is about, but he seems to be upset with you. Maybe you'd better leave." She walked over to the stunned woman. "I'm sorry. I've never seen him behave that way before."

"No problem. I'm outta here—gladly. He's one scary cat!" She said as she hurried out through the door.

"What happened?" Michael asked when he and Savannah were alone in the room.

"I don't know," Savannah said. "He saw Alyce and went crazy."

"Well, that's not like him. I wonder if he's in some sort of pain. Here, let me get him so you can take a look."

"Okay, but just don't let that girl back in here."

Michael took a step toward the cat and then changed his mind. "Savannah, let me see your arm." She held it toward him and he said, "I'm going to send Bud in to clean it and put a dressing on it. Let's do that before you finish with Rags." He looked around her and saw that the cat was still huddled under the chair. "He'll be all right there for a few more minutes."

"Okay," she said. Then, "Oh Michael, don't forget we're having guests in this evening."

"Oh yeah, what time?"

"Around seven."

***

"Happy birthday to you, happy birthday to you."

"Come on you guys, how many birthday parties is a guy supposed to get?" Michael asked.

"Depends on how well loved he is," Savannah said. "Now just blow out the candles, will you?"

Margaret looked over at Michael. "You've already had a birthday party? And we weren't invited?"

Savannah responded, "Oh we just had an early gift-opening with Adam. He made a present for his dad and wanted to give it to him. We had cake and ice cream last Saturday. So who wants chocolate cake and rainbow ice cream?"

"Rainbow ice cream?"

"Sorry, that's what the birthday boy wanted," Savannah said apologetically. "Oh wait. I also have a little Oreo cookie ice cream in there."

"I'll just have cake," Max said turning up his nose.

"Cake and Oreo ice cream for me," Margaret said.

About that time, Lexie sidled up to Michael, her nose sniffing toward the cake on the platter Savannah held.

"No chocolate for dogs, girl. Sorry about that." He then said, "Savannah, do you have a treat in there for our oldest daughter?"

"She's not your oldest, is she?" Max asked. "Isn't Buffy more elderly?"

"Yes, I guess she is. Okay then, our largest daughter." He patted Lexie and hugged her to him. "Come on, I'll get you a treat, girl." He got up and headed toward the kitchen. Before he entered, he noticed something sitting on the buffet in the dining room. "What's this?"

"What?" Savannah asked.

"Someone's keys."

"Oh yes," she said. "I found those at the clinic yesterday morning. I forgot all about them until Rags dug them out from between the seats on our way home this afternoon. I'm going to give them to Craig."

"Where is Rags?" Margaret asked. "I haven't seen him tonight."

"Yeah," Savannah winced. "He isn't feeling well—little urinary tract infection."

"Awww, sorry to hear it," Max said. "Is he here? Or at the clinic?"

"Here," she said. "We had him at the clinic today, but he had a meltdown of some sort."

"What?!?" Margaret exclaimed. "Rags? The coolest cat in town?"

"Yes," Michael said. "He went berserk right there in the examining room—caused such a ruckus it could be heard in the waiting room. Not sure how many people took their pets and went home."

"Oh Michael," Savannah said, "nobody walked out." She looked over at Margaret. "But it was pretty scary. He even scratched me up some." She held out her bandaged arm for her aunt to see.

"Well, what happened?" Margaret asked.

"I think it had something to do with our new girl, Alyce. He took one look at her and just lost it."

Margaret frowned. "Why? Did she remind him of someone or something? Why do you think he acted that way?"

"I don't know; maybe I ought to contact Caroline—the cat psychic."

"Well, he's okay now," Michael said. "We just won't let her near him, that's all."

"But wouldn't you like to know why he would react to her that way?"

"I guess. But I think I'd rather just keep him away from her."

After Savannah finished serving the dessert in the living room, she walked over and picked up a package off the dining room table. Here Michael. Happy birthday, honey." She bent down and gave him a kiss on the lips.

"Well, thank you. Is it something you made?"

"No."

"It's not a re-gift, is it? This wrapping paper looks familiar."

"No, Michael," she said a bit impatiently. "It looks familiar because I have a roll of it and I've wrapped several birthday gifts in it already."

"Oh. So what is it?"

"Open it, silly."

Michael began tearing into the colorful paper and quickly uncovered the item. "It's a… camera? Do we need surveillance cameras?" He looked up at Savannah. "Hey, not a bad idea. I can put one out by the corral and one by the dog run…"

"No, it's not a surveillance camera, it's a camera for your computer."

"For his computer?" Margaret said with a laugh. "Is he going on the dating channel? Will we see his naked butt on his Facebook page?"

"Nooooo, you guys. It's so he can talk in real time with Adam. I gave Marci one to hook up for Adam, too, so they can see each other and talk to each other any time."

"Really?" Michael said as if disbelieving such a thing existed. "Did you hear that, Max? Now how cool is that?" He grabbed Savannah and hugged her to him. "And how thoughtful is my wife?"

"So you like it?" she asked.

"I love it. I am absolutely…well, this is the best gift ever. Thank you, honey."

"Open our gift," Margaret said, handing him a gift bag.

He smiled. "A pretty bag. Thank you, guys."

"Open it, Michael," Margaret said, feigning impatience.

"Okay." He looked over at the couple and asked, "It's not a kitten, is it?"

"No," Max said.

"How do you know? You didn't wrap it," Margaret said, good-naturedly.

"Well, if it was a kitten, I would have heard it meowing on the walk over here, wouldn't I? And Lexie would have been nosing around it. No, Michael, there's no kitten in there. All of ours are accounted for."

Michael peered into the bag and removed the tissue paper. He reached in, pulled out the item and stared at it, a puzzled look on his face. "It's a…"

"It's a pencil and pen holder," Margaret said.

"Well, thank you guys. Really. Nice of you."

"Look at it, Michael," Margaret demanded.

He held it up and examined it more closely, and that's when he noticed Adam's smiling face on all four sides of the pencil holder. "Ohhhhhh, it's Adam."

"Yes," Margaret said. "We've been doing photo sessions when he comes to help us with the kitties." She stood and walked over to where Michael sat. Pointing, she said, "Here he is with Big Boy. Here's a shot with him and little JoJo. Those are the golden girls, Molly and Lolly. And here he is holding his kitty, Tiger. He wanted a picture with his kitty on it, too, so I got Marci to email me one."

"I love it, guys. I really do. You are all so thoughtful…all of you."

Savannah put her hand on her husband's arm. "Oh Michael, I think you're going to cry."

"Yes, I just might. I just might. I'm so… touched. Thank you again."

"You act like you've never had a birthday party before," Margaret said after sitting down next to her husband.

Michael was silent for a moment before saying, "Not many, actually. At least not with friends—just a meal of my choice for supper and maybe a new pair of shoes or a shirt for school. Savannah has told me about the celebrations you all had when she and Brianna were growing up. I missed out on all that."

Max leaned forward and stroked Buffy's fur as she walked past. "Well, Michael, I'd say you're getting it now."

***

"Where are you going to put your pencil box, Michael?" Savannah asked as they prepared for bed that evening. "In the study, in the office?"

"I'm thinking about the study next to the computer. Or near the phone in the kitchen to replace the pencil holder we have in there. What do you think?"

"It's up to you," she said disappearing into the bathroom.

"What are you doing in there?" Michael finally called out. "I'm waiting for my birthday kiss."

"I'm almost ready," she said.

"Ready for what? Are we going out someplace?"

The door to the bathroom opened, the light went out, and Savannah stepped into the dimly lit room wearing a low-cut, slinky, black negligee; her hair was pulled back on one side and hanging partially over one eye in soft layered curls. She stopped and leaned against the door jamb, a sultry look on her beautiful face.

"Wow!" Michael said in a low voice. "You look scrumptious. Come get in bed so I can unwrap you."

"First, you get to unwrap this," she said walking over slowly and handing him a small box wrapped with pretty paper and a bow.

"I'd rather open this," he said reaching up and putting his hands around Savannah's waist and then running them down over her hips.

"Okay. But first you have to open this."

"If you say so," he said impatiently. "What is it? You know, nothing can top what I've already received from you, Adam, Maggie, and Max. Nothing."

She smiled. "I think you'll beg to differ in a few minutes."

"I don't think so," he said while pulling the bow and paper off the little box. He opened the lid, moved some tissue paper aside, and froze in place. As if in a daze, he stared down into the box. Finally, he blurted, "Booties?" He looked up at Savannah, who had a big smile on her face.

"Yes."

He lifted the yellow booties out of the box and held them up. "Booties? Does this mean…?" he started.

"Yes, Michael. It means that I want us to have a baby."

"Now?"

"Yes. As soon as possible. That is, if you still want to…"

"Want to? Absolutely, I want to more than almost anything. Oh, Savannah," he said, reaching up and pulling her down into the bed with him. "Now you have given me everything I could ever ask for. Thank you, honey."

"Sooooo, shall we get started?"

"Get started?" he asked.

"Making that baby, silly."

"Oh yes." He reached up and turned off the bedside lamp.

***

"Who's visiting us so early?" Michael asked as he pulled on his jeans and a tee and rushed to the front door.

"Michael Ivey?"

"Yes," Michael replied, a puzzled look on his face. His eyes darted from one to the other sheriff's deputies who were standing outside the door of his home.

"You're under arrest for the murder of Peter Gamble."

Chapter Seven

"What?" he said out loud.

Savannah gasped when she walked into the living room and saw a sheriff's deputy preparing to snap a pair of handcuffs on her husband's wrists. "No!" she screamed. "NO!"

"He'll be at the main jail ma'am, if you want to call him a lawyer."

"It'll be okay, Savannah. Call Sondra. I'll be all right. It's just some sort of mistake." He then pulled back from the deputy. "Can I at least put on a pair of shoes and grab a jacket? It's cold out there."

The deputies complied and then Savannah watched as they escorted her husband out and helped him into the backseat of a patrol car. Just then Savannah's phone rang. She looked at the screen and then wailed into the receiver, "Oh Auntie, they've just arrested Michael."

"Well, damn. I saw the cars over there and wondered what was going on." She paused. "Arrested him, huh? Un-friggin-believable! Why? Do you know?"

"No. There must be new evidence, I would imagine. Listen, Auntie, I have to call Sondra. I want him out of there as soon as possible. What time is it, anyway—oh, six-forty-five. Probably too early to call." She then shook her head and said, "I can't believe this is happening to us. It's crazy."

"I know, Vannie. Just try to stay calm. Let us know how we can help. Anything, okay?"

"Sure, Auntie. Thank you so much. I'll talk to you later."

***

It was nearly eight by the time Craig arrived. "Hi Dr. Mike," he said as he entered the interrogation room where Michael sat in a chair at a six-foot table. A uniformed sheriff's deputy stood against the wall in the back of the room. Craig placed a briefcase on the floor and then stood staring at the unlikely prisoner.

"Craig, can you tell me what's going on? Why am I here? I'm being arrested for murder? That's crazy."

"Michael, calm down. I'm sure there's been a mistake here someplace, but…" he paused. He then reached down and took something out of his briefcase and laid it on the table in front of them. "We found this on your property, Michael. It checks out as the murder weapon."

Michael stared over at the object and shook his head. "Well, I've never seen it before." He looked up at the detective. "It's not mine, Craig."

"Are you sure?" Craig asked, raising one foot and resting it on the seat of a chair.

"Yeah, I'm sure. That's not my knife. You have my knife. When do I get it back, by the way?"

Craig ignored the question. "Well, Michael, take a look at this." He turned the blood-stained knife over and pointed through the plastic bag to a spot on the blade. "It has your initials on it."

"What?" Michael squinted to see the initials. "MI," he said. "Jees, someone really has gone to a lot of trouble to incriminate me; that's all I can say." He sat back in his chair and looked intently at the detective. "Anything of mine with initials on it, Craig, is engraved MMI, never just MI."

"MMI, huh? What does it stand for?" he asked removing his foot from the chair, scooting it toward him, and sitting down.

"Michael Matthew Ivey. I use the M initial on my checks—everything." He rose briefly and dug into his pocket. "Here, this is my name tag for work. See, Michael M. Ivey." He pulled out his wallet. "All of my credit cards have my middle initial."

"I see," Craig said staring over at Michael while rubbing his chin. He then said, "We talked to the guy at the engraving shop. The owner wasn't there. It was a new kid and he didn't know nothin' about tracking records. It's the only engraving shop for miles, so the work was probably done there, unless the knife came from somewhere else—it was a gift from one of Savannah's relatives in LA, for example… Would they use the M initial or not?"

"Heck, I don't know," Michael squirmed in his seat. He glared across at Craig. "It is not my knife. I've never seen it before."

"I want to see my client." Craig and Michael turned toward the door as Sondra Blair walked in. When she spotted Michael, she headed toward him and asked, "Michael, what's going on?"

"Maybe I can explain," Craig said. "A known enemy of Michael Ivey's was found dead at his veterinary clinic—murdered—and a knife with the initials MI has been discovered on Dr. Ivey's home property. We have arrested him for the murder of Peter Gamble."

"That's preposterous," she said. "This man is an upstanding, well-thought-of citizen in this community. He has no record anywhere and you cannot place him at the scene at the time of the crime, now can you?"

Craig thought about it and said, "No, we can't."

"Did you find his prints on the weapon?"

"No."

"So what you have is circumstantial? Would you say this is true, Detective?" She swished past Craig, walked to where Michael sat, and stood behind him. "So you don't really have any concrete evidence, do you, Detective?"

"Can't say that I have," Craig said with a hint of a smile.

"Then I suggest you let this man get back to his family and work."

Craig leaned back in his chair and said, "Well, we haven't booked him yet. I don't think he's a flight risk. Maybe you're right, Ms. Blair. Let's give the case more time to incubate. Ivey, go home, will ya."

"Sure will, Cra…er, Detective. Thank you." He turned to his attorney. "And thank you, Sondra."

"Yes, Michael. Now I'd like to see you and your wife in my office sometime today. Can you arrange that?"

"Yes; how's the noon hour or after office hours—five-thirty?"

"Make it six." She then turned to Craig and said, "Can I compare notes with you, Detective? I'd like to know more about your investigation, if you don't mind."

"Sure," he said, staring over at her for a moment. "There are some things I can share. Let's go into my office."

Sondra Blair made copious notes as Craig responded to most of her questions, but she was aware that he was holding back. *That's fair in an active investigation,* she thought. After speaking with Craig for forty-five minutes, Sondra excused herself. The two shook hands and went their separate ways.

She left his office feeling that she had enough information to discuss the case with

Michael. She thought it strange that she had been gearing up to represent Michael Ivey—the victim in an assault case—and now may be representing that same client as the accused in a murder case.

***

Savannah had seen three patients so far Thursday morning, checking her cell phone after each one—hoping for a message from Michael or Sondra Blair. The third time was the charm for her. It was nine-thirty when she saw Michael's text. "I'm on my way to work. All is well. Love you."

She glanced out the window just in time to see him pull into the parking lot and waited for him to appear at the back door.

"Hi, honey. I'm so glad to see you! Come tell me what happened," she said as she led him into her office and closed the door.

He wrapped his arms around her and hugged her to him, burying his face in her neck. After several moments, he pulled away and smiled weakly at her. She stared into his eyes as if searching for the answers she so desperately wanted. "They found the murder weapon on our property."

"Where?" she asked, her face contorted into a scowl.

"I don't exactly know. But the thing has the initials MI on it." He turned away and ran his hand through his hair. He shook his head and said, "Someone has gone to a lot of trouble to implicate me, Savannah."

"But they let you go. You didn't have to put up any bail money, did you?"

"No. But they don't want me to leave the area. I'm still some sort of suspect."

Savannah reached out and rubbed his back. "I am so sorry, Michael. This is just awful." She turned toward her desk, leaned her palms on the desktop, and said, "I'm so sorry this is happening." Unsuccessfully fighting back tears, she whispered, "I'm so scared for you…for us." He walked over and wrapped his arms around her. She faced him and asked, "What do we do next?"

"We have a meeting with Sondra Blair this evening after work. In the meantime," he worked hard at a genuine smile, "what do you say we just take care of our patients?"

She wiped at her eyes. "Okay," she said in a weak voice. She then took in a deep breath as if willing herself to be strong. "We don't have many patients this afternoon, so I'm going to run some errands, later. What time is our appointment?"

"Six. Let's try to get out of here by five, go home and feed the critters, and maybe have a bowl of that soup you made, before we meet with her. Sound okay?" Michael asked.

"Perfect," she said. "I'll feel better knowing we have a plan—that there's something we can actually do." She stared down at the floor and shook her head. "I just hate feeling helpless in all this." She reached over and kissed her husband lightly on one cheek. "I'll see you later," she said while running one hand along the side of his face.

She started to walk away when Michael grabbed her wrist. He looked deep into her eyes. "It'll be okay. We *will* be okay."

***

Craig Sledge pulled into the Ivey Veterinary Clinic parking lot around mid morning. He parked at the outer perimeter and exited his unmarked car. In typical detective fashion, he began to scan the area with his eyes. *Employees' cars, no doubt,* he thought to himself. *Maybe a few clients' cars...a mud-splattered monster truck, a few SUVs, Dr. Ivey's vet truck, a dull red pickup that's seen better days, and an older black sedan with tinted windows. Could it be?* He walked over to more closely inspect the car. After squatting down to examine the tires, he walked around to the front of the car and peered inside through the windshield. *Nothing out of the ordinary,* he thought. *A large coke cup from a fast-food store in the cup holder, food wrappers and a discount store bag on the passenger seat, a leather jacket lying across the backseat...what's this?* He walked to the back of the car and studied the back window. *In Memory of, Jason Merrick, 1987-2010* .

Craig looked around to see if he was alone. He then took out his cell phone and snapped a few photos of the car—especially the back window. That done, he reached into his jacket pocket, retrieved his pad and pen, and noted the license plate number. He then walked into the waiting room of the veterinary clinic. He nodded to an older woman who sat next to a cat carrier and acknowledged a couple with a frightened little dog on a leash. "Hello. Good morning," he said as he made his way to the receptionist desk. "Scarlett, right?" he asked.

"Yes?"

"Detective Craig Sledge," he said, discretely displaying his badge.

She looked at it and then made eye contact.

"Can you tell me who drives that black Toyota out there in the parking lot?"

"Uh, no." The petite freckle-faced receptionist said, shaking her head back and forth slowly. She strained to look out the front window to see which car Craig was talking about. Just then, Lisa walked in from the back, carrying an armful of charts. Scarlett acknowledged her, "Hey Lisa, do you know who drives that black car out there?"

Lisa, a heavyset woman in her mid thirties, glanced toward the window and said, "It could be the new girl, Alyce."

"May I speak to her, please?" Craig asked.

Lisa glanced over at him. "Um, sure," she said, while placing the charts on Scarlett's desk. "I'll go get her."

"Just ask her to meet me out front, will you?"

Within a few minutes a thirty-something woman with long stringy brown hair and a plain face walked up to him. "You want to see me?"

"Yes. I'm Detective Craig Sledge," he said, flashing his badge. "Is this your car over here? The black Toyota?"

"Yeah," she said hesitantly. "What about it?"

"Are you the only one who drives this car?" he asked, looking her directly in the eyes.

"Yeah!"

"You haven't loaned it out and it hasn't been stolen anytime recently, then?"

"Uh, no, why?"

"Well, it looks a lot like a car that's been involved in some crimes."

Alyce took a step back. Her eyes darted from side to side. She fidgeted with something in her hands. "What are you talking about, man?"

"Have you tried to snatch any dogs, lately? Or slash any tires?"

"No, man," she said, staring down at her hands.

The newest rooky on the squad would see right through this gal's shell. She is guilty as sin of something. Just look at her squirm. Now let's see if she'll tell me what she's guilty of.

He started to speak when Alyce looked up. She grimaced. "You know, in that neighborhood where I live, things go missing in the night. Maybe someone took my car when I didn't know it. There's a lot of crime in this town, you know." She shook her head in an attempt to flip her hair away from her face. "Yeah, I'll bet someone's been driving my car. I noticed my gas tank was low the other day when I went to go someplace. Someone's probably been hot-wiring my car."

Craig stared at her for a moment. And then he asked, "Who's Jason Merrick?"

Alyce let out a breath and slumped a little. "A friend of mine."

"How'd he die?"

"Overdose."

Craig looked hard at her. "Figures," he said.

"Hey, what's that supposed to mean, man?" she asked with a scowl. She glanced up at him, making eye contact for a split second. "If you don't have any more stupid questions, I need to get back to work."

Craig thought about it and then said, "Naw, that's it. But you better believe that if you were involved in those crimes I mentioned, I will be back. I will find you."

Alyce tightened her lips as if willing herself to keep quiet. Finally she said under her breath, "Yeah, you just do that, big man." With that, she turned and walked back to the clinic.

***

Michael and Savannah arrived at Sondra Blair's office at six o'clock sharp. "Come on in," she invited. She led them into a spacious office that Savannah noticed was well-decorated. The couple sat in matching overstuffed library chairs across the desk from Sondra, who sank into a leather executive office chair. The attorney leaned forward and said,

"Well Michael, it appears you've fallen into a bit of bad luck. So tell me what has happened so far."

Sondra listened while Michael caught her up to date on the events of the last few weeks since he had spoken to her about representing him in a trial against Pete Gamble. "And can you verify your whereabouts the night Mr. Gamble was killed, which they say was…" she looked through some papers on her desk, "sometime between one and two o'clock on Tuesday morning, June nineteenth?"

"I was home with my wife. We were home together. We didn't go anywhere that night," he said. He grimaced. "How does someone prove something like that?"

"Good question. But there are many angles to come from—talking to neighbors…if you have a landline, maybe phone records, and so forth."

Michael laughed. "Yeah, our closest neighbors are Savannah's aunt and uncle."

Sondra leaned forward and looked directly at Michael. "Michael did you do it? Did you stab Pete Gamble to death?"

"No," he said scrunching his face up in protest that anyone could even ask him that question. "Absolutely, not. And it's not that I wouldn't want to see him hurt or even dead. He was causing us some serious worry and even expense with his shenanigans. But this is not the way we handle things." He thought for a moment and then looked the attorney straight in the eyes. "No, Sondra. I did not do this."

She leaned back against her chair. "I believe you, Michael." She pulled a folder from a pile and slapped it on the desk, opened it and fumbled through some papers. "So what do you know about Alyce Drummond?"

"What?" Michael asked. "Uh, she's an employee—she's new." He looked over at Savannah and shrugged. "We don't know much about her, really."

"What does she do for you?"

"Cleans and disinfects pens."

"How long has she worked for you?"

Michael looked over at Savannah and asked, "When did we hire her, honey?"

"Last week sometime. I can look it up at the office and let you know."

"Why?" both Michael and Savannah asked at once.

"Craig Sledge called me this afternoon. He thinks she could be somehow involved. But so far, they don't know her connection, if any."

Michael heard Savannah gasp. He looked at her and asked, "Hon, are you all right? You look a little pale."

"Yeah," Savannah said scowling. "It's just that…well, I ran into Cindy today." She looked over at Sondra and explained, "She's our employee who is out on maternity leave. Alyce took her place. Cindy told me something that might be relevant to this case, actually."

"Really?" Michael asked, turning to face his wife.

"How so?" Sondra probed.

"She said that she met Alyce a little over a week ago while she was having lunch with some of the gals from the clinic. Cindy thought it was odd when this stranger came up to her in the parking lot of the restaurant and asked if she worked at our office. Alyce wanted to know what type of work Cindy did. She said the girl quizzed her on some of the details of her job—how often she had to clean the cages, what types of chemicals she used, what was the procedure for preparing a pen for a patient. Cindy said that Alyce must have overheard her and the other gals talking about her maternity leave and was interested in applying for the temporary job."

"And you thought this was strange or significant how?" Sondra asked.

"Well, I realize that jobs are hard to come by these days," Savannah explained. "But Cindy said she was a little creeped out by the way this gal approached her…like maybe she'd been stalking her. I mean, how else would she know where she worked? It struck me as odd, too, when I got to thinking about it. Who chases a stranger down to ask about the job they're leaving?"

Sondra gave Savannah a sideways look and asked, "How did Cindy know it was Alyce you hired in her place?"

"Oh, she came in one day to pick up her last check and saw her there."

Sondra sat back in her plush chair and stared at something behind Savannah for a few moments. And then she leaned forward and asked, "Had Cindy seen this girl…Alyce before?"

"I asked her that," Savannah said. "She didn't think so."

"Well," Sondra said, "she could be a plant."

Savannah shivered—looked over at Michael.

"Who did the hire?"

"Huh?" Savannah asked.

"Which one of you interviewed her?"

"I did," Michael said.

"Any red flags?"

Michael shifted in his chair and cleared his throat. "As Savannah and I discussed, it seemed fortuitous that she showed up when she did. I asked how she learned of the job, but don't recall getting a straight answer. She said she had worked as a volunteer in a shelter and knew about disinfecting pens. She even mentioned the chemical solutions we use and indicated that she understood the importance of being thorough." He thought about it for a moment and then said, "But from the sounds of it, this could be because Cindy unknowingly prompted her."

"What was her hire date?" Sondra asked, pencil poised.

"You know, after thinking about it, I'm pretty sure it was a week ago Wednesday."

"Okay, June thirteenth," Sondra said making a note. "Pete Gamble was killed six days later—the morning of June nineteenth." After scribbling more notes, the attorney looked up at Michael and Savannah and said, "Did you know that it was probably her car involved in the dognapping incident last…," she flipped through the pages on her pad and then opened it and continued, "a week ago Monday?"

"What?" the Iveys said in unison.

She rifled through the file and pulled out a piece of typing paper with a photo printed on it. "Detective Sledge faxed this over to me this afternoon. Is this the car you saw that night?" she asked as she showed it to them.

"Yes, sure looks like it," Michael said. "But it is a rather common-looking car." He studied the photo. "That dark back window with the writing on it—that's exactly as I remember it." He handed it to Savannah.

"That could be it," Savannah agreed. "But I'm not totally sure," she said while scrutinizing the photo. "I didn't get as close to it as Michael did."

He grimaced. "So this is Alyce's car?"

Sondra squinted in his direction. "You haven't seen this car parked at the clinic before?"

He shook his head. "I guess I just don't notice those things. Besides, Savannah and I usually park in back. Employees and clients park out in the front area." He thought for a moment and then asked, a bewildered look on his face, "Why would she want to take Lexie? I don't get it?"

Sondra ignored his question. She tapped on the photo with a pencil. "According to forensics, the wheelbase measurements and partial tire print they got at your house after your tires were flattened could have come from this car." She hesitated. "But as you say, it is a common type of vehicle."

Michael leaned forward. "So you think she vandalized our cars, too? But why?"

Sondra looked from one to the other of her clients. "Guys, her involvement could go even deeper. Just so you know, she is our focus right now in this investigation," she said.

Michael looked over at Savannah and noticed that she was crying. "Oh honey. It's all going to be okay."

"Michael," she said through sobs. "I want her out of the clinic. She tried to take Lexie. I'm sure of it. Why else would Rags react so strongly to her?" She took a shallow breath. "Maybe he saw her punching holes in our tires that night, too."

"Rags?" Sondra questioned.

"Our cat," Savannah explained. "Rags saw the dognapper that night when he or she took our dog." She sniffed and then continued, "We think he saw someone or something outside the night our tires were slashed. Then, when he saw Alyce at the clinic yesterday, he went crazy."

Sondra asked flatly, "How so?"

"You have to know Rags. He doesn't flip out. He's a calm cat. But when he saw her, he just lost it—he even scratched me trying to get away from her." She touched her bandaged arm.

Michael said, "We knew something was wrong—that there was a reason for his behavior." He looked down; shook his head. "It never occurred to us that he saw Alyce sneaking around at our home trying to do damage…"

Sondra made some notes. Then, looking in Michael's direction, she said, "I guess you were arrested this morning based partially on the found murder weapon—a knife with the same initials as yours."

"Yeah," Michael nodded.

"Detective Sledge said he talked to the owner of the engraving shop today."

Michael took in a deep breath. "What did he say? Is that where the engraving was done?"

She referred to her notes. "His records show that an intern did engraving on a knife fitting that description on June fifteenth. The kid no longer works there. But the note says 'gift.' Someone named Marjory Madison brought the knife in and had the engraving done. Ring a bell?"

Michael stared at the attorney. "Unbelievable," he said. "Marjory Madison? No. I don't know anyone by that name. Something is way wrong here. Things do not add up."

"Or someone is doing a really clever job of framing you, Michael. Who do you think would want to do that?"

Michael thought for a moment. He then looked Sondra in the eyes. "The only person I know who would be that vindictive or crazy is dead."

Savannah wiped her eyes with a tissue. "I want Alyce out of the clinic, now!"

"Let's don't be hasty," Sondra cautioned. "I believe her purpose has been served. I doubt that she is of any danger to you at this point. But if you feel at risk having her there, by all means, fire her. I'd just like a little more time to see if we can unravel the crime before she runs scared on us. I think Detective Sledge is on board with this.

So what do you two think? How do you feel about leaving her where she is for now?"

The couple looked from one to the other and then Savannah asked, "How long?"

"Do you mean how long will it take authorities to discover what her involvement in all this is and find out who her accomplice or accomplices are?" The attorney frowned. "It's hard to say." Sondra looked into Savannah's eyes. "We have a few possible leads. I don't expect it to drag out—as long as we don't spook Alyce. She's our focus right now. As I said, she'll lead us to any others who might be involved. And the detective is still looking into motive."

"Honey," Michael said, "I'm willing to let her stay for a little longer as long as we know the authorities are making progress in their investigation. How do you feel?"

"It's unnerving to think that we may have a murderer working for us. And it seems to me that whatever her motive, it doesn't involve us—except to implicate us." She turned toward Sondra. "Isn't that right?"

"That's how it looks to us."

Michael let out a sigh. "Okay, I guess we'll play along as long as it seems safe for us to do so. Okay, Savannah?"

She nodded, not at all sure she was making the right decision.

***

The following morning, Michael and Savannah walked into the diner. As they glanced around, they spotted someone waving at them from a booth toward the back. "It's Craig," Michael said. "Looks like he wants us to join him. What do you say, hon?"

She wrinkled up her nose and said, "I guess." But what she really wanted was to run far away from the reality of the last two weeks. It seemed that everywhere she went and every waking moment focused on Pete Gamble. Even her dreams revolved around the ugliness of the tragedy; and the uncertainty of it all kept her awake at night. She just wanted it to be over.

Craig greeted them cheerfully, "Good morning, guys. Won't you join me?"

"Hi Craig," Michael said, standing back and allowing Savannah to scoot into the booth. She smiled weakly at the detective and slid across the seat.

Craig looked over at Michael and then Savannah. "Aren't you out early this morning?"

"Decided to have breakfast here before going to work," Michael explained. "It's early for you, too, isn't it?"

"Not really. I don't get much sleep when I'm working a case."

"Just coffee and oatmeal with blueberries," Savannah said when Frank approached their booth.

Michael hesitated and then said, "How about scrambled eggs and a biscuit. Oh yes, and coffee."

"Anything new to report, Craig?" Michael asked. "We could use some good news."

"Well, I can't tell you everything we're working on," Craig said as he looked from one to the other of his tablemates. But I can tell you that we have a lead on the kid who did the engraving on that knife. I want to have a little talk with him—see if he can give us a description of this Marjorie Madison."

"Well, let me know what you find out, will you?" Michael said.

"Sure." Craig took a swig of coffee and then asked, "So did your attorney tell you that we suspect Alyce of being a part of this?"

"Yes," Michael said, shaking his head in disbelief.

"What are you going to do about her? I mean in light of what we suspect about her so far?"

Michael took a deep breath and let it out in a long sigh. "I guess we're going to let her ride it out and see what happens. I mean, if her mission is complete, she will just leave. If she doesn't leave, maybe she wasn't actually involved."

"Oh, by the way, guys, did Alyce sign anything or fill out a job application with you? I'd like to get a sample of her writing."

"Sure, we can provide that for you. Just come by the office. I'll leave a copy in an envelope at Scarlet's desk."

Craig looked intently at Michael. "This case seems to have a lot of angles. It's taking us in unexpected directions."

Suddenly Savannah jumped. "Oh my gosh, I almost forgot." She grabbed her purse and opened it. "It's been so darned crazy," she said shaking her head a little. She pulled something out of her purse. "Keys," she said, holding them up and dangling them in front of Craig.

"Keys?" he asked.

"Yes, I found them in the dirt in the parking lot at the clinic the day…well, when the body was discovered."

"Oh really?" Craig's eyes lit up.

"Yes, and it looks like the key to our clinic right here."

"Well, I'll be. A key to your clinic, huh?" While examining it, he asked, "Do you know which of your employees is most likely to carry a key ring with a skull and crossbones on it?"

"Alyce?" the three of them said in unison.

***

That morning just before noon, Craig Sledge walked up to the front door of the veterinary clinic with the set of keys in his hand. He stuck one of the keys into the lock and tried to turn it. It wouldn't budge. He tried a second key. It wouldn't go in. He looked at the three other keys on the ring—one was obviously a car key and one looked like it might go to a post office box. The last one, he thought, probably went to the lock in a storage space—a padlock. He opened the door and walked into the lobby. "Good morning, Scarlett."

"Hello. Detective, right?" the pert brunette responded.

"Yes; Detective Sledge. He held up the set of keys that Savannah had found and asked, "Are these yours?"

"No," she said.

"Do you have a set of keys with you?"

"Yes," she responded.

"May I see them?"

Scarlett looked at him for a moment and then walked down the hallway and disappeared. She returned with a wad of keys in her hand. She held them out for Craig to see.

He took them from her and looked at each key, comparing them to some of those on the other key ring. "So this goes to your car, right?"

She nodded.

"Which one goes to this office?"

Scarlett took the keys, rifled through them, and then picked up one and held it, letting the others drop to the bottom of the key ring.

Craig compared that key to those on the other ring. "Well, it looks just like this one," he said scrutinizing it carefully. "Only this one didn't work on the front door."

"That's because it goes to the back door," she said.

Just then, a woman walked into the waiting room carrying an empty cat carrier. "Oh, hello Mrs. Whitaker, we have your kitty ready. Let me get her for you." Scarlett started to turn toward the hallway and stopped. She looked over at Craig, picked up her keys, and walked off.

Craig watched her leave and then exited through the front door and walked around to the back. He tried one of the keys on the ring in the back door lock and found that it worked. *So this is an employee's key to the office,* he thought. *But who?* He walked back to the front of the clinic and through the front door. He found Scarlett putting on her sweater. She had her purse and keys sitting in front of her on her desk. "Are you leaving?" he asked.

"Yes, it's lunchtime. We usually close to walk-ins between noon and one," she explained.

"Scarlett, before you leave, can you tell me who these keys might belong to?"

She looked at the ring of keys again, shook her head, and said, "No, I can't."

"You haven't seen them before?"

"No," she said with a shrug.

"Tell me, did anyone come in this week without their keys—that you know of?" he asked.

"I don't think so…" Scarlett started. And then she said, "Hey, wait a minute. I heard them talking in the back about some lost keys. But that was a couple of days ago and I was real busy at the time. Lisa, I think it was, came up and asked me if I'd seen any car keys. I told her, 'no.' I think they might have been Alyce's—the new girl. I saw her through the window out in the parking lot later having a smoke and she was sort of scuffing up the dirt with her shoes like she was searching for something."

Craig looked at her and then asked, "Is Alyce the kind of girl who would carry a ring of keys with a skull and crossbones on it?"

"Heck, I don't know. She's new," she said rather impatiently. And then she said, "She does have some tattoos—and not the dainty girly kind, either, if you know what I mean. I saw her take off her sweater and put on her lab smock one day. Lots of ugly tattoos." She stared off into space and then said, "Yeah, I guess I could imagine her carrying a key ring with a skull and bones." She looked down at the keys. "Those sure could be hers."

"Is she here this morning?"

"No. She has gone to lunch," she said picking up her purse. She walked toward the front door and opened it. "I really have to go now. I have an appointment." She held the door open for Craig. "…if you don't mind."

"Oh sure. Sorry if I held you up." He walked out the door ahead of her and then turned. "Thank you for your time, Scarlett." He climbed into his unmarked car, pulled out his notepad, flipped through a couple of pages and then read, "Alyce Drummond, 8334 Foxtail Place, number 102." He left the pad open, set it down on the seat next to him and drove off, making a mental note to pay Alyce a visit that evening.

***

It took him only minutes to reach the apartment building from the station, where he had chosen to work late. And it didn't take long for Alyce to respond to his knock. In fact, she seemed quite eager to open the door and welcome someone. As it turned out, that *someone* wasn't Craig Sledge.

"Oh," she said, as her smile quickly disappeared. "You're not who I thought…"

"Obviously," Craig said with a smirk.

"What do you want?" she asked, setting her jaw in defiance.

"I think I found something that belongs to you."

"What?" she asked, more than a hint of defensiveness in her tone.

He held up the ring of keys.

Her face lit up for an instant and then she turned sullen—looked suspicious. "What is that?" she asked.

"Well, I'm pretty sure they're your keys, ma'am," he said. "Don't you recognize them?"

"Noooo," she drew the word out. "I don't think so."

It was then that Craig noticed a skull and crossbones tattooed on her left ring finger. He looked at the door lock. "Then none of these keys will fit your door here, right?"

Alyce wrapped her arms across her chest, pressed her lips together, and glanced quickly from side to side. Then, lifting her chin and standing up straighter, she shook her head and said weakly, "No."

"Well, let's see." He isolated one of the keys and stuck it into the door lock. "Maybe you're right. It doesn't seem to fit."

She relaxed a little.

"But what about this one?" he asked. He pushed it into the lock. "Bingo," he said as he twisted the key back and forth and watched the bolt move in and out. "Well, isn't that strange?" he said looking over at her. "What are the chances of someone else's key ring having your house key on it?" He stared at her for a moment and then said, "Ms. Drummond, I'd like to come in and ask you a few questions."

"And if I refuse to let you in?" she asked.

"I'll just take you down to the station and talk to you in a jail cell," he bluffed.

She let out a sigh. "Okay, but just for a few minutes. I have to meet someone." She opened the door for him to enter and then stepped out through the doorway and looked up and down the street. When she re-entered the room, she was tapping on the screen of her phone as if texting a quick message to someone. She motioned with her head toward a chair and Sledge sat down. She perched on the edge of the sofa across from him. "Okay, so what do you want to know?" she asked.

"Where did you lose the keys, Ms. Drummond?"

"Um, I'm not sure."

"Well, did you use them to go to work yesterday?"

She thought about it before saying, "No."

"Thursday?"

"Um Maybe."

"What about Wednesday? Did you have them that day?"

"I don't remember."

"Did you drive anywhere today or yesterday?"

"Yes. I have an extra car key."

"What about your house key?"

"Under the mat."

"And these other keys? What do they go to?"

She took the ring from Craig and identified the keys, "My storage unit, the laundry room…" She set the keys down.

"What about that silver key right there?"

"Which one? I told you, the laundry room."

The detective sat back in his chair and looked at the young woman. *Does she think I'm dense?* "I know that key fits the back door of the veterinary clinic, Alyce. Now tell me how you lost these keys or…" he hesitated, "who you gave them to."

"Where did you find them?" she asked.

"No you don't. You go first." He leaned forward. "Where did you lose them?"

Alyce suddenly perked up. Raising her eyebrows so they disappeared into her long fringe of bangs, she said, "The car thief has probably been using those keys to drive my car at night."

Sledge frowned and looked confused. "What?"

"Remember I told you someone might be stealing my car and driving it around when I'm sleeping or working? They've probably been using that key right there."

"When is the last time you had them in your possession?"

She thought for a few moments. "I don't know. I guess over the weekend."

Craig's eyes wandered over the series of tattoos on her upper arms and chest. *Yes, she is into tats.*

She was still talking, "Someone must have taken them out of my purse or I dropped them somewhere. As I recall, I drove to work Saturday. I was the first one there, so I unlocked the door with my key. But when I went to leave, the vet tech… uh…Bud, was still there, so he locked up. And when I went out to get in my car, I couldn't find my car keys."

"Did you go back in and look around inside?"

"No, Bud had left by then and I didn't have a key to get inside."

Craig squinted his eyes and scratched his head. "How did you get home, Ms. Drummond?"

"Um, I told you I have a spare key."

"That you carry in your purse?"

"Yeah."

Craig looked at her for a long time and then said, "Why is it I only believe part of what you're saying?"

"It's the truth, dude," she said. "I lost those keys and I don't know where—must have been at the clinic, though…unless…."

"Unless what?"

"Unless someone took them out of my purse. Yes, that's probably it. Someone lifted them out of my purse while I was at work."

"Who might that be?"

"One of the other employees? We all keep our personal stuff in a closet in the back. Or maybe someone who used our restroom—one of those creepy delivery guys, maybe. They come in that back area where we put our purses and coats. It could have been anyone, man. I'm just lucky they didn't use my house key to get at me, know what I mean?"

"Yeah, I know what you mean," Craig said, humoring her.

"Can I have my keys back?" she asked. "Or are they evidence?"

"Evidence?" Craig perked up. "Why would you think of these keys as evidence, may I ask?"

"Uh, just a figure of speech. I didn't mean nothin' by it," she said, nervously running her fingers back and forth across her lips. She then clasped her hands together in her lap, smacked her lips, and said, "Well, I hope you find the guy who took them and arrest him."

"Yeah, we'll do that."

"Can I have my keys?"

"I'll tell ya what," he said, "I'll let you have your laundry room key." He slid it off of the ring. "…and your storage unit key. I want to keep the ring with these keys on it."

"What? Why?" She sat forward in her chair, a frown transforming her rather plain face. "You can't do that. They belong to me!"

"I can do that and I will," he said.

"But how will I get in to work?"

"How have you been getting in to work?"

"Um, I wait for someone to open the door. But I'm supposed to be there early sometimes. I need my own keys."

Craig studied Alyce's face for a few seconds and said, "Well, you don't have to worry about that until tomorrow, right?"

"I work until noon."

"I'll bring either this key or a duplicate to you sometime tomorrow. In the meantime, make arrangements to have someone let you in tomorrow morning." He stood to leave and noticed that she was sitting there, staring down at the keys in her hand with a blank look on her face. "I'll let myself out," he said. "Thank you for your cooperation." He then stopped and addressed her again. "If it comes to you who might have *taken* these keys of yours, please let me know. Otherwise, we may decide to charge you with contempt or interfering with a criminal case or being an accomplice to murder," he said with emphasis.

***

The next morning after picking up a cup of coffee, Craig visited a hardware store and had a key made. Then he drove over to the clinic. "Oh hello, Alyce," he called out when he saw her walk through the hallway that opened out into the waiting room.

She stopped and looked in his direction. He held up her key ring.

"Uh, thanks," she said after walking toward him and reaching out for the keys.

Craig pulled his hand back, looked her in the eyes and said, "Don't plan to leave town." He watched her to see how she would react. *She looks like a scared rabbit underneath that tough exterior,* he thought.

***

Sunday morning, the Iveys walked into the diner and saw Craig sitting alone in a booth. He stood to greet them. "We're going to have to quit meeting like this," he said, motioning for Michael and Savannah to join him. "Actually, I was about to leave, so you can have the booth to yourself." He looked at his watch. "I have a meeting with Damon in a little while."

"I heard you were spending time with him. How's he doing?" Michael asked.

"Pretty good, actually. He and his mom are getting along, which is good to see. He's even on good terms with his little brothers." He thought for a minute and then said, "It's amazing to me what a difference it can make when someone comes off drugs. Life actually takes on a new meaning."

"Damon isn't exposed to drugs inside?" Savannah asked.

"Well actually, yes," Craig said. "He says he can get them if he wants them. He seems to be taking the program we're working seriously and claims he does not want to go back to the life he was living. I hope he's sincere."

"Well, good luck with him. I'm sure Iris is thrilled with his progress and his potential. Speaking of Iris," Savannah said looking around, "where is she this morning?"

"Good question," Craig said. "I thought she was on the schedule. I expected to see her here." He motioned for Frank to come over. "Where's Iris?" he asked.

"Oh, you didn't hear? She had to take her son to the hospital."

"What?" Craig said. He reached for his cell phone to check for missed calls.

"I wonder what happened," Savannah said, her brow creased with worry.

Craig pushed a button on his phone. "I'll see if she'll answer."

"Iris. Where are you? Frank said…" He listened for a minute. "Oh God. I'll be right there, Iris."

Craig dropped the phone into his jacket pocket and looked over at Savannah and Michael as if in shock. "They suspect that Brett has overdosed. Iris is at the hospital with him in Straley."

Chapter Eight

"I got a call from Iris," Savannah announced from the front door as she struggled to carry in several bags of groceries later that afternoon.

Michael rushed to give her a hand. "What did she say?" he asked.

"She thinks he'll be okay," she said as she rushed toward the kitchen and set the bags on the counter. She turned to face Michael. "It seems that Brett went to a party last night and ingested something. From the sounds of it, they don't think he purposely took anything, but all of a sudden, he started convulsing. He passed out and the idiot kids at the party thought he was dead or dying. They didn't want to get in trouble, so they took him out and dumped him near the park. Iris thought he was spending the night at this kid's house; they were supposed to go fishing yesterday. Well, one of Brett's friends must have sobered up enough to think somewhat sensibly and he got a ride over to where they'd dumped Brett. He got worried when he saw Brett and called 9-1-1. Iris got the call around four this morning. It appears that it wasn't a minute too soon. Brett had a rough day, but he was coming around when I spoke with Iris this afternoon and she thinks he can come home tomorrow."

"How awful. Iris must have been scared to death," Michael said.

"Yes, she sure was. She said Craig was wonderful—a great support for her and for Brett. Craig even helped out with Chris—picked him up from some event he was attending and took him to the hospital to be with his mom and brother. Evidently, Brett gave Craig the name of the guy he thinks brought drugs to the party. Craig is going to check him out."

"So what does Damon think about all this?" Michael asked.

"I don't know if they've told him yet. It doesn't sound like Craig got a chance to see him today, after all."

Michael suddenly reached for his cell phone, looked down at it and said, "It's Craig."

"Hello, Craig. How's Brett?"

"Doing okay, we think. It was a rough go."

"So I heard. How's Iris?"

"She's an amazing woman, Michael. She's doing gr
said, "Say, Michael, we were wondering if we could come by this evening—Iris and I.She has something for yo
"…so do I."

"Sure, we'd like to see you. Come by anytime. Wait," Michael said, "Savannah is motioning to me. He spoke into the phone again, "Craig, Savannah has made some Texas hash and wonders if you two…and Chris…would like to come for dinner. We'll eat in about an hour."

"Texas hash?" Craig said with enthusiasm. "My favorite. Let me ask Iris." He returned to the phone and said, "Sounds great. We'll see you in an hour. Oh, and it'll just be me and Iris. Chris has homework and leftover pizza to munch on."

Iris and Craig arrived at six sharp. They stepped into the house when Michael opened the door. "Hi Lexie," Iris said, bending down and ruffling the dog's long Afghan fur. "You're such a pretty girl." She then looked around the room. "Where's my Buffy?"

"Oh, probably in a hidey-hole somewhere. But you know she'll come out to see you before the evening's out."

"I love that little cat." Iris smiled.

"And she loves a warm lap," Michael said.

Savannah strolled into the room. "Hieveryone." She hugged Iris and then Craig.

"Love your lounging outfit," Iris said. "That color is so good on you." Then she said, "What am I saying? I haven't seen a color yet that doesn't look good on you." She scrutinized Savannah for a moment before saying, "Except maybe a bright-yellow."

"Well I'll stay away from yellow, then," she said with a smile. "What colors do you avoid, Iris?" she asked while gazing over at her friend's smart ensemble—plum designer jeans, a fine-knit, cream-and-plum print sweater and, of course, matching platform heels.

Iris thought about it for a moment and said with a laugh, "I don't think that color's been invented, yet."

"How's he doing, Iris?" Savannah asked, hesitantly.

"They said he has a lot of sleeping to do, yet—so we left him to it." She smiled and clasped her hands together under her chin. "He's going to be okay. I'll go back early tomorrow and, hopefully, bring him home sometime later in the day." She reached out and touched Savannah's arm—looked over at Michael, "Thank you both for caring and for letting us hang out with you tonight."

"And for making Texas hash," Craig said, winking over at Savannah.

Later in the evening, while Savannah and Iris cleared the kitchen table, the two men retired to the living room. "Michael, I didn't want to bring it up at dinner because I'm sure that you two are up to your eyeballs in this thing. But I spoke with the kid who did the engraving on that knife. Sure does sound like our girl, Alyce, was the one using the alias Marjory Madison. I got the signature from the engraving company and our handwriting experts compared it with the sample you gave me. Looks like a match."

"So what does this mean?" Michael asked.

"Not sure yet. We are working on her connections—finding out just who she is and what her part is in this whole thing."

"Who wants coffee?" Iris asked as she entered the room carrying a cup and saucer in each hand. Savannah was right behind her.

"Iris, don't you ever get tired of serving coffee?" Michael chuckled.

"Not when there are tips involved," she quipped.

"Well, here's a tip," Michael said with a smile, "don't bet on the horses."

"Yikes," Savannah said. "Peaches. Did you feed her, Michael?"

"Yes, I did," he said, a smug look on his face.

"Oh thanks. I forgot all about her. Poor mare. I hope to be able to ride this weekend. I think I'm healed enough if I don't do too much posting." Savannah set down two cups of coffee and went back into the kitchen. She returned with a tray holding a sugar bowl, cream pitcher, napkins, and teaspoons.

Once everyone was settled, Iris held up a gift bag and handed it to Michael. "Happy late birthday, boss, friend, all-around good guy."

"Well thank you, Iris," Michael said sincerely. "How nice of you. Now what could this be?" He reached into the bag while smiling over at Iris. He lifted something wrapped in striped tissue and began tearing into the paper. "Feels like a book."

Everyone sat silently, watching Michael.

When he got the wrapping off, he looked down at the object and said, "Well, how cool is this? Iris, where did you find it?"

"Online, of course," she said.

"What is it, Michael?" Savannah asked. She was sitting on the sofa, her legs folded under her. Rags was lying up against her, watching everyone.

Michael held the gift up for her to see. "It's an all-Afghan calendar." He turned to Lexie, who was hovering nearby. "Look, girl, here are some of your relatives." He addressed Iris and Craig, "This is great, guys. Thanks a lot." He thumbed through it. "Here's one that looks a lot like her."

"Oh, here she comes," Iris said with a smile. She leaned over toward the floor. "Come on Buffy. Come see Aunt Iris."

From across the room, the little cat looked up at Iris with big blue eyes. She sat down and began licking her fur. She then looked up at Iris again and walked toward her, jumping into her lap and curling up. "You are such a cutie, Buffy," she said while petting the long-haired beauty. She looked over at Savannah and said, "Now if I ever decide I want a cat…"

"Don't get any ideas. You can't have that one." Savannah became contemplative and said, "You know, I'm awfully sorry that Mrs. Armstrong died, but I am so happy that the family gave Buffy to us."

"Well, Michael used to have her more than old Mrs. Armstrong did, didn't you, Michael?"

"Yeah, she boarded with me pretty often. She's a good girl, aren't you, Buffy?" he said smiling over at the cat.

"And Rags really loves her," Savannah said. "They sure seem devoted to one another."

"That's because Lexie and Walter have eyes only for each other," Michael said.

Everyone watched the animals for a while—and when each cat and dog seemed to have found their comfort zones and settled down, Michael asked, "So Brett can come home tomorrow?"

"Yes, we think so," Iris said. "That was a close call and a wakeup call for him."

Michael shifted in his seat. "I didn't know he was doing drugs, Iris."

"I really don't think he was," Craig said. "I believe that someone may have talked him into trying something at this party or he got it accidently and the stuff these kids got hold of was bad. Some of the other kids were pretty sick, but it didn't affect them as seriously as it did Brett." Craig cleared his throat and leaned forward. "You know, I saw Damon late today. He already knew about Brett and was furious."

"How did he know?" Savannah asked.

"Word gets around in these joints," Craig said. "He thinks he knows who sold the kids the stuff and he gave me some names." He set his coffee cup on the table next to him. "You may be surprised to know that one of the names that came up was Pete Gamble."

"Really?" Michael said frowning. "He was involved in the drug scene?"

"Yes, I guess in a pretty major way."

"How does someone who is involved in drugs run a fairly successful, legitimate business?" Michael asked.

"Well, Pete inherited the business from an uncle. And I don't think it has been all that successful in recent years. Besides, drug lords like having legitimate businesses to hide behind."

"He was a drug lord?" Savannah asked, raising her eyebrows.

"That might be a bit of an exaggeration," Craig said. "But it seems he was doing a lot of distribution." He paused. "Damon gave me several other names, too. He seems to think that some of these punks could be after him and they purposely sold or gave Brett and his friends bad stuff. Damon thinks he knows who it was. But if we start approaching these two-bit dealers, this could put Damon in danger."

"Even while he's in prison?" Savannah asked.

"Maybe even more so in prison," he responded.

"Craig is going to take him to a safe place before he starts investigating," Iris said.

Michael cocked his head in Craig's direction. "Out of jail? You can do that?"

"Yes, he's up for a furlough and is eligible for early release, anyway. Since he'll be under my supervision, my request was granted. I have a cabin in the mountains. I'm taking him up there for a few days or a week while we see if we can clean up the streets of Hammond once and for all."

"Once and for all?" Michael said with a chuckle. "That sounds like a pipedream to me."

"Well, yeah. It is wishful thinking and somewhat unrealistic. But we can certainly put a dent in their penny-ante operations; that's for sure."

"And save innocent kids from what Brett's going through," Iris said, dabbing at her eyes. She sat up straight and said with a slight smile, "By the way, Dr. Mike, I won't be in to clean this week, if that's okay."

"Why?" Michael asked.

Her smile widened. "The boys and I are going to the cabin to be with Damon. Craig will be coming back and forth."

"Oh, no problem, Iris."

Savannah addressed her friend with a smile. "Hey, that sounds great, Iris. I'll bet you're looking forward to that."

"Sure am," she said, her face aglow with joy.

"More coffee anyone?" Savannah asked as she stood to clear away the plates.

"No. None for me. Thanks," Craig said. And then he asked, "Uh Michael, how's Alyce doing this week?"

"Interesting you should ask. We were talking earlier this evening about her. The first week she was with us, she seemed fine. But there's something missing this week. I think we'll actually have a legitimate reason to let her go." He scratched the back of his neck. "Not sure what's going on with her. It's like she's preoccupied. Kind of jumpy, actually, don't you think, Savannah?"

"Yes. Yesterday, she had just come in after taking a cigarette break. I asked her to prepare a pen for a new boarder and she just looked at me kind of blank, like she didn't understand a word I was saying."

"Hmmm, you might have a druggie on your hands there," Craig said.

Savannah scrunched up her face. "Oh, I hadn't thought of that. And you heard about Rags's reaction to her, didn't you? He freaked out when she came into the room where he was."

"Yeah, that was odd." Craig leaned forward in his chair. "Well, as it turns out, Damon knows her. He was surprised to learn that she was working for you. Said she usually works in sleazy bars as a cocktail waitress and she sometimes dances at strip clubs. He said he has never known her to have a regular job."

"Well, that's interesting. Maybe she's turning over a new leaf…or trying to," Michael said.

Savannah laughed. "Ever positive, as Auntie Marg says."

Craig looked askance at Michael. "I don't think so. But I guess anything's possible."

***

The headlines in Tuesday evening's paper blared: "Raid Results In Arrests."

"Did you see this?" Michael asked when Savannah walked through the door of their home.

"Yes, I stopped by to see Auntie; and Max showed it to me. I guess Craig's operation was successful."

"Says they arrested a dozen people on all variety of charges," Michael said. And then he motioned to her. "Come here, I want to show you something."

"What?" Savannah asked as she zipped up her purse, set it down and walked over to the sofa where Michael sat.

"Here, look at this guy."

"Well, I can't see much of him. What about him?" she asked. "Is it someone you know?"

"Oh, I think he may have paid us a visit at some point—but no, we don't know him. At least, I hope not."

"You're talking in riddles, Michael."

"Look at what he's wearing, Savannah."

"Ohhhhhh. Could it be? Oh my gosh, Michael. It looks like the same fabric as the swatch Rags had at the clinic that night. We'd better call Craig."

"Wait—let's look at the online newspaper. Maybe we can bring it closer and see the fabric better. Do you remember what it looked like?"

"I sure do. Exactly."

Once Michael brought the photograph up on the computer, Savannah stared into the monitor. "Yes, that's it, Michael—I can see it clearly. That's the fabric from Rags's swatch. I'm calling Craig right now."

"What did he say?" Michael asked when Savannah had hung up the phone.

"He seemed glad for the reminder. In fact, he was a little excited about it. I guess he'd forgotten about the fabric."

***

"I want to talk to one of the men we picked up last night," Craig Sledge told the sergeant in charge of the jail.

"Which one, Detective?"

"Gus Ramirez."

The sergeant looked down at a list. "Oh, we just let him go. He had a public defender and made bail."

"Crap!"

"Why do you want him?"

Craig looked over at him and said, "Well, someone let a cat out of a bag and I want to talk to him about it."

"Huh?" the sergeant cocked his head slightly and rubbed the back of his neck.

"Just don't rent out his cell to anyone else. He may be needin' it." With that, Craig turned on his heels and walked back to his office. "Gonzalez, let's go. We have a possible perp to nab."

After driving around for an hour in the area where they'd originally picked up the man named

Gus Ramirez, Ramon Gonzalez said, "Sledge, we've been past this block eight times. He's not here."

"Well, he could be in the club or the tat parlor. Let's go see if we can find him there." They parked and walked into Clive's Tattoos. "Have you seen Gus tonight?"

"Nope," the tattoo artist said without looking up.

"Are you sure?" Craig said pulling the plug on the tattoo gun he was using.

"Yeah, man, I'm sure. Now quit interferin' with my business, man."

"Do you know where he might be this time of night?"

"Don't know—he'll probably be at the club later."

Once outside, Gonzalez said, "Sledge, why don't we go get dinner and then do a stake-out. No one goes to the clubs before nine."

"Yeah, I guess. I'm just eager to take a good look at this guy."

"Where do you want to eat? Your favorite place?"

Craig looked confused for a moment and then said, "Oh, the diner? Naw, she ain't workin' tonight."

"You sure are sweet on that gal, aren't you?"

"She's a great gal." Craig didn't want to tell his partner that he had Damon at his cabin and Iris and the boys were out there waiting for him. *Looks like I won't return until late tonight,* he thought. *I'd better call*. "Iris, how is everything?"

"Good. We're having a nice time getting reacquainted. When will you be here?"

"I'm on a hot trail, so it may be late."

"They're expecting rain tonight. Drive carefully, will you, ya big lug?"

"Sure, anything for you. Do you need me to bring anything tonight?"

"Just you," she said. Then her tone accelerated, "Hey the boys went fishing today. We're cooking up some trout for dinner. Craig, you should have seen what fun they had out there on the river together. I don't know how many times I cried from pure joy today. Thank you for giving me this wonderful gift," she said while looking at the three boys, who were in the kitchen cleaning their fish and trying to freak each other out with fish parts." She smiled. "We'll be here when you get here. Good luck with your…hot trail."

Chapter Nine

A couple of hours later, Craig and Ramon Gonzalez parked across the street from Club Macho, watching for Gus Ramirez. "Is that him?" Gonzalez asked, looking from the man he saw on the street to the mug shot in his hand.

"That's him," Craig said, "and he's wearin' just the right attire."

"What?"

"Just hang tough. You'll find out in a few minutes. Let's go get him."

"Gus Ramirez?" Craig asked as he approached the man standing outside Club Macho.

The thickset Hispanic man spun around, dropped the joint he was smoking, and said, "Yeah, who wants to know?"

"Detective Sledge," Craig said, flashing his badge. "This is Sergeant Gonzalez. We want to ask you a few questions."

"About what, man? I paid my bail."

To Gonzalez's surprise, Craig reached over and began rubbing the fabric of Ramirez's lapel between his thumb and fingers.

"What do you want?" Gus said, slapping at the detective's hand and taking a step back.

"Just settle down, Gus," Sledge said. "I want to check you out." He looked the man up and down with a wide smile on his face and said, "Yep, you look mighty fine tonight. Just the way I hoped to find you." He thought for a moment and then said, "Let's go in the restroom, shall we?"

"What? Are you some sort of pervert? No, I'm not going in any john with you guys." He looked from one to the other and began backing away.

Craig reached out, grabbed the man, and bent one arm behind him. Pushing him along in front of him, he asked, "Where's the bathroom in this place?"

"In the back," Gonzalez said, himself somewhat perplexed by his partner's actions.

"Is there a back entrance?"

"Yeah."

"Good, let's go around back."

"Sledge, what are you doing?" Gonzalez asked in a hushed tone.

"You'll see, Gonzalez. Just stay with me here. In just a minute, you'll see this guy's true colors."

"Lock the door," Craig instructed his partner once the trio was inside the restroom. He cuffed Gus and then stood back and looked intently at him.

Craig couldn't help but notice beads of sweat running down Gus's ruddy face and disappearing into his thick black moustache. "What do ya want, man?" he asked. "What are ya gonna do? I'll have your badge, you try anything funny with me, you pervert."

Sledge reached over and began handling the lightweight, brown tweed shirt-jacket Gus wore. He examined it from top to bottom. Finally he found what he was looking for. "Ah, Gus, it appears that your dress suit here has a tear in it. He reached into his pocket and pulled out the swatch Savannah had given him several days before and fingered it so that Gus could see it.

Gus's eyes grew large. "What's that, man? What do you want with me?"

"I want you to turn around and face Gonzalez, there."

Gus didn't budge, so Sledge took his right arm and swiveled him around. He held the swatch next to the hole near the bottom of the loose-fitting jacket and said, "Bingo. Do you see this here, Gonzalez? Perfect match, wouldn't you say?"

"Yeah," Ramon Gonzalez said, not quite understanding the significance of the discovery.

Sledge reached over and took the cuffs off Gus. "Now pull down your pants," Sledge ordered.

"No!" Gus shouted. "No! I'm not gonna let you…"

"Let me what? Get your mind out of the gutter. I just want to look at something."

"Don't you need a warrant?"

"No, but you'll need a feeding tube if you don't do as I say."

"Okay man, okay." Gus unfastened his baggy slacks and looked at Craig.

"Drop 'em." And if it will make you feel any better, I want you to leave your shorts on—if you're wearin' shorts." He raised his voice, "Just drop your pants."

Gus complied and Sledge put the cuffs back on him, his hands behind his back. Craig then squatted down and looked at the back of Gus's right thigh. "Oh, Gus, what happened here?" he asked as if he was actually concerned.

"Uh, what do you mean?"

"I see a gnarly scratch—looks like you got a pretty good gouge here, maybe a week ago. Looks a little infected." He stood and turned Gus around so he could look him in the eye. "So what happened? Were you hopping over a barbed-wire fence or something?"

"Yeah," Gus said, sweat pouring out of his forehead. "Uh, yeah. I got caught on a damn fence…when I was out in the country…fishin'. Yeah, that's it, I was fishin' and had to climb over a fence."

"Well, it looks to me more like…" he got in Gus's face and continued, "a cat scratch. Don't you think so, Gonzalez?"

Gus started yelling. "No man. There was no cat. I don't know what you're talkin' about."

"Well, how is it that the cat had this piece right out of your jacket there? And the piece is missing from right where this scratch is?"

"This aint' my shirt, man. I borrowed it from a homeless guy."

"Ramirez, pull your pants up." He uncuffed him so he could comply and then quickly cuffed him again. "Okay, let's go."

***

"Sorry for calling so late, Michael. Just thought you'd like to know, I have someone in jail for the murder of Pete Gamble."

"That's great news. It's never too late to hear good news. Wake me up anytime you can tell me something like this." He then paused. "Who is it? Anyone we know?" He looked over at Savannah, who had propped herself up on one elbow on her pillow.

"I doubt it. Name's Gus Ramirez. Not sure if or how Alyce fits in, yet, but I imagine it has to do with a drug deal gone bad. We'll know more in time. Right now, I'm headed out to the cabin to join Iris and the boys. Oh, by the way, Michael, would you tell Savannah that it was her cat that solved the case?"

"How's that?" Michael asked, a puzzled look on his face.

"Just tell her he left his mark on the guy, that's all."

"Sure will. Have a good night. And drive carefully. It's pouring out there."

"Tell me about it. I'm almost to the turn-off to the cabin. I'll probably lose power on my phone soon. Good night, Michael."

***

The headlines in the Wednesday evening paper read, "Arrest Made In Pete Gamble Murder." The story went on to say that the authorities believe there will be more arrests and they aren't sure if they have the ring leader or not.

"So Rags saved the day again, huh?" Margaret smiled while staring over at the big cat. "Just look at how nonchalant he is about his part in the investigation. I'm telling you, he ought to be in a movie or at least on a talk show."

"What's he going to say?" Savannah laughed.

"Oh, they'll get an interpreter—a cat whisperer—to interview him."

"Funny, Auntie." Savannah thought for a moment, then said, "It really is pretty remarkable how much help he has been to the sheriff's department since we came here. He ought to be their mascot."

Margaret giggled. "If they could only see him now, all stretched out there on his back looking like some sort of lawn ornament. They'd think twice about choosing him as their mascot."

"Stop it! He's cute!" Savannah said.

"Is that what you call it?" Margaret glanced toward the doorway to the kitchen where the two ladies sat visiting. "Now there's cute—look at that beautiful cat. Come here, Buffy."

"That's because she reminds you so much of Layla—your beautiful faux Persian."

"That she does," Margaret said, picking up the fluffy little cat and helping her get settled in her lap.

Suddenly, Lexie, who had been asleep near the side kitchen door on her bed, lifted her head and pricked up her ears.

"Michael must be home," Savannah said, peering toward the living room.

Lexie stood up, shook her whole body, and then trotted off to greet her master.

"Hi ladies," he said when he walked in. He bent down and kissed Savannah on the lips and patted Margaret on the shoulder. "What's going on?"

"Just talking shop," Margaret said.

Savannah turned toward her husband, "Oh Michael, did you ever hear from Alyce?"

"No. I think she has quit. I had Scarlett arrange to have the locks at the clinic changed and I brought home the employment applications we accumulated before Alyce came on the scene. We can go over them together, maybe tonight."

"Okay. Now, honey, sit down and eat; Craig's coming over in thirty minutes. Says he has some news."

"Gosh, what could be better than having the murderer locked up? That's the news I was most interested in."

Savannah stood and walked over to the stove. "He says they have motive and he wants to share it with us before it hits the papers."

"What's for supper?" Michael asked, while straining to see what Savannah was dishing up.

"Auntie brought over some of Max's veggie pasta. We already had a bowl. Would you like some wine with it?"

"Mmmm, looks good." He glanced over at Margaret. "Tell Max thank you." He thought for a moment and then said, "Yeah, I'll have some of that fancy wine in one of your…our…fancy glasses," he winked at Margaret.

"I'm glad to see that you use them, Vannie." Margaret smiled.

"I sure do. I love them. They were the best wedding gift ever."

"How many have your broken?"

"None," Savannah responded indignantly, as she poured some sparkling cider into her empty glass. "Want more Gewürztraminer?" she asked her aunt.

"Sure. Why are you drinking that kids' stuff?" she asked.

"Just limiting my alcohol intake, that's all. One small glass of wine once in a while is enough for me."

"Humph, you're no fun."

"Oh yes she is," Michael countered while rushing to swallow a mouthful of veggie pasta.

Savannah smiled adoringly at her handsome husband.

Knock, knock

"Oh, it must be Craig. I'll get it," Savannah said jumping up from her chair and walking into the living room. "Hi Craig," Savannah said, giving him a one-armed hug around the neck.

"Hi. How's everything with you this week?"

"Pretty good. Is Iris back from the cabin?" she asked.

"Yes and Damon's back in the cell, under guard. All is as it should be at the moment, I guess."

"But you've been working pretty hard, from the sounds of it," Savannah said, leading the detective into the kitchen.

"What do you mean?"

"You're being quoted all over the paper and on the radio," she explained.

"Yeah, not my favorite thing to do," he said. "But it goes with the territory."

Craig entered the kitchen behind Savannah. He waved at Michael and then patted Margaret on one shoulder as he walked to an empty chair at the kitchen table.

"Want some veggie pasta?" Savannah offered. "Max made it."

"Ooooh, sounds tempting. But Iris and I have plans this evening. We're actually going out to eat somewhere other than the diner."

"Cool. How about a glass of wine or a cup of coffee?"

Craig looked at the bottle sitting on the counter and then over at the coffee pot and said, "Better make it coffee. I'm driving tonight."

"So what's up?" Michael asked as he wiped his mouth and dropped the napkin into the empty bowl in front of him. "Savannah said you have more news."

He looked straight on at Michael and said, "Alyce and Pete Gamble were lovers."

Savannah, who had picked up Michael's bowl and set it in the sink, whirled around. "What? Oh my gosh, that's too weird."

Margaret and Michael sat stunned, eager to hear more.

"They have children together. He treated her pretty badly; there was so much chaos that the kids were taken away from both of them. The kids live with Alyce's mother somewhere south of here. According to his rap sheet, there was lots of domestic violence and, from what I hear, only some of it was reported."

"Domestic violence? That doesn't surprise me. Pete was a dark man," Margaret said.

"Well, according to the guy we're holding, Gus Ramirez, Alyce sought solace in a friend of Pete's—a guy known as the Weasel. And it was the two of them who plotted Pete's murder. They'd wanted to do it for a long time and when he assaulted you two, they saw this as an opportunity to do the deed and frame you."

"Well, I'll be," Michael said. He stood and began pacing.

"Ramirez says it was Alyce's idea to take your dog. She figured the more reason you had to hate Pete, the more likely it was you'd be considered a suspect in his killing. As for the keys, she had given them to the Weasel and he must have dropped them as they were making their getaway the night they killed Gamble. They saw a light go on in your rental and left in a hurry without locking the clinic door."

Michael stopped near the pantry and stared across the room. "Yes, certain times of the year—in certain weather—that door is hard to close. It will pop back open if you don't lock it. Been meaning to fix that." He looked over at Craig. "So was he killed right there at the clinic?"

"Yeah, did my cat witness another murder?" Savannah asked.

"No. Gus said they waited for Pete out in the parking lot of his store and jumped him with a stun gun. They tied him up and hauled him out to a field near the old dump. They stabbed him there—well, Ramirez says it was the Weasel who did the killing. He says the only reason he was involved was to give the Weasel a hand in snatching and then moving Pete's rather heavy body. That's what he got paid to do." He chuckled. "I imagine you two paid his fee."

"What?" Michael said as he walked over to his chair and sat down, his eyes fixed on Craig.

"Well, it appears that Alyce was the only one working, so she was probably paying him out of the salary you paid her," he said with a grin.

"Holy cow," Margaret said. "Sounds like something I'd see on one of my detective programs, not that would happen right here in our town."

"Doesn't it?" Savannah agreed.

"Oh, Ramirez claims he has a video on his phone of the Weasel doing the killing."

Michael poured himself another glass of wine. "Sheeesh. That's sick." He turned toward Craig. "Have you seen it, yet?"

"Naw. It's in the evidence room. Someone will check it out."

"Is Alyce in jail?" Savannah asked. "She didn't show up for work yesterday or today."

"She could be by now. They were supposed to pick her up this afternoon."

"So what did you find out about the murder weapon?" Michael asked.

"Just as we thought. According to our snitch, Alyce had the engraving done, the Weasel used it and another knife to do the job, and Gus snuck up to your property and tossed the engraved one out his car window, hoping the authorities would find it. Which they did. The other knife hasn't shown up. Gus thinks it's still out in that field. If so, we'll find it."

"That poor sucker," Michael said quietly.

"After all these people tried to do to you, the only thing you can think about is poor Pete?" Savannah said. "Michael, you really are something special."

"Well, it would be pretty awful, don't you think?"

"Sure," she agreed. She then turned her attention toward Craig. "Thank you so much for letting us know about this, Craig. You can bet that we'll have a better night's sleep tonight than we have had in…well, a couple of weeks."

"Me too," Craig said with a wink. "I've been pulling for you guys all along and it feels good to get to the bottom of it. I'll be able to relax once everyone's in jail and have been convicted."

Michael shot a piercing look at Craig. "You mean those two aren't in jail yet?"

Well, let me check—Craig pulled his cell out of his pocket and made a call. When he finished, he said, "It's a done deal. They were picked up in her car just outside the city limits. Looks like they were running. There were suitcases in the trunk. They found a nice supply of drugs in the car, too." He smiled. "So that's more drugs and druggies off the streets."

"How many did you round up in your operation this week, Craig?" Savannah asked.

"Looks like around a dozen, maybe more, where the charges will stick. The courts are going to be busy this month," he said with a chuckle. "And Damon is pleased as punch to know that the streets are a little cleaner and safer for his younger brothers. He may be released early. Did you know that?"

"I heard that," Savannah said. She then looked concerned. "Do you think he's ready?"

Craig thought about it for a moment and said, "With the support that kid has now and his good taste of positive sobriety…well, positive in some ways—jail ain't such a positive thing—I think he'll be okay. He's talking about starting fresh somewhere else. It's always a bad deal for a newly sobered guy to come back to where all of his drug connections are. Damon knows that and is thinking about moving down toward the bay area and getting' a job as a cook while taking online journalism courses and doing some freelancing. He's working on a novel for young adults."

Chapter Ten

"Bad news again, Michael."

"What, honey?" he asked, yawning and stretching as Savannah climbed into bed and cuddled next to him.

"I'm not pregnant."

"Oh, bummer. But it will happen. We've only been trying what, for three months?"

"Yes. I guess it's time to see a doctor—to see if either of us has a problem. What do you say?"

***

"Well, I like the doctor's recommendation, don't you?" Michael asked as they left the obstetrician's office, an impish smile on his face.

"What?" Savannah asked.

"Keep trying," he said, laughing.

"Yes. Best prescription I ever got," she said. "But he also wants us to go on a fertility diet. Oysters for you and lots of good healthy, whole foods for both of us. I guess it's as good a time as any to give up alcohol and coffee. It hadn't occurred to me to do that *before* getting pregnant."

"Like you drink a lot of alcohol and coffee…"

"Well, I do enjoy my glass of Gwurztereener in Auntie's pretty wine glasses," she said, purposely hacking the word. "And my one or two cups of coffee per day—I'll miss that."

"Well, you don't have to give up using the pretty glasses, honey. We'll just fill them with herbal tea or lemonade." He looked thoughtful for a moment. "Oysters, huh?" he said, making a face. "Never been a big fan." He smiled. "But I'd eat grasshoppers if it meant we could have a child."

***

It was early December, nearly six months after Savannah and Michael had decided to have a baby.

"Maybe we're trying too hard, Michael."

He rolled over toward her in bed. "What?"

"I've been reading that sometimes when a couple adopts or they get otherwise less focused on having a baby, they get pregnant."

"Hmmm, I'm sorry, Savannah. I can't imagine even pretending not to be interested in loving you."

"Well, you don't have to do that, silly. But maybe we should stop wanting a baby so much and just get more interested in something outside of ourselves."

Michael thought about it for a while, then said, "You know, the other day you mentioned having your sister come to stay while she's on break from medical school. Maybe it would do you good to take some time off work and just do girlie things with Brianna and Maggie and maybe Iris for a week."

She rose up on one elbow. "Do you mean it, Michael?"

"Yes. I think it would be good for you to get out of the clinic and on your horse more. We've had some unseasonably great weather lately. Maybe Brianna could borrow a horse from Bonnie and you could ride somewhere together. You could go shopping…things like that."

"That would be so much fun. I like the idea. I just talked to Mom a few days ago about Brianna. She said she seems kind of stressed lately. She could probably use a vacation." She thought for a minute and said, "Yes, I'm going to call her first thing in the morning and see if I can get her to come. I can really take time off work?"

"I don't see why not. I can handle things for a week by myself. Bud can fill in."

"Okay, then. I'll see if I can make it work."

***

A few days later, Michael asked, "So, when is she coming?"

"Who?" Savannah teased.

"You know who—your sister. Now don't play with me, lady."

"She's driving up tomorrow. Isn't it exciting? Auntie said she wants to come out and play with us, too. Oh, I'd better go start freshening up the guest room. Which one is most ready for guests, do you think? Where are you going to be working?"

"I want to continue working on the nursery, so that's off-limits right now. And Adam will probably come next weekend. So how about the old master bedroom—your aunt's old room upstairs. She would have her own attached bath and everyone could have their privacy. I think she'll love the way you decorated it, don't you?"

"Yes, perfect." She rushed toward her husband, grabbing him around the neck in a tight hug. "Thank you Michael. I am so excited, I can't even tell you. It's been a long time since I've hung out with my girlfriends." She started to turn and walk toward the stairs. "Even if they are my relatives." She laughed.

Michael smiled broadly as he watched Savannah walk away. *Sheesh, I love seeing her happy,* he thought.

***

"She's here!" Savannah yelled to Michael, who had come home early from the clinic to work on the nursery—not that there was any rush to get that particular room done. In fact, there was no rush at all, yet. But when he surveyed the projects he had on his to-do list, this was the most appealing to him. The first thing he wanted to do was add more electrical outlets.

"Hi, Bri—sooooo good to see you. Thank you for coming. Ooooooh, you look good, girl."

"Hi, Sis. Your invitation came just at the right time, I've been dying of boredom in LA," Briana said, feigning extreme annoyance. She cocked her head, a smile taking over her pretty face. "Gosh, it's good to be here and to see you."

"Your hair has grown. Are you straightening it now or have you lost your curl?"

Brianna patted her overnight bag. "Got my straightener right here."

"Is that all you brought with you?" Savannah asked.

"No, there's more in the back." She motioned to the back of the white Lexus.

"Nice car."

"Yeah, I couldn't wait like you did to get a house. I've been enjoying my inheritance the way Dad meant for me to. Paid cash for the car, you know. No car payments."

"Well, we have house payments. But the inheritance sure helped." She became solemn for a moment. She looked to the heavens and said, "Thank you Dad. Love you!"

Brianna smiled. "Amen to that."

The two sisters walked around to the back of the car and Brianna opened it with the push of a button.

"Classy. I'll bet you have heated seats, too."

"Sure do."

"No kidding. Look at you, girl. Living the good life."

"Mmmm, yeah, I guess that's what most people consider it."

Michael stepped out onto the porch. "Hey there, Sis," he called out to Brianna. He walked out to greet her, bent down and gave her a hug.

"Holy cow, man, what do they put in the water here? You look great, Michael—taller, healthy. Both of you, in fact."

"It's your sister's cooking," Michael said.

"Well, whatever it is, it's workin'. Good to see you, Michael. Thanks for letting me come."

"We've been looking forward to your visit. Can I bring something in?"

"Yeah, there's another bag in the back. Thanks."

Savannah bubbled over with excitement. "You're going to be in Auntie's old room. Wait until you see what Michael has done with it."

"Well, Savannah did the decorating," Michael explained. "I just made a lot of sawdust."

"You got that right. He's a sawdust-maker." She laughed.

"It's beautiful. Just great. I may never leave this place," Brianna said, spinning slowly around the room—taking it all in.

"I'd love to see what else you two have done here." She looked over at Michael. "I hear you're quite the weekend renovation warrior."

Michael and Savannah laughed.

"Come on, let's do a tour," Michael said. He chuckled. "They're free on weekdays." He led the way across the hall. "This is Adam's room."

"This is great. I'll bet he loves it. Does he come here much?"

"He'll be here this weekend."

"Can't wait to see him. He is such a doll."

"Michael has completely redone our bedroom and bath." Savannah looped her arm in her sister's. "Come on I'll show you."

"Beautiful. Is it too late to change rooms?"

"Yes," Michael and Savannah said in unison.

"In here is the nursery," Michael announced. "This is where I'm working now."

Brianna gasped and turned quickly toward Savannah. "Are you PG?"

Savannah shook her head and put her hand on her stomach. "No, not yet," she said sounding a little melancholy.

"Well, there's my favorite boy," Brianna said as she spotted the big grey-and-white cat winding his way through the doorway into the unfinished nursery. She walked over to greet him. "Hi Rags. How've you been, huh buddy?"

Just then, Savannah noticed a scattering of sawdust near the wall where Michael had been working. "Looks like I'm behind with my job," she said as she picked up a broom that was leaning against the far wall and started to sweep the dust into a pile.

"Well, while you do your wifely duties, I'm going to unpack," Brianna said. "I want to hang the wrinkles out of my clothes."

"Cool. I'll meet you on the porch in a few for lemonade. We can let Rags play outside." Brianna picked up Rags and held him like a baby. "Does he still steal stuff from the neighbors?" she asked.

"No," Savannah said, looking over at her cat. "We keep a closer eye on him out here. He can't go out by himself—too many predators. Besides, Auntie and Max are our closest neighbors." She laughed and said, "I'd hate to see what he'd bring home from those old folks who live at the end of the lane—dentures, adult diapers, Bengay… Now, he takes things out of women's purses and he even pulled a wallet out of a man's jacket pocket once." She leaned toward her sister as if to tell her a secret. "Oh, and he took off with Iris's hormone replacement pills."

Both girls laughed. Savannah said, "When I called to tell Iris he had them, she asked if he'd swallowed any. I told her I wasn't sure. She said to check him for boobs and a vagina." Both girls doubled over laughing before Brianna lowered Rags to the floor and headed down the hall and up the stairs.

"Get out of there, Rags," Michael scolded. "We don't want to lose you in this maze of walls."

***

This brings us full circle to that December day when Rags found the mysterious note in the wall.

Savannah peeked into the nursery and found Michael still seated on the sawhorse, deep in thought. She walked over, put her arms around him, and said, "Michael…I…" Just then they heard a voice.

"Hey, where are you guys?"

"It's Auntie. I knew she couldn't stay away." Savannah laughed as she gave her husband a quick peck on the cheek and turned toward the open nursery door. "We're in here," Savannah called.

"Is she here?" Margaret asked upon entering the small room.

"Yes, she just went up to unpack."

"So what are you two doing? Working?"

As Savannah began to tell her aunt about their eerie find, Brianna returned to the room. "Hi, Auntie. I thought I heard your voice." She rushed over to give her a hug.

"Hi, Bri. You look great, girl. Love your hair long and straight like that. Makes you look thinner."

"I looked fat before?"

"Nooooo. But this style does streamline you." She looked over at Savannah and asked, "What's that you have in your hands, Vannie? Looks old."

"Yeah. Rags just found it in the wall."

"What?" Margaret's flawless skin suddenly turned pale. "What is it?"

"Not sure. I was just going to look at it again when you came in. This seems to be some sort of message." Savannah set the box down on the sawhorse next to Michael and unfolded the paper. "Looks like it's written in German."

Margaret became quiet.

"How do you know it's German? Ever read German, Vannie?" Brianna laughed.

"I've seen German writing before," she said indignantly.

"Can you read it?"

"Noooooo."

Michael held up the box they had found. "This was in the wall, too."

Margaret gasped and everyone looked over at her.

"What's wrong, Auntie?"

"Well, it's probably just as well that you found it."

"Found what? What is it?"

"What's in the box, Michael?" Brianna asked.

"A broken eggshell."

"Eggshell?" Brianna repeated looking confused. "Why would someone store an eggshell in the wall?" She walked over and peered into the small box. Margaret stood back, staring apprehensively toward the others.

"Do you know what this means, Auntie?" Savannah asked.

"Well, only partially. Remember, I told you there was something in the house. I didn't know exactly what it was—didn't expect it to be a broken egg. But the rumor passed down through the generations says it's a gypsy curse."

Savannah and Michael caught each other's eyes.

"What?" Brianna said. "You've got to be kidding."

"The story is that when old Jed Forster's dad was building this house, a band of gypsies came through. I guess the old man didn't quite cotton to them—thought they stole a hog from him or something. Anyway, he got angry with them and the gypsies, before they left the area, claimed to have cursed the house. This was around 1900."

"Wow! That's quite a story, Auntie. Something out of the books I used to read as a kid," Savannah said. She looked over at the box. "Never thought I'd be living one of those stories, though," she said almost inaudibly. She then looked up at her aunt and her sister. "What do you think it means?"

"Well, I read those stories, too, Vannie," Brianna said. "And I even met a gal in college who was into some of this voodoo stuff. I think an egg has to do with fertility. This egg, however, is broken, so this would mean lack of fertility—infertile—unfertile."

Michael and Savannah looked at each other. Tears filled Savannah's eyes.

When Brianna saw how her words had affected her sister, she said, "But I could be way out in left field. Let's find a German somewhere and have them read the note. Okay, Sis? Let's do that before jumping to any conclusions." She thought for a minute and then said, "Heck, the egg may have been whole and it broke with all of Michael's hammering or there was an earthquake or something."

"Yes, good idea," Margaret said. "Let's don't get upset until we know what it means. Come on now, how about dinner at our place tonight? Max is cooking," she added, in an enticing, sing song manner.

"Oh, that's right, he used to be a chef," Brianna said. She looked over at Michael and Savannah. "Sounds great. Okay with you two?"

They nodded.

Savannah tucked the note in her pocket and took a deep breath in an attempt to shake off the sense of doom that had washed over her. "What time?" she asked.

"Come over any time. If you show up before dark, we can show Bri around the place."

Still feeling a bit off kilter, Savannah hesitated and then, determined to collect herself, she said, "How about if we freshen up and we'll come over around four thirty. Okay with everyone?"

"Yes." Margaret nodded. "What time is it now?"

"Just about two thirty," Savannah responded. "That will give us time to find a German."

"Bud," Michael said.

"What about Bud?" Savannah wanted to know.

"He took German in college."

"You're kidding. I had no idea," Savannah said. She then added, "Hey, isn't his name Bogart? That's German, isn't it?"

"I think it is," Brianna agreed.

***

Michael walked out to the porch where Savannah, Briana, Lexie, and Rags were gathered. "Bud said he'll meet us at the clinic at four and see if he can read the curse thing."

"Don't call it that until we know that's what it is, Michael," Savannah scolded.

"You're really taking this seriously, aren't you?" he asked.

"No. I just don't want to jinx anything."

"Jinx a curse?" Brianna laughed. "Now that's rich."

"It may just be a joke that one of the construction workers played while they were building the house," Savannah reasoned.

"They didn't have construction workers in those days," Michael explained. "They had neighbors come in and do a barn-raising thing."

"Well, neighbors play jokes, too," Savannah reminded him.

***

"Nice place," Brianna said as they pulled up in back of the clinic.

"Yes, it is a great place. Michael planned it out well. Oh there's Bud just driving in."

"Hey Bud," Michael said as he stepped out of Brianna's Lexus.

"Hi, Dr. Mike, Savannah. Nice wheels," he said. Suddenly, Bud's eyes focused on something past the couple. Savannah turned to see her sister sliding out of the driver's seat and said, "Oh Bud, this is my sister Brianna. Come here Brianna; I want you to meet our right hand here at the clinic."

"Hi. I remember you from the wedding," Bud said.

"Oh yes. I think we danced, didn't we?"

"You must have made quite an impression on her, Bud, if she doesn't remember whether you danced with her or not," Michael teased.

Both Brianna and Bud blushed.

"Well, Bud, I told Savannah that you can speak some German. We have a challenge for you." He held up the yellowed piece of paper and asked, "Can you read this for us?"

Bud took the letter in his hands. He studied it for a few moments and then his demeanor turned somber. He looked up at Michael and then over at Savannah. "Where did you get this?"

"Oddly," Michael said, "we found it in the wall of our house, along with a broken eggshell."

Bud seemed stunned for a moment. He swallowed hard and said, "It's a curse, guys… if you believe in such things. A gypsy curse." He watched their reaction and took an extra look over at Brianna. "You know, there were bands of gypsies living in this area around the turn of the century—the 1900s."

"That's about the time the Forster house was being built," Michael said.

"What kind of curse is it?" Savannah asked hesitantly.

"Fertility. It says here that nothing on this property will be fertile, the land or the animals or—" He looked over at Savannah and added, "the humans."

Michael could see that Savannah was upset. He put his arm around her and squeezed her to him. "That's only if you're into witchcraft and stuff, right?"

"Not really," Brianna said with wide eyes. "According to my witch friend, curses are real and can do damage." She then asked Michael, "Can you grow things on your land? When's the last time you had a good crop?"

"Savannah laughed nervously. "Well, we've never planted a crop."

"Oh."

"But there are ways to break curses. Didn't your witch friend tell you that?" Bud asked.

"Yeah, but who wants to drink eyeball stew and eat gremlin guts?" Brianna laughed.

"You guys are freaking Savannah out, now," Michael warned. "Honey, they're just making fun of the note."

Savannah turned to face Bud and Brianna. "Well, thank you for the bad news," she said flatly. Do either of you witch hunters know where we can go to find out how to reverse the curse?"

"I'll do some checking," Bud said.

Brianna glanced over at Bud. "So will I."

Bud looked in Brianna's direction for a moment and then said, "A…how about…I mean… maybe we could check together. I have a good source right here in town."

She looked him in the eyes and then glanced quickly up and down his body before saying, "Well, I suppose we could." She shrugged. "Yeah, why not?"

"What are you doing tonight?" he asked.

"Gosh, Bud, you're eager. She just got here," Michael said.

Bud looked down at his boots. "Oh sorry. Just seemed like there was an urgency with this situation, that's all."

Michael thought for a few moments and then said, "Bud, why don't you join us for dinner at Max and Maggie's this evening after you do rounds. Then, if you want to go out together, you can go after dinner. Savannah and I have had a busy week and wouldn't mind going to bed early. All right with you, Brianna?"

"Sure," she said, shrugging her shoulders again.

***

An hour later, Brianna and Bud returned to the Sheridans' kitchen with Max after having toured the cattery. "So, how do you like our place?" Margaret asked.

"It's great!" Bud said. "I had no idea you had such a cool facility here—especially that tunnel where the cats can go outside and be safe in wire pens. Max, you're a genius."

"Incredible," Brianna added.

"Well, thank you." Max bowed in their direction, a big smile on his face. "We do enjoy the work."

"Well, most of it," Margaret agreed. "It is heartening to see a cat transformed from a street urchin with no place to go and no one to love him into a lap cat in a safe home."

"Ah yes," Max agreed. "That's what it's all about for us."

Margaret addressed the couple with a new subject. "What would you two like to drink? We have red and white wine, herbal sun tea, beer…" she suggested.

Brianna looked around at what the others were drinking. "No wine for you tonight, Vannie?" she asked.

"No," she responded. "The sun tea is really refreshing."

"I'll have a beer," Bud said.

Brianna pointed to a bottle of chardonnay sitting on the counter. "White wine for me."

After everyone was served, Savannah looked over at Margaret. "Auntie, I want to know more about the curse and the gypsies. Bud tells us the letter talks about a curse to render everything and everyone on the old Forster property infertile."

"What? I didn't know Bud could read German."

"Yeah, two years in college. My ancestry is German, so I wanted the experience," he explained, sneaking a quick glance in Brianna's direction.

"Hmmm," Margaret said as if genuinely impressed. She then addressed Savannah. "Infertility, huh? Let me think about it. As I recall, when Jed's mother and father built the place, Jed was five and his older brother, Clem, was seven. As the story goes, Jed's mother Abigail yearned for a girl. But despite their plans, including building that home for a large family, she didn't get pregnant again. I never thought about it being for any other reason than…" she hesitated "…they just never had another child."

Michael noticed Savannah's mood shift. She was obviously troubled by this information. But just as obvious was the fact that she wasn't going to let it go. "Who else lived in the house?" she asked.

Margaret thought for a moment and then continued, "Well, after their parents passed, Clem lived in the house because Jed travelled with his job. Jed met his wife in Colorado and they had Tom's dad, Tom senior, and James. When Clem's wife died, he didn't want to live there anymore." She looked down at her glass of wine, took a sip and then said, "Come to think of it, Clem and his wife never had any children. Jed and Ella May moved in with their two boys."

"So did they have any more children?" Savannah asked, her voice shaking a little.

"What?" Margaret said, while reaching out to pet a cat that had strolled up to her.

"Did they have any more children?" Savannah insisted.

"Actually, no." She lifted Layla onto her lap and began smoothing the fur around her pretty Persian face. She looked up at Savannah, a serious look on her face, and said, "You know, there has never been a child born to anyone living in that house."

Savannah's eyes welled up. Michael looked over in time to see her face contort into a mask of terror just before she burst into tears and rushed out of the room. Michael followed her, reaching her just as she stepped out onto the deck outside the back door. He held her for what seemed like hours, and she sobbed into his chest.

***

"I'm sorry about my blubbering last night, Michael," Savannah said as she walked with him out to his truck the next morning.

"No need to apologize, honey. I know how much it means to you to have our baby. That crazy witchcraft thing was a kick in the stomach for me, too. But I don't think it's real, do you? How could it be? It's just a bunch of hocus-pocus that someone made up over a hundred years ago, for heaven sakes. It has nothing to do with us."

"I suppose so. That's what I want to believe. I guess I've just been under a lot of stress and I've been so disappointed month after month."

Michael took Savannah's chin and raised her face so he could look into her eyes. He spoke softly. "We will have a baby. You can count on it. It's just that the right one hasn't chosen us, yet."

She smiled at the thought.

"Now you go have a great time playing with your sister and forget all about that old curse. Will you?"

She nodded.

"Okay, now," he said, kissing the end of her nose, "go have fun."

Savannah waved goodbye to Michael, Lexie at her side. Once in the living room, Savannah noticed that Brianna was walking slowly down the stairs. She watched her younger sister stretch and yawn. Lexie spotted their guest, too. She ran over to Brianna and danced around her legs as she continued her descent.

"Do you guys get up this early every morning?" she asked, rubbing her fingers deeply into her eye sockets and then blinking at her sister. She bent down and greeted the dog. "Hi Lexie. Nice to see you, too. You are such a pretty girl." She looked up briefly at her sister. "You know, Lexie makes me want a dog. They're so full of unconditional love. Not like a cat." She looked over and saw Rags, who was sitting in the middle of the coffee table. "Not like cats…" she said in a rather accusatory manner. "They're too aloof for me. I want a constant show of affection."

"Oh baloney," Savannah said as she headed toward the kitchen. "Coffee?" she called over her shoulder.

"YES, please," she yawned again. As she followed Savannah into the kitchen, she couldn't help but ask, "What do you mean baloney?"

Savannah poured a fresh cup of coffee and added hot water to her herbal tea. "I mean, you are about as aloof as…Rags."

"How do you figure?"

"Well, do you remember JugHead and how he mooned after you? You'd ditch him every chance you got?"

"JugHead?" Brianna questioned, running her fingers through the top of her thick dark hair to discourage stray strands from tickling her forehead. "Do you mean Jeremy? Oh my gosh, Vannie, he was a stalker!" she exclaimed.

"Stalker? He thought he was your boyfriend. You dumped him without letting him know, remember?"

"Couldn't he tell I was over him? Anyway, that was in seventh grade."

"What about Georgie Peyton? When he wanted to make out, you were off chatting it up with the neighbor kids."

"They were building a science project!"

"I remember you telling me that one of your boyfriends quit dating you because you were more interested in the movie he took you to see than in him."

"Well, I guess maybe I am careful who I smooch with." She pondered the concept for a minute and then wrinkled up her nose. "I really don't like smooching all that much."

"Well, I'd say you haven't found the right smoocher, yet," Savannah teased.

"Come here, Lexie," Brianna said. "I'll smooch with you—you are such a cutie." She leaned over and ruffled the long fur on top of the dog's head. She stood up and stared at Lexie for a moment. "She reminds me of a girl I know. Her hair is the same color—only out of a bottle—and she parts it down the middle just like Lexie's." She laughed. "She has a nose like Lexie, too—long." She motioned, running her fingers alongside her own nose and out about a foot in front of her face.

Savannah laughed. She walked over to the refrigerator and pulled out a bowl of fresh fruit. "What do you want to do today, Sis?"

"I don't know. What is there to do here?"

"Whatever it is, I think Auntie wants to join us. We can take you on a tour of town and maybe do a little shopping and have lunch out. There's a nice Italian bistro with patio dining."

"Sounds good to me." Brianna stared out the kitchen window for a moment before saying, "Oh, I think your horse is hungry. I can see her looking over here."

"Thanks for the reminder. I'd better go take care of her. Wanna come?"

"Sure."

"Here are some clogs you can wear—gets kinda muddy out there this time of year." Savannah looked over at her sister, who was staring down at the shoes. "Yeah, they'll be a bit sloppy on you. Just wear your slippers with them."

"She reminds me of a horse I used to ride at camp," Brianna said as they approached the corral. "She always tried to run home at the end of a trail ride. I hated that horse."

Peaches raised her head up and down and whinnied softly.

"You've hurt her feelings," Savannah said, patting the horse on the neck and murmuring to her.

"Sorry, Peaches. But that mare was nasty." Brianna stepped out of Savannah's way while she tossed hay into the feed bin. "She once stepped on my foot…on purpose! Do you remember that?" she asked.

Savannah walked over, turned on the faucet, and watched as the water trough began to fill with clean water. "Yeah, I do remember something about a broken little toe. You had to wear my shoes for a while to give your toes more room."

"Yes. Now, if that wasn't embarrassing."

"Embarrassing, huh?"

"Well, not only were your shoes too big for me, they were ugly."

"Ugly?"

"Yes, you wore boy shoes. I was into girly shoes, patent leather with bows."

"My shoes weren't ugly, they were… serviceable."

Brianna laughed. "Yeah, serviceable if you were a combat soldier or marathon runner." She changed her demeanor and said, "But I have to say, I like your grown-up style."

"My grown-up style?" Savannah asked.

"Yes, you have some cute shoes in that closet of yours. I loved those you wore to Auntie's last night."

"Well, thank you. Feel free to borrow some if you break your toe while you're here. Otherwise, I guess you still wear a petite size seven, right?"

"Yes, seven wide, I'm afraid. And what size are yours?" she asked as she looked down at Savannah's rubber boots and the clogs she wore over her house shoes.

"Still a ten…narrow." She reached over and gave her sister a little playful punch, you still five-feet-five?"

"And a half," she straightened her posture. "You still seven feet?" she laughed.

"Five-nine-and-a-half in my stocking feet. I have a gal friend who's taller. Well, you met her at the wedding."

"Oh yes, Iris. How is she?"

"Very good. Happily in a relationship," Savannah said while turning off the water spigot.

"She was cool. I liked her," Brianna said as they headed back toward the house—Lexie racing out in front of them and reaching the porch first. They stepped into the kitchen and began to put breakfast together, when Brianna asked, "How tall is Bud—about five-eight?"

"Yeah, about that, I'd say."

"So if I wear my stilettos, I'll be taller than him."

Savannah stared over her sister. "Do you have a date with Bud?"

"Well, could be," she said coyly.

"Really?" she asked, a questioning grin stretching across her lips.

"I like him. We have things in common."

"What, besides your interest in gypsy curses?" Savannah wanted to know.

"We both went to medical school."

"He went to veterinary school."

"He finished? Why isn't he practicing—I mean in his own practice?"

"Oh, lots of reasons, I guess. He's comfortable just working as a vet tech right now."

"He's cute. Does he date much?" Brianna asked.

Savannah set a bowl of fresh fruit and a plate with home-baked apple muffins on the table. She sat down and looked over at her sister. "I wouldn't know. I don't recall him ever talking about a steady girlfriend."

Brianna dropped down into a chair and leaned forward with both arms on the table, frown lines evident in her face. "He's not gay, is he?"

Savannah laughed. Don't panic, I don't think so. It seems like he was interested in a young gal who used to bring her horse to us sometimes. Don't know why it didn't work out. Or maybe it did. He doesn't bring his personal life to work."

"Okay then," Brianna said, settling back in her chair, "I'll just have to do my own detective work."

Savannah stared at her sister while taking a sip of tea. "You really are interested, aren't you?"

Brianna looked up. "Is it okay with you?"

"Sure. We think Bud's a great guy. Solid, reliable, stable. Uh-oh."

Brianna stopped in mid-bite. "What?"

"Doesn't sound like your kind of guy. Don't you usually date the bad boy?"

"Maybe I'm ready to change all that. Too much drama with those guys. Maybe I'm ready to settle down like you and Michael."

"We'd better get some breakfast in you. I think you're losing it, girl. I've never heard you talk like that before. Here, let me feel your forehead."

"Stop it and eat your breakfast," Brianna snapped. And then she looked over at the clock on the stove. "When's Auntie coming over?"

"She'll be here around ten. You have plenty of time to get ready."

"Hi Rags, watcha got there, boy?" Brianna bent down to see what Rags had brought her—and then she began shouting. "Oh, no you don't! Give me that, you naughty boy!"

"What? What's he got?" Savannah asked, leaning over to get a look at her cat who, by then, had raced past the pantry through an open door to one of the downstairs bathrooms. Brianna was hot on his trail. "Give me that. Raaaaaggggs, bring that back here now."

Savannah began to laugh as Brianna attempted to grab the cat, who had done a three-sixty and was heading for the staircase, still carrying the object in his mouth.

"Darn it," Brianna said. "Savannah do something. Tell your cat to drop it, will you?"

Still laughing so hard she could barely speak, Savannah finally managed to ask again, "What is it?"

"My birth control," Brianna said indignantly. "He took it right out of my overnight bag. The thief."

"I told you to keep things like that locked up," Savannah said, still trying to control her laughter. "Come on, I'll help you corner him."

By the time the two had returned to their breakfast, both of them were laughing. "I guess I learned my lesson. I will use those drawers up there and keep my purses and luggage zipped. I don't want to lose my birth control—that's for sure." She looked over at her sister. "Does he ever get yours?"

Savannah became more serious. "Well, I haven't been using birth control since June. And still we're not pregnant."

"Oh that's right," Brianna said. Suddenly, she laughed out loud.

"What's so funny?" Savannah sat back in her chair and stared over at her sister.

Brianna shook her head with a big grin on her face. She said, "I'm sorry, Sis. But I wouldn't be so depressed about all of the fun you and that dreamy husband of yours are having trying to make a baby." She giggled.

"Oh stop it." Savannah slapped at her sister, a half smile on her face. She said, "Yes, it has been great. I have to tell ya." Then her mood darkened. "But we really want a baby. And now that curse has me freaked out."

"Don't worry, Bud and I have a plan."

"A plan?" Savannah perked up and then looked over at her sister suspiciously.

"Yes. He knows someone we can talk to who might be able to help."

Savannah explained, "We've already been to doctors. Is that the kind of help you mean? The doctors say we're both just fine."

"No," Brianna said. "I mean help breaking the curse."

Savannah leaned forward, her elbow on the table and her chin crutched in her hand. "You really believe in that, don't you?"

"Don't you? If you didn't, you wouldn't be so upset. You must have some level of belief."

Savannah looked off into space. "I'm trying really hard not to acknowledge it. But I guess a part of me is scared stiff that it's true." She looked intently at her sister. "How much faith do *you* put in these things?"

"I believe in being careful and thorough. Bud and I want to find out more about this particular curse and we are meeting with someone to talk about it this evening."

Chapter Eleven

That evening, Savannah picked up the phone. "Hi Mom, good to hear from you. How are you…and Bob?"

"We're good," Gladys said. "Are you girls having fun?"

"We sure are. I love having Brianna here. We went shopping with Auntie today and had a leisurely lunch at a bistro. Great fun. Tomorrow, we're going riding!"

"Horseback riding? Does Brianna know about this?"

"Yes, I promised her a nice gentle horse. Belongs to a friend of ours. We're taking a picnic lunch. I tried to get Auntie to go, but she claims she has too much work to do."

"Now there's something I can't even begin to picture—my sister on a horse."

"Yeah, I don't think we're going to see that picture anytime soon."

"Is Brianna there?" Gladys asked.

"No, she's out on a date."

"A date? My, that girl works fast. Who's she dating?"

Savannah thought for a moment and then said, "Well, maybe 'date' isn't the right word. She just went someplace with our vet tech, Bud to…do some research." She wasn't ready to tell her mother about the curse or the fact that she was trying to get pregnant—not yet. She hoped she wouldn't be sorry that she had told Brianna. This was something she felt was personal between herself and Michael, and it didn't seem right letting others in on her private life. Even though she asked Brianna to keep their secret for now, she wasn't sure her sometimes scatterbrained sister could do it. She tended to speak out of turn when it was least expected.

"Is he a nice boy—this Bud?" Gladys asked.

"He's a nice young man, Mom—he's twenty-eight or so. Same age as Brianna. She's not dating boys anymore, is she?" Savannah laughed.

"No, I guess not. It's hard to believe you girls are so…grown up."

"Thought you were going to use the 'O' word for a minute."

"'O' word?"

"Old."

"Oh no, honey. That word applies only to people in my age group and your aunt's."

"Don't let *her* hear you say that," Savannah warned.

They both laughed.

"Mom, call back tomorrow if you get a chance and you can talk to Brianna. We should be home from the ride by dinner time. Speaking of dinner, Michael just came in and I'd better go finish fixing ours. Love you."

"Love you, too, Vannie."

"Your mom?" Michael asked as he took off his shoes and wriggled his toes. Michael loved wearing flip-flops and wore them most of the time, but drew the line for work. He often took his work shoes off and either went barefooted or slipped on his flip-flops as soon as he got home. And this routine held true no matter the season.

"Yes, it was Mom," she said.

"She always calls on the landline phone, doesn't she? Why is that?" Michael asked.

"I don't know—old-fashioned, I guess. She calls on my cell once in a while. And she has a cell phone, but uses her landline most often." She walked over to where he sat on the sofa.

"So how was your day?" she asked, slipping down next to him, sliding her arm around his neck, and resting her head on his shoulder.

He reached over and squeezed her thigh while leaning his head down to kiss her on the forehead. "Good. No emergencies. Everything went smoothly. I missed you, though." He turned to face her. She sat upright and he kissed her on the lips. He then looked around and asked, "Where's Brianna?"

"Out with Bud, would you believe?"

"Oh," he said before taking her face in his hands and kissing her again. When he pulled away, he noticed they were not alone. "Hello there, Miss Buffy. How are you this evening?" He reached over and petted the cat.

"You sweet thing," Savannah said smiling down into her clear blue eyes. "I'll bet you guys are hungry."

"Yes we are," Michael said. "What's for dinner? And what's up with Brianna and Bud?"

Savannah stood and headed toward the kitchen. Michael followed. "Dinner is whatever you want it to be. And I guess so are Brianna and Bud," she quipped over her shoulder.

"What kind of answer is that?"

She turned to face him. "Well," she laughed before explaining, "it's sort of a potluck dinner. I brought home leftovers from our lunch at the Bistro, we have leftovers from last night, and there are a couple of homemade chicken pot pies in the freezer, if you'd rather."

"Oh, *I* have to decide…after working all day?" He laughed. "Isn't that why I married you, to have someone decide what's for dinner?"

"Are you kidding me? Really?" she said playfully. "You married me for my brain?"

"Isn't that what most women want to hear?"

"I don't know if you've noticed," she said in her most sultry manner, "but I'm *not* most women."

"You sure aren't," he said, moving toward her and pinning her against the counter, forcing a passionate kiss on her. "Hey, I know what I want for dinner," he said giving her a come-hither look.

She stared into his eyes, a smile on her face. "I like your way of thinking, handsome—just let me feed the gang and I'll be right there."

He pulled her to him. "Meet you in the boudoir."

***

The next morning, Savannah's friend and riding buddy, Bonnie, drove over with her horse trailer and picked up Peaches. Savannah and Brianna met her at the stable. While Savannah saddled her horse, Bonnie introduced Brianna to Wilson. "We used to use this gelding in a program for children with disabilities," Bonnie explained while brushing a wayward curl from one of her chocolate-brown cheeks. "He's just about the most dependable horse on the property."

"Sounds just my speed, then," Brianna said. She walked over to look the horse in the eye. "Hi, Wilson. Pleased to meet you. I hope you don't mind if I climb up on your back. I brought you an apple."

"You don't have to bribe Wilson." Bonnie laughed. "He's quite the gentleman."

"Well, you can tell what kind of guys I've been hanging out with, then, can't you?" Brianna said with a chuckle.

"Are you sure you won't join us, Bonnie?" Savannah asked.

"Naw, I have a student coming this morning and I promised my husband I'd take his horse through his paces. He needs a little tune-up in the arena."

"Sure do appreciate you coming out and picking up Peaches," Savannah said.

"It's great to see her again and I'm glad old Willie is getting some exercise. He doesn't get out much unless you bring Charlotte over."

Savannah gave the cinch on Peaches's saddle one last pull before tying off the leather strap. She led her mare over to where Brianna was brushing Wilson. "Here, let me help you put that saddle on, Sis," she said while tying the lead rope from her mare's halter to the hitching rail.

"Thanks, I'm likely to get it on backwards or upside down," Brianna confessed.

Once the horses were saddled and the riders mounted, the sisters took off down the dirt road toward the trail Savannah had ridden with Bonnie numbers of times. Bonnie's Queensland heeler, Bella, chose to trot along, so they packed her collapsible bowl and an extra bottle of water in the saddle bags. After they'd traveled for a while, Savannah suggested they stop, check the cinches, and have a drink of water. They poured some for the dog, too.

"So how was your date last night, Sis?" Savannah asked after handing Brianna a bottle of water and taking a swig of her own.

"Not a date."

"Oh, then how was your non-date?"

Brianna looked up at a blue jay in a nearby tree and said, "Really kinda fun, actually. Bud is a cool guy." She then looked over at Savannah and asked, "Have you met his family?"

"Um, well, I guess I've met his mom a few times when she has come in to get something for their cattle or dogs. That's all. Why?"

"Then you haven't met the grandma?"

"No, I don't think so."

"She's a kick," Brianna said slapping her own thigh.

"So you went to his house?"

"No, we went to his grandmother's house."

"Why?"

"Bud wanted to talk to her about your German letter and the curse thing."

"Oh really?" Savannah's interest was definitely piqued. "What does she know about curses?"

"It seems, Big Sister, that this woman either was or is a witch herself—a German witch."

"What?"

"You didn't know that?"

Savannah thought for a minute and then said, "Well, I guess I knew that the family was into some sort of unusual remedies and potions, but I didn't connect it to witchcraft."

"How's that?" Brianna asked.

"Let's mount up and I'll tell you as we ride."

"Okay, now which foot do I put in the slot… er, stirrup, first?"

"Left foot from the left side of the horse."

"Oh, okay." She looked the situation over and then led the horse to a rock. She climbed up on the rock and mounted from there. "Ah, much easier."

"You're funny." Savannah laughed.

"Yeah, don't you make fun of me, girl—you with those long legs of yours. Not everyone walks on stilts like you do, you know." She looked around. "It is so beautiful up here. Is the weather always this nice?"

"Yeah, except when it rains. It can get kinda messy. And it can get cold."

"Does it rain a lot?"

"More than in LA, I can tell you that."

"Well, I vote to have weather like this every day of the year."

"I'm with you. It is a gorgeous day for December."

"So, what about Bud's family and their potions?" Brianna asked.

"Last year, there was a calf born on one of the ranches and he was having a hard time of it. Bud was there for the birthing and I guess he got kind of attached to the little guy. We treated the calf for what we thought ailed him, but he didn't improve much. He just wasn't keeping pace growth-wise with the others of the same age. He wasn't thriving. One day, Bud asked us if he could bring something from home to use on the calf." She wrinkled her brow and shook her head a little. "…a poultice of some sort. We told him it was okay with us. We thought we were going to lose the calf anyway and what Bud had in mind wasn't going to be ingested. We said that if the owner agreed, we were all for anything he thought might work. Well, he brought this poultice. He said his grandmother whipped it up for him out of some rather unusual items, as I recall. And both Michael and I were astonished to see the calf begin to improve."

"Did you ask Bud what it was?"

"Yes, he just said it was designed to ward off evil spirits or something like that. Didn't resonate with me. I thought it was some sort of woo-woo stuff. I didn't understand it—didn't know if I wanted to."

"And did the calf live to become someone's steak dinner?"

"Noooo," Savannah said, frowning. "The owners weren't all that interested in keeping a calf that wasn't in tip-top health and Bud asked if he could take him. The little steer still lives on Bud's parents' property." She looked over at Brianna. "Doesn't Bud live on that property, too? And the grandmother?"

"I haven't been to Bud's family's ranch, but I understand that Bud has a small house on the back forty, so to speak. Oma—the grandma—lives in town in an apartment." Brianna thought for a minute before saying, "Well, it may have been that Oma cast a spell on that calf or broke one with her poultice. She knows all about curses and things. She was quite familiar with yours, by the way," Brianna said.

"Good grief, how many people know about this? I really didn't want it advertised all over town. It's private and kind of weird."

"Don't worry, Oma and Anika are sworn to a sisterhood or witch-hood oath of some sort," Brianna explained.

"Anika?"

"She's a friend of Bud's grandmother. Oma sent us to Anika along with the letter."

Savannah turned to look at her sister, who trailed behind. She rested her right hand on the back of the saddle and asked, "So what did she say?"

"Well, Bud and I had a good laugh about it afterward, because she kind of talked in riddles. She never came right out and said much of anything that you could hang a hat on."

"Was she a fortune teller or what?" Savannah asked.

"Uh, I suppose something mysterious like that. I'm not sure. But she was familiar with this curse. She said it was used a lot by gypsies in the old days. She said it is a fairly easy one to break and she…well, she was all flamboyant, you know, putting on a sort of show for us. Not only that," Brianna said laughing, "she had this bird that kept coming over and sitting on top of her head. It was hard not to bust out giggling during the session, but Bud and I sure laughed afterward. The people in the diner probably thought we were crazy or something because we couldn't stop laughing." She looked off into space for a moment as she recalled the evening.

Savannah reined Peaches in so Brianna and Wilson could catch up. Once her sister was next to her, she asked, "Sooooo, how do we break it? What did she tell you?"

"She didn't tell us much. She gave us something."

"What?" Savannah insisted.

"A little piece of honeycomb and a couple of leaves."

"What? What are we supposed to do with them?"

"Heck if I know. When we took these things back to Oma, she said basically that this is something the one affected by the curse must work out. And then she repeated, 'Bees. Leaves. Bees. Leaves.' That's it," Brianna said with a shrug. "Then Bud brought me home." She twisted her body in the saddle toward Savannah and said, "He wants me to go to his place for dinner tonight. Savannah, you don't mind, do you?"

"Mind what?" she asked as if suddenly shaken out of a stupor.

"Bud wants me to have dinner with him tonight."

"Sure, whatever you want. That's fine."

Savannah urged Peaches forward and Wilson followed along. *Bees and leaves.* Savannah ran the words through her mind again and again. *Bees and leaves.*

***

"Dinner for two again tonight? I wouldn't even know we have a guest in the house. I never see her," Michael joked while seasoning a couple of rib eye steaks to put on the grill.

"Yeah, she runs off with Bud every evening."

He stopped and looked at Savannah. "Now who would have thought?" he said. "Bud and Brianna. Brianna and Bud. Never in a million years."

"Why?"

"Huh?"

"Why do you find it hard to think of Bud and Brianna as a couple—not that they are a couple," Savannah said, tilting her head to one side.

"Well, for starters, when's the last time you saw Bud with a girl type? I've never even seen him flirt and believe me, there have been opportunities for flirting when we've been together someplace."

Savannah turned sharply toward Michael, the knife she was using to chop vegetables for the salad still in her hand. "What opportunities for flirting?"

"For him to flirt, not me. I'm spoken for, remember?" He held up his left hand and pointed to his wedding ring.

Savannah thought about it for a minute. "Maybe he's just shy. Or so interested in his work that he doesn't want to be distracted."

"Well, I'd say he's distracted this week," Michael pointed out. He stopped sprinkling garlic salt on the meat and turned toward Savannah. "Do you know what he said to me today?"

"What?" Savannah was all ears.

"He asked if Lisa could take over for him this weekend because he'd like to make plans to go out of town. Now when is the last time Bud has gone anywhere or asked for anyone to cover his rounds?"

"Hmmmm, do you suppose he and Brianna are planning to go somewhere? She didn't mention it to me."

"I think that's what he had in mind. But he didn't come right out and say it." Michael picked up the pan with the meat in it and headed for the kitchen door. "I'm going to put these on the grill."

"Want a beer, hon? I'm finished with the salad. I'll bring you one if you want and we can sit on the swing and watch the sunset."

"Sure!" he said enthusiastically.

"Come on, Lexie. Wanna go out?" Savannah said. "No, not you, Rags. You just sit up on the window perch Dad built for you and watch from there tonight, okay?" She motioned toward the perch and Rags climbed up the series of levels to the top, where he could sit comfortably and observe the goings-ons in the yard. "Good boy," she said.

"Uh-oh, Lexie, come back here," she called as she saw the dog take off out the door like a bullet.

"It's okay, it's just Dottie," Michael said. "Lexie will be back in a minute." The couple watched as the dog drew ever closer to a little black-and-white speckled rabbit. When Lexie was a few feet away, she came to a screeching halt. She took a few steps toward the rabbit, who simply kept eating the green grass and weeds on the far side of the expansive lawn. Lexie sniffed the rabbit and nudged him with her nose. When there was absolutely no response, the dog turned on her heels and trotted back to the porch to join Savannah and Michael.

"Is that rabbit deaf and blind?" Savannah asked. "He doesn't even flinch when Lexie comes barreling down on him."

"I think he just has the dog's number. He knows she won't hurt him. You know, they've been playing this same scenario out for months now."

"That's one strange bunny. It's a wonder he's still around with all of the real predators we have out here."

"Isn't that the truth?" he laughed.

When Michael sat down on the porch swing next to Savannah, she turned toward him and said, "Michael, Bud and Brianna visited a witch or gypsy or something last night and talked to her about our…uh…curse."

"Yeah? What did she say?"

"Something about bees and leaves."

"What?"

"That's all she would say. Said it is for us to figure out from there." She shook her head. "I just don't get it. What does it mean? Maybe I can get some answers on the Internet. What do you think?"

"I think you're taking this much too seriously."

"You do? And to what do you attribute the fact that we aren't pregnant yet?" she snapped.

"I don't have any answers; you know that. And I'm as disappointed as you are that it hasn't happened yet."

"I don't think so, Michael."

He looked stunned. "Why would you say that?"

"I'm disappointed for you, I think, more than I am for me. So I am doubly disappointed." She started to cry. "I feel like I'm letting you down. I so want to give you a child." She sobbed into her hands.

"Come here, sweetheart." He put his arm around her and pulled her to him. She leaned her head against his chest and continued sobbing.

"Just so you know—yes, I want our baby—lots of our babies. But this isn't what my life is all about. My life is about you—about us. I could not be happier. My life is perfect. A child would be most welcome. It would just enhance the perfection we already have together."

He pushed her away from him slightly so he could look into her face. "Honey, I am not disappointed in you. Sure, I want us to get pregnant and I had hoped it would be soon. But this is not what I'm living for. And I don't want you to make this your central purpose or…or, honey, we might begin to lose us in your obsession."

"You think I'm obsessed just because I want so much to give you a baby? Is that what you think—I'm being obsessive? I guess you just don't understand, Michael." She stood up and walked over to the kitchen door. "You know, I'm just not very hungry. I'm going to bed."

Now what did I say wrong? Michael wondered. *I've really blown it. I've never seen Savannah act this way. All I wanted to do was to take some pressure off her so she could relax and enjoy what we have and I seem to have done just the opposite. I feel so awful. I've never had Savannah pull away from me like this. If only…*

Chapter Twelve

"I'm really glad you agreed to come with me this weekend, Brianna. When my dad started talking about me taking a trip to the wine country to look at a horse, I wasn't too interested. And then when you came along, I thought it might be a fun trip to share with you." Bud looked over at her and said, "You do make things fun. I don't think I've laughed as much all year as I have with you just this week."

"Yeah, we are a couple of laughaholics," she quipped.

"Laughaholics? Now that's a new one on me."

"That's 'cause I made it up." Brianna got serious. "Bud, have you thought any more about that curse and the bees and leaves thing?"

"Yeah, I can't figure it out. I've never been much into that stuff. I guess I kinda took it for granted, growing up with it. But it wasn't something I wanted to get involved in, except for the folklore remedies." He glanced over at Brianna and nodded. "Now that interests me."

"That's because you're involved in medicine and the science field, don't you think?"

"Yeah, probably. Does that interest you?"

"Oh yes. I'm fascinated with anything scientific or mystical, actually. I could sit and listen to your grandmother all weekend."

"Hey, I should have brought her along."

"That would have been fun, only…"

"Only what?" he asked.

"Oh, I was just thinking that…what if we wanted to make out or something?"

"Make out? Where did that come from? I mean…"

"Bud, I do believe you're blushing."

"Well, I do believe you are a bold woman."

"Yeah, I guess I am." *Should I tell him what I've been thinking? I've thought about kissing him since the first day I met him and saw those kissable lips of his. And, even though we've been together every night since I got here, he hasn't tried to kiss me. All I could get out of him was a nice strong hug the night we went out to dinner. What's up with this guy? Is he a gentleman, shy or...surely, he's not gay.*

"Don't you want to kiss me? I thought maybe that's why you brought me on this trip—for the opportunity to kiss me. Hey, we are going to share a room tonight, aren't we?"

"Um, yeah, we actually have a suite, so it's two rooms. I stayed at this place with my folks once. They know the couple who own it and they get a good rate. Does it sound okay to you?" he asked looking over at her briefly.

"Sounds nice. Sure."

"The view is great—it overlooks rolling hills with grapevines. It's actually a winery and they've added this bed and breakfast with all suites. Pretty classy. Oh, and there's a Jacuzzi in each suite."

"Sounds really nice, Bud. Can't wait to see it." *He's shy. I think he's just a late bloomer and he's shy around girls...er women. That's what I think.*

Bud was deep in his own thoughts, *Gosh she's pretty. Her skin is flawless. She has the sexiest figure. I wonder if she has seen me looking at her; staring at her. I'm not usually one to be so instantly taken by a woman. But this one is way different. She's exciting and beautiful. I love being with her. I wonder if she's serious about wanting to kiss me. 'Cause I sure want to kiss her. It's practically all I've thought about since I met her. But the timing just didn't seem right. I've been so awkward in the past when it came to kissing a girl and I don't want to blow it this time—not with this woman. She may just be the one.*

Brianna was enjoying the small talk as the couple traveled north. With each subject, she learned something new about Bud and had the opportunity to share something about herself. She was surprised to discover how similar their childhood dreams and interests had been, considering what very different people they were now. Or were they? He was certainly every bit as dedicated and devoted to his profession as she was to hers.

After driving and talking for about four hours, he announced, "We're here."

"Where?" she looked all around.

"This is the vineyard. The winery and inn are just up the road a ways. Pretty, isn't it?"

"It's beautiful. Lovely country. So different than Los Angeles…or Indiana."

"I'll bet. I've never been to either place."

Brianna looked at him in disbelief. "Really? I mean I can understand Indiana. Who goes to Indiana, unless you're enrolled in a university there? But you've never been to Los Angeles?"

"Nope," he said as he pulled his Ford Explorer into a driveway. Soon, a large Tudor inn came into view. They parked in front of it.

"This is gorgeous," Brianna said as she twirled around the room, trying to take it all in. "The décor, the view—look, we can sit out there on the balcony and watch the sunset. Where's the Jacuzzi?" she asked, excitedly.

Bud stood leaning against the door to the suite, his arms folded in front of him, watching Brianna with a big smile on his face. "Probably in the bathroom," he called after her, although she had already disappeared through the doorway.

"Wow, that's luxury," she said as she walked back into the room with her arms wrapped around herself, a dreamy look on her face. "I can't wait to get in there and feel all of those jets all over my body," she said.

"Want to take get in the Jacuzzi before we watch the sunset? I'll go get us a bottle of wine in the gift shop."

"No, I don't want to miss the sunset," she said. She looked over at Bud. "I feel like a kid in a candy store—so much to see and do and experience. She then walked over to him, put her arms around his neck and hugged him. "Thank you for bringing me here. I'm having such a good time and this…" she said, motioning with one arm, while keeping the other one wrapped around his neck… "this is an amazing perk." She felt Bud slip his arms around her waist. He pulled her around so she was facing him.

"I'm glad you came." He stared into her eyes for a moment and then slowly moved toward her until his lips touched hers ever so lightly.

"Mmmmm," she said.

He pulled back. "Excuse me?"

Nothing," she said just before kissing him back—quickly at first. And then she gave him a lingering kiss that left them both a little weak in the knees.

"I'll go…" Bud started, his voice a bit froggy. He cleared his throat. "I'll go get that wine now and a couple of glasses." He started to turn and then looked back at her and said, "Don't go anywhere."

"Are you kidding? I'll be right here waiting for you. You can be sure of that." She winked.

***

Earlier that same morning at the Ivey household:

"Adam's here," Michael called out.

Savannah finished drying the last of the breakfast dishes. She checked to make sure the coffee was still hot and then she walked toward the living room. She watched as her husband gathered up his little boy in his arms in a giant hug. He then greeted Marci, Eric, and little Rose. Savannah smiled. She was so glad she had come to her senses (or that her hormones had passed their crises) and that she and Michael had made up last night after her crazy outburst. *Poor guy, what must he have thought? Yes, it had to have been a hormonal thing and stress, perhaps. Whatever it was, I will not let it happen again. I never want to see that kind of hurt in Michael's eyes again.*

"Hi Marci, Eric. Come on in. I have fresh coffee and muffins."

"Oh, muffnins," Adam said. "Savannah makes good muffnins." He looked back at his parents. "Come see my room," he said, excitement in his voice. "Where's Rags? He probably wants to see Mom and my other dad, too."

"His other dad," Marci repeated, shaking her head. "He has two dads and that's just the way he wants to keep it," she said.

"I think it's great, don't you?" Savannah smiled. "How many little boys have two such devoted dads that he loves equally?" she said as the two women followed Adam and his two dads up the stairs. Lexie walked next to Marci, trying to get a better look at the child she held in her arms. Rose leaned over reaching her little hand toward the dog.

"I just hope it doesn't hurt Michael's feelings that he still calls Eric, Dad," she confided.

"Not at all. I can tell you that he is happy that Adam has Eric in his life."

"Mom, come see my room," Adam called from the top of the staircase.

"We're coming, honey," she said as she set Rose down and held her hand, helping her walk the rest of the way up the large staircase. Lexie reached over and licked the four-year-old's face and Rose giggled.

"She's not wearing her glasses today." Savannah noticed.

"Well, she broke them. Sometimes I think she does it on purpose," she said, a knowing look on her face.

After taking a tour of Adam's room, greeting all of the animals—including Peaches—and visiting over coffee and muffins, Adam waved goodbye to his mom, "other dad," and sister.

"What shall we do first?" Michael asked.

"Can I take Rags out to play?"

"Well that's a nice idea," Savannah said. "It's been a while since he has been outside."

"You mean he hasn't got to go visit Peaches?"

"No."

He frowned. "I bet he misses Peaches." His face lit up. "Can I put his harness and leash on?"

"Yes, that's a good idea, buddy," Michael said. "We don't want him getting away from us."

"Can I hold the leash?" Adam asked.

"You sure can."

Savannah watched as Michael helped Adam strap the harness on Rags and hook the leash to it. She followed them outside and smiled when she heard Peaches whinny at the sight of them walking toward her. *She's probably most happy to see Adam because he always gives her apples and carrots. But she does seem to be rather fond of Rags, too. And he sure likes hanging out with her.* Suddenly,

Savannah looked beyond the corral at the barren land. She strolled out there and stared for a moment at the dried-up fruit trees planted here and there. She walked up to one of them and snapped the tip off a branch. She stepped over to another tree. *Most of these trees were here long before I came and I don't remember any of them bearing. What's wrong with this soil? What's wrong with this land? Is it the curse? But there is no curse on Antonio's garden,* she thought as she ambled over to the raised beds their long-time gardener so lovingly tended. She stared down at the lush eggplant plants, kale, and cabbage. She looked over at the thriving rows of cauliflower and broccoli. *Why is his garden a success? I must ask him. He grows some of the best and biggest tomatoes around all summer long.*

She glanced at her watch and then turned toward the corral. "Michael, I'm going in to work now. You boys have fun. I'll be home in time for lunch."

"Okay, hon. Have a good day," he said as he watched Adam feed Peaches some carrot tops. He then called after Savannah, "How about if us guys fix corn dogs for lunch?" When he remembered how diligently Savannah was watching her diet, he added, "And a watercress, spinach, tomato, and gorgonzola sandwich on rye."

Savannah smiled. "Perfect. I'll see you two soon."

***

"That was a killer shunshet," Brianna said. "I mean sunset," she corrected herself with a laugh.

"Are you shlurring your words, Brianna?" Bud asked. "'Cause it shounds like you are."

"Yeah a little."

"You only had one glass of wine."

"A big glass and on an empty stomach." She turned and pointed at him in a scolding manner. "You didn't feed me lunch. That's the problem."

"I didn't? Oh my gosh, I guess I was so anxious to get us here, I plum forgot to stop for lunch. I'm sorry. Will you forgive me?"

"Only if you'll kiss me again," Brianna said, looking at Bud and making no attempt to conceal her flirtatious mood.

"Sure will." He leaned in her direction and then stopped, stood up, and walked over to the railing around the balcony. "No, I don't think I will."

Her smile faded. "Why not?"

He squinted in her direction. "You've been drinking, young lady, and I don't want to take advantage."

"Oh please Bud, take advantage," she pleaded. "I only had one glass of wine."

"One *big* glass," he reminded her.

She walked over to him and said, "I will absolutely not regret anything that happens here this evening. I promise; okay, Bud?"

Although he tried, he couldn't resist her. He was ever so aware of her sumptuous body next to his. He looked down at her full lips. No, he was past any possibility of resistance. He grabbed her and kissed her hard.

"Wow!" she said when he let her go. "Wow!" She pulled him to her again. After kissing one another over and over, Brianna moaned and pulled away. "Bud," she said.

"Yeah?" he was obviously a bit unsteady and out of breath—weak with passion.

"Let's get in the Jacuzzi."

"Did you bring a bathing suit?"

"Nooooo," she said, peering at him from under feathered bangs.

"Oh," he said looking from her toward the door where the Jacuzzi waited—the thought of it tempting every fiber of his body. "Okay," he said as he walked over to the sofa, sat down, and started pulling his shoes and socks off. Next, he pulled his T-shirt over his head as he headed toward the bathroom and the Jacuzzi. He reached over to turn on the water. "Do you like it hot?" he asked.

"I like it just about any way I can get it," she responded while unbuttoning her light-weight cotton blouse. Bud watched as she unfastened her capris and let them drop. She stepped out of them and tossed them on a nearby chair. She then stood in front of the mirror and pulled her hair up, wrapping it in a loose knot. Bud was mesmerized as he stared at her lovely womanly form and the dainty skimpy undergarments she wore. *If I'd known she was wearing such sexy underwear,* he thought, *I would have been so distracted while driving, I might have crashed the car.*

"It's taking a long time to fill," she said, leaning over the edge of the tub and watching the water run into it. Bud stood bare-chested, staring down at her. After a few minutes, she looked up at him. *Man is he ever toned and taut. He's actually quite gorgeous—something that's not obvious under the clothes he usually wears.* "It's full enough, don't you think?" she asked.

"Uh-oh." He looked over. "Yeah, I guess it is." He stood up, turned away from Brianna and slipped out of his jeans. Brianna did not turn away.

Chapter Thirteen

The following day, Brianna and Bud woke up in each other's arms. "Good morning, beautiful," Bud said, brushing a curl off Brianna's forehead.

"Hi," she said sleepily. "What time's it?"

"Do you need to be somewhere?"

She thought for a moment, looked around the room and then at Bud, and said, "As a matter of fact, no." She wrapped her arms tightly around his neck.

"Mmmmm," he said as he pulled away from the kiss. "Don't get me started again. I have a horse to look at, remember?" He kissed her once, twice, three times on the lips and then moaned, "I really have to get up or…"

"Or what, cowboy?" she asked.

"You know what," he said kissing her one more time before climbing out of bed quickly lest he succumb to the temptation to stay there all day.

Brianna rolled over and watched as Bud grabbed his clothes and headed for the bathroom.

***

"Good bye beautiful room, Jacuzzi, view, winery… I hope to see you again," Brianna said, giving the room one more look on her way out the door with her overnight bag. "And dinner last night under the stars…it was wonderful," she said. "And so were you." She grabbed the front of Bud's shirt and pulled him in for yet another kiss.

"I'll give you all day to quit that," he said with a chuckle.

She looked up into his eyes. "I wish we had another whole day."

"We'll have others, Brianna. At least, I'd like to."

"Promise?" she asked.

"Oh yes. I want to see a lot more of you."

She turned toward him on the way out the door and said, "What more is there to see of me?"

They both laughed.

Once the couple had loaded their two small overnight bags into the back of the SUV, Bud pulled out a square device with a small screen and affixed it with a suction cup to the windshield, at the left of the steering wheel.

"What's that?" Brianna asked, crinkling up her nose.

"GPS," he responded while pushing some of the buttons.

"Oh brother," she said. "Don't you know how to read a map? Those are the most ridiculous and annoying things ever invented. I knew someone who used one and he had these conversations with that woman in there all the time—even argued with her when he didn't want to go where she said to go. I hated that thing."

"You have one in your Lexus, don't you?" he asked as he programmed the device.

"Yeah, but I rarely use it."

"Well, I like GPS technology. It's amazingly accurate." He started the car and looked over at her. "Did you know that your cell phone has GPS? I find it to be incredibly useful for all types of travel. It's a great system."

Brianna flashed him a disgusted look and shook her head.

After they'd been driving for a few miles, Bud asked, "Are you hungry?"

"Sure am."

"Wanna stop here for breakfast?" he motioned to a restaurant up ahead.

"Sure. As long as they have hot coffee."

"How far away is the horse we're visiting?" she asked after they were seated and had placed their order.

"According to the GPS, about thirty miles northwest. So not too far."

"What will the horse be used for?"

"Dad's looking for another ranch horse."

"Oh, a working horse?"

"Yeah, pretty much."

"What will his job be?" she asked.

"It's a mare. She'll be used for round-ups, branding; things like that."

"Does your dad treat horses well?" she wanted to know.

Bud looked at her, cocking his head, a lock of his wavy dark-blond hair trailing alongside his temple. "Yes," he said. "He's very good with horses—has a gentle way with them."

"So he doesn't whip them and stuff to make them mind? I've seen guys do that and it always makes me mad."

He shook his head and said, "Oh no, he doesn't believe in mistreating any animal." He thought for a moment and then said, "He's the reason why I decided to become a vet—Dad and Grace."

"Well, you're not a vet, are you? I thought you were a vet tech."

"Oh, I have my license, just haven't officially put it into practice, yet. Too much responsibility, still, at my folks' ranch."

"Who's Grace?"

"She was my first dog. We had dogs on the ranch—working dogs. And I liked them fine, as well as the cats and horses and cattle. But Grace was my first pet dog." He seemed to be in another world for a moment as he brought her memory into focus. He looked at Brianna and said, "She was the most beautiful border collie mix and smart, too. Mom and Dad gave her to me for my eighth birthday and we were best pals until…" He took a deep breath.

Brianna stared hard at Bud and asked quietly, "How was it that she made you want to be a vet?"

"Well, she was only six years old when she died; she was hit by a car. I was the first one to find her. She was hurt real bad and I wanted so much to be able to help her, but there was nothing I could do. I swore then that I would never let another animal die if I could help it. I was fourteen when she died and I've been focused on being a veterinarian ever since."

Brianna reached out and rested her hand on Bud's, massaging it with her thumb.

He took a deep breath, looked her in the eyes and asked, "So what made you want to be a doctor?"

"I'm afraid I don't have such a touching story. I've just always been interested in science."

"Oh, one of those brainy math and science students?"

"You might say that. When a junior high counselor suggested that I could become a doctor if I wanted, I thought, 'why not?' And my path has been leading in that direction ever since."

"What will you specialize in? Have you decided?"

"Yes, I'd better have made my decision by now. I graduate in the spring. I want to be a geriatric specialist."

"Why?" Bud asked, his brow crinkled.

"Why not?" She laughed. "I just think this is an area that, for many years, was neglected. And I think there's a lot we can learn and more that we can do for our elderly." She looked down at their hands, and said, "Bud, I think there's a lot to be said for outlook. So many doctors today are focused on some of the wrong things when it comes to treating the elderly. We need more positive reinforcement and less major surgery, if that makes sense. I mean, putting a ninety-year-old man through major elective surgery just doesn't make much sense to me. Sure, I believe in quality of life and I'm not against surgery. But I think some of our doctors today are frivolous in their recommendations where the older generation is concerned."

Brianna tilted her head. "You're staring at me," she said. "Are you even hearing a word I'm saying?"

"Yeah, you like old people and doctors are frivolous," he said flippantly. He turned serious. "You know, I really like your hair curly like that."

She displayed her palms, smiled and said, "This is the real me. I'm afraid I have curly hair."

"So yesterday I was with an imposter?" he said laughing.

The couple pulled away from the table and watched as the pert waitress placed two plates in front of them. She poured more coffee into their cups and then retreated. Brianna looked down at her veggie omelet and fruit bowl with lust in her eyes. "Mmmm, looks good," she said.

"Not as good as my meat-lover's meal," Bud said.

"Ewwww, all of that cholesterol and nitrates." She paused and said, "It does look good, though."

Bud glanced up at her. "So, do you eat healthy all the time, or are you just showing off?"

She smirked. "Humph, if I was showing off, it appears that it would be wasted on you."

"Yup," he said as he dipped his heavily buttered biscuit into a bowl of gravy and took a big bite.

***

"I need to stop for gas before we head out to parts unknown," Bud said, glancing to his left before making a right turn into a quick-stop market. He pulled up to a gas pump, stepped out of the car, slid his credit card into the slot, and began pumping gas.

Brianna pulled a bill out of her purse and she stepped out of the car, too. "I'll be back in a minute—want to get a bottle of water. Want anything?" she asked before walking away.

"Yeah, water sounds good, thanks." He dug into his pocket and pulled out a five dollar bill. "Here," he said.

Shc slapped her hand in his direction. "I got it."

Brianna slipped through the automatic sliding door of the little market as it opened, looked around, and spotted the water bottles toward the back of the store. She walked up to the cooler, studied the sizes, brands, and prices, and then opened the door and removed two bottles. Just then she heard a voice from somewhere behind her: "Give me the cash."

She spun around in time to see a man standing at the checkout counter pointing what appeared to be a gun at the clerk. The heavyset man behind the counter stared in terror at the gunman. He stepped back from the counter as if he wasn't sure what to do.

"Put the money in the bag. Now. Hurry!" the gunman said, glancing out the windows as if searching for someone.

The clerk looked past the gunman toward Brianna, who was frozen in place. She could see that he was trying to figure out what to do—sound an alarm, pull out a weapon of his own, perhaps, or give him the money. Brianna just hoped he would make the right decision and the gunman would leave without incident. As far as she knew, he wasn't aware of her. She wanted to keep it that way. But when the gunman saw the clerk look in her direction a second time, he turned quickly and saw her. He backed away from the counter. Keeping the gun aimed at the clerk and in a position to where he could see both of them, he growled, "Get over here where I can see you." She hesitated. "Now!" he ordered.

Brianna walked slowly toward the counter and stopped. She looked out the window and saw that Bud was still pumping gas. "Just give him the money," she said to the clerk.

"Yeah, do like she says," he told him.

"I don't have much yet. It's early in the day," he said.

"Don't matter. I'll take what ya got. Now get it!"

The clerk pushed a button on the cash drawer. He reached in and grasped the bills, stuffing them into the bag the gunman had tossed on the counter.

"That's all?" he asked.

"Yes. Like I said…"

"Is there a safe here? What about a bank deposit ready to go to the bank?"

The clerk shook his head. "No."

"You'd better not be lyin' to me," he said. He took the bag of money and then looked over at Brianna. She held a twenty-dollar bill in her hand. She had left her purse in the car. The man snatched the bill from Brianna's hand and looked her up and down. "Got anymore on ya?"

"No," she said, through gritted teeth.

"Let me see." he reached over and patted the front pockets of her jeans.

"Don't you touch me, you slime," she

snarled. Just then, saw the sliding door open and Bud walked into view. The gunman spun around and pointed the gun at Bud. "Git over here," he demanded.

Bud held his hands out so the man could see them and walked over next to Brianna. "What the hell do you want, man?" he asked.

"I want your money. Give me all you got and don't try to hold out."

Bud gave him a sarcastic look and then reached into his front pocket, pulled out a few bills, and handed them to the guy. The gunman looked down at what he held in his hand, "A hundred. Cool. Got any more where that came from?"

Bud shook his head. "That's it man. Now you'd better leave before the cops get here."

"What cops?"

"The cops I called when I saw you through the window holding that gun."

The gunman became visibly nervous. He turned and quickly glanced around outside. "Shit!" he said. He ran to the sliding doors and looked to the right and the left and then he rushed back toward the counter. "My ride left me," he said as if sounding defeated. He looked out at Bud's Explorer. "Is that your car?"

Bud grimaced and nodded.

He looked over at Brianna and back at Bud, "You two together?"

"Uh…" Bud wasn't sure what to say. *What does this jerk have in mind? How can I keep Brianna safe?*

"Well?" the gunman demanded.

"Yeah, we're together," Brianna said.

"Well, you're gonna be my ride."

"No I'm not," Bud said.

"Oh yes you are." He then reached over and slammed the pistol over the clerk's head. Brianna watched in horror as the large man fell slowly to the floor, blood trickling from a wound on his head. The gunman grabbed Brianna and put the gun against her ribcage. She dropped the bottles of water. He turned to Bud, "If you know what's good for you and you don't want your woman hurt, you'll do as I say. Now move." He motioned with the gun toward the door.

Brianna stumbled over the bottles of water as the gunman pushed and pulled her along with him toward the front door, behind Bud. She could only hope to see the cops drive up before they reached Bud's car. But no such luck. *Maybe it was a bluff when Bud said the cops were on the way. I sure hope not.*

Bud looked over at Brianna and saw that the robber still had the gun pointed at her ribs. He pushed it into her and she winced. He looked at Bud and said, "Git in and drive."

Bud scanned the area with his eyes—he saw no one who could help. Reluctantly, he opened the driver's door and climbed in. The gunman put the gun in his waistband and opened the backseat door. He shoved Brianna in and then climbed in after her. Bud eyed them through his rearview mirror, a scowl of determination on his face. *I will get Brianna out of this safely. I will. There's too much I want to share with her. It can't end here, it just can't.*

"Turn right," the gunman demanded.

Bud complied. After they'd gone a few blocks, he reached down and felt his cell phone in his pocket. Not wanting to be obvious, he inched it up from the bottom until he was able to work it out the top of his pocket and into his hand. He glanced down and hit the button for 9-1-1. He set it to *speaker* and then turned down the receiver volume, easing the phone onto the floorboards beneath him.

"What are you doin'?" the gunman growled.

"Scratching my leg, what do you think?" He glanced into the rearview mirror and asked, "Okay, where are you taking us?"

"Just drive, will ya? I'll tell ya where to turn."

"Did it ever occur to you that you just committed an armed robbery back there at the 7-Eleven on Fletcher?"

"So what? Needed the money."

"You may have killed that clerk when you hit him with the butt of your gun."

"Then he ain't gonna follow me, is he? And he won't be callin' the cops, neither."

"And now you'll have a kidnapping charge. When you get caught, you're going to be in a whole lot of trouble." Bud thought for a minute and then said, "You know, I may run out of gas in this dark blue Explorer."

"You just got gas back there at the station."

"You mean where you kidnapped us five minutes ago? I tried to get gas, but the cap was locked and I couldn't get it off. I came in to ask for help getting it off."

"Crap," the gunman mumbled. He looked over at Brianna and said, "And just when you and I had a chance to get acquainted. Guess I'll have to bail and find me another ride." He leered over at Brianna and said, "Maybe I'll just take you with me. I could use a little fun."

Bud could see Brianna in the rearview mirror. She was coiled up against the right side back door, fear on her face. "The lady just may be getting out at the next stop, jerk," Bud said, catching her eyes in the mirror. Just then, he turned the car sharply to the right, throwing the gunman off balance against the left rear door, and then he slammed on the brakes. "Jump out, Brianna!" Bud yelled. She scrambled toward the door, jumped out while the car was stopped, and ran right into the arms of a police officer who was just stepping out of his patrol car. Bud escaped out the passenger door, remembering to take the keys with him. He ran around the car, grabbed Brianna and pulled her aside, saying to the officer, "He's in the backseat. He's armed."

"You two get behind the squad car." The officer motioned. He pulled the gun out of his holster, crouched behind the front of the car and aimed toward Bud's car. "Throw your weapon out," he called.

The gunman hesitated just for a moment before tossing his gun out onto the pavement.

"Come out with your hands up," the policeman ordered.

"Aww right, man. I'm comin'. But I didn't do nothin'. These guys were just givin' me a ride home. My buddies left me hangin' as a joke."

"Yeah, armed robbery and kidnapping isn't much of a joke. Just then, a second police unit arrived and one officer jumped out to help the first while a third one began halting traffic. Once they had the gunman cuffed and secured in the backseat of a squad car, the first officer walked over to Bud and Brianna, who were sitting on a curb. Bud had his arm wrapped around her and she was leaning into him.

"Are you two okay? Do you need paramedics?"

"Yeah, we're fine. He didn't hurt you, did he, Brianna?"

"No. Just scared the bejeebers out of me. That's all. I've never looked down the business end of a gun barrel before. Creeeeepy."

"Well, ma'am, you have your husband to thank for your life. He's one clever dude. We have his whole conversation with this perp on tape."

"Really?" Brianna stared over at Bud. "How?"

"I just called 9-1-1 on my phone and let them hear what was going on."

"But how did they know where we were?"

He looked her in the eyes and said, with a slight smirk on his face, "GPS technology."

Chapter Fourteen

The next morning, Savannah stood at the kitchen counter pouring a glass of orange juice when she heard a voice behind her.

"Morning, Sis."

"Well, hi there. What time did you get home last night?"

"Late," she said while helping herself to a cup of coffee. "Thanks for giving me my own key while I'm here. Sure don't want to wake up the whole household when I come in late. She looked out toward the living room. "Is Adam here?"

"Naw, we had to take him home last night. He missed seeing you. He said, 'Brianna's cool. She let me scoop my own punch at the wedding and get two pieces of cake.'"

Both girls laughed. "He is a cutie," Brianna said. "I missed seeing him, too."

"Did you have a good time with Bud? How'd it go?"

"Oh Savannah," she swooned. "We had the best time. He is so much fun to be with."

Savannah glanced up at her sister. "Bud? Really? I guess I haven't seen that side of him."

"Well, you've missed something," she said while slipping into a kitchen chair, both hands around the warm coffee mug. There's a whole lot more to this guy than most people seem to know."

"No kidding, like what?"

"Oh…" she sighed. "Where do I start?"

Savannah looked over at her sister, who was reaching her hand out, trying to lure Buffy toward her. She sat down opposite Brianna and asked, "Well, what did you do—anything fun?"

"Ex-rated," Brianna said with an impish smile.

"Really?" Savannah looked stunned.

"Oh yes. We stayed at this winery. We had a gorgeous suite with a Jacuzzi. It was the most heavenly night ever."

"Brianna! I've never seen you like this. He really must have made an impression. I've noticed the girls in the office flirting with him, but he never shows much interest." She leaned in and said, "I think some of them kinda wonder about his sexual preference."

"Whose sexual preference?" Margaret asked as she appeared in the kitchen doorway.

"Hi Auntie. She's questioning Bud's sexuality," Brianna explained.

"Your tech?" she asked as she poured herself a cup of coffee and joined the other two at the table.

"Yes. I never have seen him express much interest in girls or women, have you?" Savannah asked.

"Well, I can tell you that he's all man." Brianna grinned.

"Brianna, how did you find this out?" Margaret teased.

"Wellllll…"

"They had a room with a Jacuzzi tub," Savannah said with a knowing smile.

"No kidding. And you got in together? With or without clothes?" Margaret asked.

Brianna cocked her head toward Margaret, a dark curl floating across her forehead. "I'd forgotten how blunt you can be, Auntie."

"Well, you started it—you said he is all man and I…er…we want to know how you know this."

"Experience," she said coyly.

"You mean you experienced his manhood?"

"Auntie…" Savannah said.

"Oh stop it, you want to know, too—Brianna, did you and Bud have sex?"

"Boy did we…" she said. Suddenly unsure as to whether she wanted to take this conversation any further, she added, "And he saved my life."

"What?" Savannah said.

Margaret flashed a menacing smile. "How?" she asked. "Did you swoon and nearly drown in the hot tub?"

"Noooooo."

"Did you strangle in your lingerie?"

"No, Auntie," she said impatiently. "We were kidnapped by an armed robber."

Savannah gasped. "No way, Sis." When she saw the look of fear in her sister's eyes, she asked, "Really? Did that really happen?"

"It sure did. It was awful—scary." Brianna looked up at Savannah and Margaret and said, "Now I know how you two must have felt when that awful man kidnapped and almost killed you." She lowered her eyes toward Buffy, who by then, was in her lap. Brianna unsuccessfully fought back tears as she ran her hand over the cat's head and the plush fur on her back. Buffy looked up at her and softly mewed. Just then, Lexie stepped out of her bed, shook herself and walked over to sniff Buffy. The little cat reached out with a paw and patted the dog on the nose.

"Better leave her alone, Lexie," Savannah said. "Come on over here and lie down."

Margaret leaned forward and looked Brianna in the eyes. "What happened, girl?"

"We stopped to get gas and this guy was holding up the station—with a gun! His ride evidently split, so he highjacked our car—made Bud drive and Bud secretly used his cell phone to call the police." She smiled a little. "He is so clever. I still can't believe it. He says there's a GPS thingy on his phone and, just by calling 9-1-1 and leaving the phone open while he talked to the kidnapper, the police caught on and found us before anything bad happened."

"Holy cow, Brianna. How awful," Margaret said.

Savannah blinked her eyes in disbelief. She stood and walked over to hug her sister. "I'm so glad you're okay."

"Me too," she said, blotting at her eyes with a tissue she'd pulled from the pocket of her lightweight denim jacket. Then she took a deep breath, looked up at Savannah, and asked, "So how was your weekend with Adam?"

"Very nice," she said as she picked up the coffee carafe and refilled two coffee mugs. "We had a kick-back weekend and I think Adam had a good time."

"What's on the agenda for today—anything?" Brianna asked.

Savannah looked at Brianna. "What do you feel like doing after your wild and crazy weekend?"

"And sexy," Margaret added. "The way she talks, she probably needs a cold shower."

"Well, let me fix us some breakfast first—how about pancakes with fresh blueberry topping?"

"Mmmm, sounds good," Brianna replied.

"Did you eat, Auntie?" Savannah asked.

"No, count me in. Sounds delish."

Savannah walked over to the counter when something outside the large kitchen window caught her eye. She turned to the others and said, "Oh, there's Antonio. You know, I want to talk to him. I'll be right back."

As she headed toward the side kitchen door, Lexie at her heels, Brianna said, "I see you have the batter ready, how about if I start the pancakes?"

"Sure. That would be great," Savannah said over her shoulder. She stepped outside in time to see the gardener heading toward the compost pile with a shovel. She called out, "*Hola* Antonio."

He nodded in her direction. "Hello *Señora* Ivey." Lexie trotted over to him and he bent down to greet her.

"Antonio, I have a couple of questions for you."

"*Si Señora*," he said, giving Lexie one last pat on the head before standing and looking up at Savannah.

"Antonio, what kind of trees are those I see out beyond the corral?"

He looked out toward the old orchard. "Apple, pear, peaches, plum, I think."

"But they don't bear fruit. They look dead. Have they ever had fruit on them?"

Antonio took off his worn straw hat and scratched his head while looking out over the sparse orchard. "No. I have not seen them grow. I once watered. No more. Maybe dirt bad."

"But how do you grow such beautiful vegetables in the same dirt?" she asked gazing toward the lush raised garden beds.

"Oh that?" he said. "Bad spirit here." He swept his arms around the yard. "Esperanza and I feel it long ago when we come here to help the Forster family. We try to make it go away. We use potions—herbs, salt. We work hard here and now we have *bonito* garden, yes?"

"Yes, you sure do. And the potions wouldn't work on the trees?"

"*Señora* Maggie no want trees fixed. Just garden."

"Interesting," she thought out loud. "So the right potion can reverse a curse—black magic."

"Bees leaves," he said with a wide smile.

"Bees leaves?" she repeated.

He nodded and walked away.

***

As the three women finished breakfast, Margaret said, "Brianna, how would you like to ride out with me to the old lumber mill your grandpa ran? There's an outlet mall there now; maybe we can find those designer shoes you like at a discounted price."

"I would love that. Want to go, Vannie?"

Savannah thought for a moment and then said, "You know, I think I'll stay here. Charlotte's coming over to play with Rags this afternoon and I'd like to take Peaches out for a little ride. She's been cooped up these last few days."

Brianna stood and carried her dishes to the counter. "Didn't Adam ride this weekend on that cute little saddle you showed me?"

"Oh yes, but Peaches doesn't get much of a workout with Adam, I'm afraid. You two go and have fun."

"Are you sure?" Margaret asked. "You seem preoccupied. Is everything okay with you and Michael?"

"Oh gosh, yes, Auntie. We're good. I'm just a little bummed after finding that…curse thing in the house. I'll be okay. Just want a little time to myself."

"I understand, Sis." Brianna reached out and hugged her. "We'll miss you." She started to walk away, then stopped and said, "Fantastic breakfast. Thanks."

Savannah laughed. "Well, you did most of the cooking." She watched as the two women stepped out the front door, both of them talking at once.

"Come on, Lexie, let's go for a ride."

The dog jumped up and danced around Savannah. She darted toward the side kitchen door and then back to Savannah. Just before Savannah could open the door, she looked down and saw Rags standing next to Lexie. "Oh no you don't, Ragsy. You can go out when Charlotte comes to play. You stay in with Walter and Buffy for now. And don't get in Helena's way while she's cleaning, will you?" She called out, "I'll be back in a little while, Helena."

"Yes, Ms. Ivey."

Savannah grabbed her phone and a bottle of water off the counter and she and Lexie headed out to the corral.

Soon the trio was happily traveling down the country road. The sun felt warm against Savannah's skin, although there was a cool breeze blowing in. *Winter is on the way*, she thought. She reined Peaches down to a walk and then took a swig of water, tucking the bottle back in the carrier Michael had bought for her. She took a deep breath and scanned the horizon, glancing from time to time at the little dog, who was bouncing back and forth across the dirt road. She waved at Harvey, one of their neighbors. And Lexie stopped briefly to play with his little corgi before racing to catch up with Savannah and Peaches. Savannah was careful not to take the dog into areas with stickers and burrs because of Lexie's long, Afghan fur.

She decided to take the orchard trail this morning—the orchardists kept the area around the trees weed-free, so it was an ideal place for Lexie to romp. She recalled a time when she had inadvertently ended up in an area heavy with foxtails, and that's when Lexie learned to ride a horse. Savannah had brought her up into the saddle with her until they'd moved through the stickers.

Once past the orchards, Savannah heard a buzzing sound. She tilted her head, trying to discern where the sound was coming from. As the buzzing grew louder and louder, she realized that what she was hearing was a bee swarm. *Been there, done that,* she thought, recalling the time she'd gotten caught in a swarm of angry bees and ended up with several painful stings.

This swarm was high in a tree off about thirty feet from the trail—a safe distance. And the bees did not seem angry; they were just busy. She stopped and watched them. "Bees and leaves," she said. What Antonio had said that morning was still rolling around in her mind, "Curse, spirits, potions, herbs, and salt. Bees and leaves. Or as she recalled Antonio saying, "Bees." "Leaves." She repeated it, "Bees Leaves. Bee Leave. Believe."

"Oh my gosh," she said out loud. "Believe!" *That's it*, she thought. *Once you know there is a curse, the way to break it is to believe it is gone and to live life as if it is gone or that it was not valid to start with. Believe*. She started to laugh.

She looked over at the dog, who was sitting in the shade of a tree staring up at Savannah. "We have to go home, Lexie. I have something I need to do." She reined the horse around and let her have her head. Savannah enjoyed a gentle lope for a while and then she practiced posting at a trot. She felt like she was smiling the whole way home. *Believe*, she repeated.

Chapter Fifteen

"What are you doing out here in this barren orchard of yours?" Brianna asked when she caught up with her sister later that afternoon. She looked around. "You ought to have Antonio take these dead trees out."

Oh no." Savannah laughed out loud. Sounding almost giddy, she said, "I'm going to make a peach pie next summer and some plum pudding." She continued to hoe around one of the trees. Then she began applying fertilizer, using a coffee can to measure it from a large bag.

"Are you crazy?" Brianna asked. "They look dead to me."

Savannah turned toward her sister and said defiantly, "You believe what you want and I'll believe what I want. I am going to have fruit on these trees next year."

"Okay, then, Ms. Black Thumb."

As if she hadn't heard her sister's comment, Savannah handed her a large package of sunflower seeds and instructed her, "Here, plant these, will you?"

"Where?" Brianna looked around, confused.

"Everywhere." Savannah motioned with both arms. She spun around and said, "I want flowers blooming everywhere."

Brianna read from the package and then asked, "Isn't it too late to plant sunflowers?"

"Maybe and maybe not. Now use some of this fertilizer and be sure to water good." She gazed across the orchard, a big smile on her face. "Oh, this is going to be so pretty out here, don't you think?"

"Sure. I guess. If they grow."

"Believe, Brianna. Believe," Savannah said grinning widely. "Here's a spade; now make little holes and drop in those seeds. I'm going to drag the hose out here and start watering my orchard." She looked over at the trees and said, "I'll ask Antonio to prune them tomorrow. I understand that you have to prune their branches every year."

It was all Brianna could do to force herself to participate in her sister's folly. She decided to humor her, however, and began planting the sunflower seeds.

"So, Brianna, what did you buy today at the outlet mall?" Savannah asked as the two women traipsed back to the house a little dirtier and a lot sweatier.

"Nothing for gardening," Brianna said. "I'm just glad I packed these old jeans and flip-flops. I didn't know you were going to make me do hard labor." She pulled her T-shirt up and wiped her face with it. "Look at me, I'm sweating. I hate to sweat." She thought about it for a minute and then said, "There's only one activity I don't mind sweating for and that's…"

"Never mind," Savannah said putting one hand up toward her sister. "I get the picture." She looked at her watch. "We just have time for a shower before Charlotte gets here."

"Oh, I'm glad I got back in time to see Charlotte. She's a neat little gal." Brianna smiled, "I love her lisp." She turned toward Savannah and said, "You know, she's just about the prettiest Downs child I've ever seen."

"Yeah, she's a delight. Fun to be with." She glanced over at Brianna, an impish look on her face, and said, "Last one to the porch is a toad."

"Croak," Brianna said as she watched her sister sprint off toward the wraparound porch.

"You're no fun," Savannah said when Brianna strolled up to the porch steps.

"Well, I know someone who would beg to differ…"

"Never mind," Savannah said, grabbing Brianna's hand and yanking her into the house. She popped her on the butt and said, "Go get a shower, will ya? You're grungy."

"You're grungy," Brianna mimicked, using a snarly tone. When she saw Savannah start after her again, she said, "Okay, okay, I'm going." She walked a few steps and then turned, "No wonder you don't have many visitors out here if this is how you treat them." She laughed. She headed up the stairs and then turned back. "By the way, Sister dear, I bought extra clothes today. I've decided to stay for a while."

"Really?" Savannah's eyes widened, her brows rising. "That's cool. I'm glad you're staying."

***

Savannah heard the doorbell just as she was pulling her wet hair back into a ponytail. "Coming, Charlotte," she called. She peered out through the stained glass side window, a habit she'd developed after the surprise visit and kidnapping by Joe Forster more than year earlier. She recognized Charlotte's form and opened the door widely. "Hi hon," she said, giving the girl a warm hug. "So glad to see you."

"Can Ragth go outthide today?"

"He sure can," she said as she closed the door. "Look, here he comes."

"Hi Ragth," Charlotte said, bending down to pet the large cat. I brought you thomething. Ith a kitty treat. Here," she said, balancing a couple of little morsels on her palm. Rags sniffed her hand. He then found the treats with his nose and sniffed one of them before taking it into his mouth, stepping back and eating it. When he'd finished one, he moved forward and gently took the other one.

"Hi Charlotte," Brianna said as she walked down the staircase. "How are you?"

Charlotte stood and stared at Brianna. "Hi," she said shyly.

"Charlotte, this is my sister, Brianna. You met her…"

"Oh yeth, at your wedding. I remember. You tried to catch the flowerth."

Brianna looked puzzled for a moment and then laughed. "That's right. I tried to catch the bouquet, didn't I?" She looked over at Savannah and said, "But my sister's tall friends got in my way."

"I thought it wath funny when you almoth fell down." Charlotte laughed.

"Your memory is too good for your own good, Charlotte," Brianna said.

"Can I take Ragth on the leath?"

"Leash? Yes, that would be okay. Let's go get his harness." Savannah turned toward the girl and said, "Charlotte, would you like something to drink?"

"No, I'm good."

"Well, how about if we each take a bottle of water with us outside?"

"Okay," Charlotte said. "Don't forget one for Ragth."

"Where is he taking her?" Brianna laughed as she watched Rags lead Charlotte out past the corral.

Savannah, a pensive look on her face, said, "Out to my orchard. Hey look at that. He's digging around one of the trees."

Charlotte turned and waved at Savannah and Brianna and they both waved back.

"That's strange," Savannah said quietly.

"What?" Brianna asked before taking a swig out of her water bottle.

"I've never seen him out in that area. Why now? Does he sense that something is different out there?"

"Yeah, he sees all that loose dirt." She leaned toward Savannah, looking her in the eye. "Don't you know why cats like loose dirt, Sis Vet?"

"I've been watching him and he hasn't squatted once," Savannah said defiantly. "He's not interested in the dirt. He likes the vibes out there. He notices that something about that area has changed. Look at him. He seems to be happy out there. He feels the good vibes."

"Pshaw," Brianna said "…good vibes. He sees it as a giant litter box, that's all." She laughed.

"Who sees what as a giant litter box?" Michael asked as he walked through the kitchen door to join the ladies on the porch.

"Oh hi, hon," Savannah said. She held a hand out to him and he walked over to her, took her hand, leaned in and kissed her on the lips.

He then followed Brianna's gaze out beyond the corral. When he spotted Charlotte and Rags, he said, "Gosh, what are they doing out in the old, dead orchard?"

"Michael," Savannah said, "it is not an old, dead orchard unless you believe it is."

"What? It's been an old, dead orchard ever since I can remember."

Brianna flashed a teasing grin at Savannah and said, "But that's only because that's what you thought you saw there. Right Vannie?"

"Well, sort of…I mean…" Savannah struggled to find words of explanation that her husband would comprehend. Finally she stood and grabbed him by the hand. "Michael, walk out here with me. I want to show you something."

"Are you coming, Brianna?" Michael asked.

Savannah was glad to hear her sister say, "No," as she pulled her phone out of her pocket and looked at it. "That's Mom on my cell. I have some things I want to tell her."

"So what's this all about, honey?" Michael asked. As they got closer to the old orchard, he said, "Well, it looks like someone's been doing some work out here. I wonder why?"

"It was me, Michael. I fed and watered the trees. I want to have Antonio prune them the way they should be pruned. I'm going to bring these trees to life out here. Not only that," she added, "this is going to be a field of sunflowers. Won't it look beautiful from our kitchen window?"

"Well, yes…I guess," he said. "But Savannah, what makes you think these trees will ever produce again? They look dead to me."

"They're not dead, Michael. Look," she said rushing over to one of the trees. "When I stripped this branch, I see green underneath. But the main reason why I think they will produce and flowers will grow is because I believe. Michael, bees leaves—believe. We just have to believe."

Michael raked his hand through his hair, looked over at his wife, and said, "But honey…"

"Hi Dr. Mike," Charlotte said. "Look, Ragth found wormth. Loth of them. They're all wiggling around under thith tree. He likth to watch them wiggle."

"Worms?" Savannah said excitedly. "Look Michael, worms. See, this ground isn't dead. There is life out here. There is no curse unless we choose to believe it."

"But what about the fact that no one ever had a child while they lived here?" Michael asked.

"Coincidence, pure and simple," she said. "Or, they simply believed they would be barren." She tilted her head. "When the gypsies put the spell on the house, they probably made it known to the original Forster family. They knew there was a curse and they believed it. With each generation, the story became somewhat diluted. Auntie knew about the curse, but the details of it had been lost to history."

He shook his head, glanced around the small orchard and then looked over at his wife. "I suppose you could be right."

"Of course I am," she said. And then she wrapped her arms around his neck and said, "Oh, Michael, I am so happy."

Chapter Sixteen

Fall turned into winter and then spring. Brianna had finished her studies in Indiana and was busy applying as a geriatric physician in a variety of clinics and offices throughout California. She hoped to find a position somewhere near Hammond in order to be closer to Bud. They were both tiring of the long-distance aspect of their blossoming relationship. And, while Bud had his veterinary license, he was rather content working part-time on his folks' ranch outside of Hammond and part-time as a vet tech for the Iveys' clinic. Although, he knew that if he and Brianna were to marry, he might have to make some changes. His dad was talking about retiring in a couple of years. Did he want the full responsibility for the ranch? Would Brianna be contented living the ranch life? He knew he needed to take inventory of his priorities while also considering her dreams and goals.

In the meantime, the clinic was getting busier and busier. One day Michael invited Bud out to lunch. "Listen Bud, I know you completed your veterinary studies some months ago. I suppose you're dreaming of a practice of your own, and you will be an excellent veterinarian. I've valued you as an employee for the last…what has it been…four or five years?"

"Yeah, something like that," Bud said.

"As you know, business is picking up. I've been thinking that we ought to hire another veterinarian. And Bud, if you would like the job on a part-time basis like you've been working, I want to offer it to you. I see it working into a full-time job in the near future—if that's what you want."

"Gosh, thanks, Dr. Mike. I appreciate your confidence in me." Bud sat back in the booth while their sandwiches were served. He looked at his plate for a moment and then said, "Can I think about it and, talk to Brianna and my folks? I'll let you know."

"Sure, Bud. Not a problem."

***

"How are the Easter plans coming, honey?" Michael asked as he slipped into his flip-flops one Sunday morning.

Savannah stepped out of the bathroom, pulled her hair back, and wrapped it in a knot. "I am having so much fun! I can't wait to have the whole family together here for an entire weekend. It'll be like I remember when I was a kid and all of us cousins came here and played. Some of my cousins have children now and Adam will be here. It is just going to be the most perfect Easter ever. We'll have horseback riding, horseshoes, and of course an Easter egg hunt."

"You're so cute when you're excited," Michael said, walking over to Savannah and tapping the tip of her nose. "So what are we going to do today? Do we have plans?" he asked, wrapping his arms around her waist and looking into her eyes.

"Well, there's a lot to do around here since our Big Sur trip. Gosh, I'm glad Bud stepped up to the plate and decided to work as a vet at least part time for us, so we can get away like that sometimes."

"Yeah, we've been so busy with the practice and finishing up some of the remodeling projects, the everyday upkeep is piling up around us. I don't know when I last washed off the porch…"

"And I've even neglected my sweet mare," Savannah said with a frown.

"Good idea to board her at Bonnie's these last few weeks, don't you think?"

"Yes. But I want to bring her home as soon as possible—the weather is getting better, the days are getting longer…and I miss her."

"Meow."

"Hi Ragsy," Savannah said as she spotted the cat rounding the corner into the room. "Yes, I'm going to feed you. Come on. Let's go," she said heading for the kitchen.

After feeding the small animals, Savannah started the coffee, poured herself a glass of orange juice, and stepped out onto the porch. She pulled her sweatshirt around her, scrunched down into one of the cushy porch chairs and began scanning the horizon. *Hmmm, don't like looking out at an empty corral. Need to bring my horse home,* she thought. She looked beyond the corral and toward the orchard she'd so lovingly tended these past months. *I haven't been out there in a while. Need to go check on things.*

She went back into the kitchen, donned her rubber boots, and walked out to the little orchard. As she approached, something caught her eye. *What's that?* she thought to herself. *A bump in the dirt.* She walked closer. *Lots of bumps in the dirt.* She knelt down and picked at the dirt on one of the bumps. Underneath she saw a bit of green poking through. *Green! It's a sprout. My sunflowers are sprouting! Oh my gosh!*

She stood up and began running toward the house. "Michael! Michael!" she called.

He swung open the kitchen door. "What?" he said, his brow furrowed in worry.

"I have sprouts," she said breathlessly.

"You have what?" he asked.

"Sprouts. My sunflowers are sprouting!"

Michael stood there, a puzzled look on his face.

"Come see, Michael," she said turning and rushing back out to the orchard.

"Well, by golly, honey, these are sprouts. And they sure do look like sunflowers."

"See Michael, the orchard isn't dead. There is no curse."

Michael wasn't completely convinced, however. It had been months since they'd decided they wanted a baby and still Savannah hadn't become pregnant. He took in a deep breath and looked around, not knowing quite what to say to Savannah. *Obviously, she is convinced, but I'm not sure I am,* he thought. As Savannah flicked the crust of soil off several sunflower seed sprouts, gleefully counting after uncovering each one, Michael looked out over the horizon. Suddenly, his eyes caught a glimpse of something. *Could it be?* He stared for a moment and then, as if somehow drawn toward it, he began walking—slowly at first and then his pace hastened. He stopped, stunned for a moment, and then he called out, "Savannah! Savannah!"

She looked up and saw him standing in front of one of the old fruit trees. He turned to look at her and called out again, "Come here; you're not going to believe this!"

Savannah hurried to her feet and rushed to his side as fast as she could go in her rubber boots. "What is it?"

"Look…leaves. This tree is full of little leaves. It's alive." He looked around. "And this tree has a shadow of green, too. Look, is that a leaf unfurling there? Savannah, your orchard is alive!" he said, laughing out loud. He looked over at her and saw tears streaming down her face. He wrapped his arms around her and held her to him while she sobbed softly.

She then pulled away from Michael, wiped her eyes, and stared at the trees. "This is incredible," she said. "Oh my gosh, Michael. There is no curse, is there? Maybe there never was." She then shook her head and said, "Then why…?"

He held her to him resting his chin on her head. "I don't know. I just don't know, honey."

Suddenly, she pulled away and said, "Michael, what is the date?"

"Um, the tenth isn't it?"

"It is? March tenth? Oh my gosh. I'm never this late." She turned toward the house, held out her hand. "Michael come with me quick."

"What's going on, Savannah. What are you late for? We don't have to go to work today."

"Just come with me." She led him into the house through the living room and into their bedroom, where she said, "Wait here."

He sat down and petted Rags, who was lying in the unmade bed. "What's up, buddy?" he asked the cat, while scratching him behind the ear.

"Okay, Michael," Savannah said, rushing into the room. "Watch and see what happens."

"Watch what?" he asked. "What is that thing?"

"A pregnancy test," she said matter-of-factly.

"What?" He jumped up from the bed and turned to face her. "Do you mean?"

"I don't know, yet. We have to watch and see if this thing turns blue. It's supposed to take three to five minutes."

He raked his hand through his hair and asked, "How long has it been?"

"Let's see," she said, consulting her watch, "one and a half."

Michael sat down next to Savannah and put his arm around her. The two of them stared for what seemed like the longest two minutes ever. Finally, she said, "It's turning, Michael. I can see it turning blue."

"Yes, it's blue—Oh my gosh, does this mean?"

"Yes, it could mean that we're finally pregnant."

"Should you see the doctor to be sure?"

"Well yes, we'll do that. But these home pregnancy tests, I'm told, can be quite accurate and you can get results immediately." They both looked down at the strip again. She said, "Blue. Definitely blue."

"Does that mean a boy?" he asked.

"No. These tests aren't that advanced." She stood up. "But Michael," she said jumping up and down, "it could very well mean that we are pregnant. We're going to have a baby."

"Wow! I'm speechless. A baby." He stood and pulled her down on the bed with him, rose up on his elbows, and said, "I am so happy. Thank you."

***

"I'm seeing the doctor today," Savannah announced. "It has been a month, and I want to make sure everything's okay."

"Can I come?"

"Well, you can if you want—in fact, why don't you come and they can do the vaginal on you."

"Naw, I'll pass on that one," he said shaking his head.

"Truly, there is no reason for you to be there today, I'm sure."

An hour later, Savannah walked into Michael's office as he studied a chart. He stood immediately upon seeing her and walked swiftly toward her. "Well?" he asked.

She didn't even try to hide her smile. "Everything is great. Yes, we are pregnant. Oh Michael," she said throwing her arms around him. "We could have a baby by Christmas. Can you believe it?"

He pulled away from her and looked deeply into her eyes. Tears of joy rolled down one cheek as he said, "Yes, Savannah, I believe."

Other books in the Klepto Cat Mystery series

Catnapped

When Savannah Jordan agrees to help her aunt while she recovers from a broken foot, she doesn't expect to walk into a mystery, become part of a not-quite-legal surveillance team, be kidnapped by a deranged stranger and meet a steaming hot veterinarian.

Beloved neighborhood cats are missing—the community can only guess at their fate—and Aunt Margaret's life is being threatened. Is it because she has a clue to the missing cats or is it something more sinister? Of course, as in all of the Klepto Cat Mysteries, Rags, an ordinary cat with a most unusual habit, has a paw in saving the day.

If you like light mysteries with only a little terror, if you're infatuated by interesting cats and if you love a love story, you must read this book.

Cat-Eye Witness

Savannah and Aunt Margaret open the old Forster home to the Hammond Cat Alliance for a fundraiser to help rehabilitate the abused horses rescued months earlier from the catnappers.

Before the afternoon is over, the collected funds go missing and someone is murdered in an upstairs bedroom.

Suspicion surrounds Iris, a local waitress and Savannah's new best friend. The only witness to the murder is Rags, Savannah's cat. With the assistance of a cat psychic and Rags's good friend, Charlotte (the young girl with Downs), the cat helps to "paw" the killer…but not before an attempt is made on Rags's life. The case is solved only after Rags comes face-to-face with the killer for the second time.

Detective Craig Sledge is new to this book, as is Damon, Iris's errant son. Sledge finds this to be one of the muddiest cases he has ever worked, with inconsistent clues and no apparent motive. He's constantly surprised, perplexed and impressed by the cat's uncanny ability to come up with clues he has missed. His fascination with the attractive Iris Clampton also mystifies the detective.

In this story, one of the rescued horses goes into labor and there's a night of high drama

at the ole corral as veterinarians Savannah and Michael work to save the foal. This experience renews Savannah's deep interest in horses and riding, which ultimately serves to help her bond with a very important surprise character who finds his way into her life and Michael's just as they prepare to say their wedding vows.

While Rags is the animal star, he isn't the only animal featured in this story. Layla is back in all of her tangerine feline beauty. And Rags makes friends with Buffy, a perky almost Himalayan cat and the inseparable duo, Walter, an all black cat and his sidekick, Lexie, a charming Afghan mix dog. Savannah's new ride, Peaches, also debuts in this story. An incident with this mare adds another dimension to Savannah's and Michael's relationship. Can he hold her with open arms?

Some say this is a love story with a mystery in the background. And it's a story of family and friendship as newlyweds Margaret and Max continue to be a meaningful part of Savannah's and Michael's world.

Undercover Cat

A popular local journalist goes missing just before she has the opportunity to turn in her story exposing unscrupulous cat hoarders. Not only is Colbi a friend of Savannah's and Michael's, Damon (now out of prison and employed by the local newspaper) has a strong personal interest in her. In fact, Damon breaks some rules and some trusts in his search for Colbi.

Is this a love connection? It's doubtful because Colbi is a strong advocate for the feral cat population and Damon hates cats—or so he believes.

Colbi's rescue is almost too late. She needs time to heal both physically and emotionally. So the Iveys invite her to recuperate in their home. Just when Colbi begins to feel safe, a body is discovered in the Iveys' orchard and Rags (their kleptomaniac cat) goes missing. Can someone in a nearby homeless camp shed some light on the evolving mystery?

The Colony Cat Caper

Savannah Ivey, a veterinarian out on maternity leave; her aunt Margaret, the founder of the Hammond Cat Alliance; and Colbi Stanton, a reporter for the local newspaper take on a cat colony at an old, abandoned building. Odd activity around the place makes them wonder if it actually is vacant; some believe it's occupied by something other-worldly. When a stranger comes to town and suggests the Alliance open the old building to a fund-raiser, everyone gets involved, including Rags, Savannah's kleptomaniac cat. He finds something that day that stirs a lot of people—both law-abiding and crooks—into action. Are the feral cats and their caretakers in serious danger? What (or who) lurks inside the old building? What secrets does it hide? And who has the key that unlocks the mystery?

34306991R00146

Made in the USA
Middletown, DE
16 August 2016